AUGUST OF THE ZOMBIES

ALSO BY K. G. CAMPBELL

A Small Zombie Problem

The Zombie Stone

AUGUST OF THE ZOMBIES

ZOMBIE PROBLEMS
BOOK 3

K. G. CAMPBELL

ALFRED A. KNOPF

NEW YORK

J
CAMPBELL

THIS IS A BORZOI BOOK PUBLISHED BY ALFRED A. KNOPF

Visit us on the Web! rhcbooks.com

Educators and librarians, for a variety of teaching tools, visit us at
RHTeachersLibrarians.com

Library of Congress Cataloging-in-Publication Data is available upon request.
ISBN 978-1-101-93163-9 (trade) — ISBN 978-1-101-93164-6 (lib. bdg.) —
ISBN 978-1-101-93165-3 (ebook)

The text of this book is set in 12-point Simoncini Garamond.
The illustrations were created using watercolor and colored pencil.
Interior design by Stephanie Moss

FEB - '22

$20.99

Printed in the United States of America
January 2022
10 9 8 7 6 5 4 3 2 1
First Edition

To Debbie and Rick, who
inspired the whole thing

CONTENTS

PART III

PART I

CHAPTER 1

THE ONES BEFORE

A ghostly band of morning mist hovered on the Continental River. From somewhere within the milky vapor advanced the sputter of a weary outboard motor. Soon a blurry shape emerged. And the shape appeared to be that of a garden shed roped to a listing pontoon: a houseboat . . . of sorts.

"Here comes Madame Marvell," said August DuPont.

The boy had eyes of the palest gold, like late-summer marsh grass, unusually large and round and rendered even larger by large, round eyeglasses. Between those and his rather small mouth, he bore a distinct resemblance to a baby owl.

Swatting away some butterflies circling his head, the boy lifted a boatswain's whistle to his lips and blew, closing and opening his fingers over the instrument's holes to create a wavering warble.

The dawn stillness should have resulted in the sound seeming piercing and conspicuous, but it was masked to some extent by the weak fog and the clamor of passing street sweepers.

The snail-paced vehicles edged along nearby Dolphin Street, their great circular brushes noisily swishing trash into their steel bellies: plastic cups and confetti and sequined masks and a million strings of colored beads—all the festive debris generated by two weeks of Carnival.

The whistle was loud enough, however, directed as it was across the water, to reach the approaching vessel, which shifted course slightly, clearly heading toward the high-pitched sound.

"Are you quite well enough to travel?" asked Belladonna Malveau. "It is not every day, after all, that a person gets walloped in the head by the paddle of a riverboat."

"The paramedic came by first thing," muttered August. "He said there's no concussion, gave me the all clear."

Belladonna studied her cousin for a moment.

"Ah!" she said, as if in revelation. "That's what's missing: your beekeeper's costume."

"I lost the helmet in the river last night," explained August. "Without it, the gloves seemed rather pointless."

"Are you *certain* you are all right? You look, well, bluer than a day-old bruise."

August threw the girl a dispirited glance.

"I'm doing fine, I guess," he said dolefully, "considering I'm the person who ruined the Grand Parade, highlight of Croissant City's world-famous Carnival, an event watched on television by millions of people."

"Oh, quit being so hard on yourself," said Belladonna consolingly. "It wasn't *your* fault."

She glanced discreetly at the gaggle of zombies nearby: a softly weeping showgirl, a small prince, and a well-dressed lady with only half a face. The bedraggled creatures swayed unsteadily on the boulders that formed the river's embankment.

"Was it not your pirate zombie," persisted Belladonna, "Jacques LeSalt, who truly caused the entire accident?"

"*Your* pirate zombie," repeated August. "That, cousin, is precisely the problem. Let me ask you this. If the float had not collided with the fire hydrant, would the masts have collapsed, drenching everyone with bubble fluid and wrecking the TV presenters' balcony, Yuko Yukiyama's xylophone, and the entire sound system?"

"I guess not," admitted Belladonna.

"And if celebrity cat Officer Claw had not flipped his lid and leaped, claws extended, onto the bald head of the driver, would the float have collided with the fire hydrant?"

"No," said Belladonna more quietly.

"And if pirate zombie Jacques LeSalt had not been on the

float, would he have mistaken foil-wrapped chocolate doubloons for his own treasure and lunged for them with a monstrous bellow, causing celebrity cat Officer Claw to flip his lid in the first place?"

Belladonna shook her head.

"And why was Jacques LeSalt on the float?"

Belladonna was silent.

"Because of me, Belladonna." August gazed upon the lapping brown water with a bleak expression. "Because, like you said, he's *my* zombie. Not that I can say why. I certainly didn't set out to collect a bunch of undead groupies, who follow me everywhere."

"Like ducklings," observed Belladonna, "trail behind their mother."

"If only they *were* ducklings! Ducklings don't smell like moldy coffins. Ducklings don't make people scream and panic, or cause havoc wherever they go. Ducklings don't drool on your arm and offer you their eyeball."

August looked down at the fourth undead member of this strange little riverside gathering, his great-great-aunt Claudette, who, blue-lipped and crooked, was drooling on her living relative's arm and offering him her eyeball, as she often did.

"Ducklings," continued August, "don't get you blamed for things you didn't do and make everyone hate you."

"I don't think everyone hates—"

"Margot Morgan Jordan called me a loser. Then a monster! The girl who plays TV's beloved Stella Starz hates me."

"Well, I'm sure—"

"This has to stop, Belladonna. I *must* retrieve the Zombie Stone. The thing, you see, is a Go-Between, a bridge between two worlds. It is the only thing that can force the zombies to return to the land of the dead, where they belong. It is the only thing that can set me free from"—August's eyes drifted to Claudette's pasty, adoring face—"all this undeadness."

"And you're sure the map can help, the one the undertaker found in Pepperville?"

August studied the newspaper in his hands, a copy of the *Croissant City Crier.*

"According to Octavia Motts," he said, "the librarian at the Pepperville Public Library, there's a mighty good chance it reveals the hiding place of Jacques LeSalt's famous treasure. We know that's where Professor Leech was headed with the zombie he stole. And the Zombie Stone. If I can figure out their route, maybe I can intercept them."

"They have a healthy head start," observed Belladonna. "Must you go to Pepperville first? Can't you make out the map in the paper's photograph of Mr. Goodnight?"

"It's too small," explained August. "And blurry. You can't make out the details or read the place-names. I need to examine the original."

"We're headed home tomorrow," said Belladonna. "Beauregard has some engagement in Pepperville, and Mama won't permit me to remain here alone. You could come with us in the limousine; you'd arrive around the same time as you would if you left now in *that*." She nodded at the approaching houseboat.

"I don't think so," said August. "Aunt Orchid has been asking some awkward questions about Madame Marvell, who for personal reasons chooses to remain incognito. Besides, do you really think your mother and brother would welcome *all* of us"—he jerked his head toward the zombies—"into the family vehicle?"

"Hmm," grunted Belladonna. "You have a point." She glanced at her cousin with good-natured, far-apart eyes of dark translucent brown, like breakfast tea.

Eyes that reminded August of a recent observation.

"The family portrait," he said. "The one in the Funeral Street music room."

Belladonna's expression changed, became more guarded.

"What about it?"

"I thought your father died when you were babies. You and Beauregard are six or seven years old in that painting. And your eyes are cornflower blue."

"They are? How odd." But the girl had turned toward the river, and her voice was prickly.

"Belladonna, are those children you and Beauregard?"

Belladonna's jaw stiffened.

Then August watched some sense of resignation pass over his cousin. Her face relaxed. Her eyelids drooped. So did her shoulders.

She turned to August.

She shook her head.

"Then who . . . ?"

"The Ones Before," said Belladonna quietly.

August was suddenly transported to the gloom of the Chamber of Jewels on that hot summer day when he and Orchid Malveau first met. He saw a woman staring at nothing, her veiled face stricken with the bleakest grief.

He remembered her words.

"The Peruvian flu was a democratic disease," his aunt had said, "claiming the lives of rich and poor alike. Men. Women. Children too."

Children too.

It was suddenly so obvious.

"She lost her husband," said August, "*and* her children."

Belladonna nodded.

"Twins. Like us. The Ones Before."

"You once said that you'd been—what was the word you used . . . 'recruited'?—recruited to be perfect Malveaus. You made it sound like you'd been hired to fill a vacancy. Is that really how you feel? Like a replacement?"

Belladonna studied her bracelet for a moment. It was a handsome piece, fashioned from pasta—rotelle, to be precise—lacquered rich blood-red.

"I had a peacock," she said, as if it were no more unusual than owning a parakeet. "Some folks don't believe they make the most affectionate pets. But when Mama was busy being all bereft and Beauregard was busy being, well, Beauregard, Salvador was always there . . . for *me*. I loved him for that, even though he was an appalling biter. We'd sit by the river and share dewberries. Salvador was just crazy for dewberries. He was my friend. And then he died."

"I'm sorry," said August.

"Afterward," continued Belladonna, "all the places Salvador used to be felt so empty. I hated that emptiness. All I wanted was to have my Salvador back. 'Bring him back!' I would sob, over and over. 'Please, Mama!' She couldn't, of course. But one day she brought home the fuzziest little black peachick. She told me he needed a mother to love him and that I needed a peacock to love. I was shocked at first. 'You can't just *replace* Salvador!' I yelled. I was frightened, I think, that if I loved the new bird, somehow it would make my feelings for Salvador less real, you know? It would make his life seem less valuable."

"And you believe," suggested August, "that you and Beauregard are Aunt Orchid's fuzzy peachicks?"

Belladonna nodded.

"I think we were twins that needed a mother to love them, and after the Peruvian flu, she was a mother who needed twins to love. She was well intentioned, I believe. But something has gone wrong. She cannot stop herself from wanting the thing she lost, so she has tried to turn us into that thing."

August considered this.

"Is your new peacock just like Salvador?"

"Why no. Matisse is most certainly his own peacock. Such a drama queen. Hates dewberries."

"And did you come to love him?"

"Didn't want to. I missed the biting. But the love just sort of bubbled up; I had to put it somewhere."

August reached out and touched Belladonna's bracelet. It appeared so bright against the black of her dress.

"Perhaps," he suggested, "*you* should try being your own peacock."

"Hmm," said Belladonna resentfully as Madame Marvell approached and cut the engine. "That sounds annoyingly wise."

The houseboat bumped gently against the rocks of the embankment. At close quarters, it was apparent that the craft was in a much-diminished state. It looked as if it had been attacked by a giant alligator and subsequently tossed around in the violent wake of a mighty riverboat. Which, of course, it had.

A chunk of its platform was missing, and of necessity, the engine was positioned off-center. Of the eight rusted oil drums

that had formed the pontoon, only six remained, and the resulting loss of buoyancy left the rear corner of the deck (which had
listed at the best of times) trailing in the water. The roof had lost
many of its shingles. The ropes securing the shed to the pallet
were frayed. Nailed to the houseboat's wall, a battered, broken
sign read "Madame Marvell, Ball Gazing, Magic—"

"I've seen boats made of folded newspaper," observed Belladonna, "that looked more watertight than that thing."

The girl known as Madame Marvell shot the young Malveau
a scowl as she helped four shaky-legged zombies board.

"She's quite seaworthy," snapped the wild-haired girl defensively.

"I certainly hope," retorted Belladonna, "you're not headed
out to *sea*." She raised her eyebrows at August as he leaped
from the embankment to the swaying deck, accompanied by his
butterflies.

"Just the swamp," the boy reassured her, "and its quiet
waterways like glass."

Belladonna nodded with a concerned frown and raised her
palm in farewell.

"Bon voyage, August," she muttered to herself as water
suddenly roiled around the outboard motor and the houseboat
lurched toward the expanse of the Continental River.

As she watched the crippled craft—visibly tilted, low in
the water—return to the mist, Belladonna was reminded of a

wounded duck. And at that very moment, as if the universe had read her thoughts, the air was filled with the nasal honking of waterfowl in flight.

What Belladonna Malveau saw when she looked up caused her brow to crease with puzzlement. The skies above were darkening with birds, hundreds—no, thousands—of them, forming great speeding triangles.

And the great triangles of birds were all speeding in the same direction.

Inland.

Away from the sea.

CHAPTER 2

AWAY FROM THE SEA

"Have you ever known a March morning to be so warm, Mr. LaPoste?"

Hydrangea DuPont handed the local mailman a glass beaded with condensation and a lace-trimmed handkerchief.

"That I have not, Miz Hydrangea," said the man, mopping his brow with the handkerchief and taking a large gulp from the glass. When he tasted the cold beverage, his itchy-looking pink nose wrinkled a little.

"It's on the tart side, Mr. LaPoste, I know," said Hydrangea apologetically. "Sugar, I regret to say, is a luxury beyond our budget here at Locust Hole. Now that the last of DuPont's Peppy Pepper Sauce has finally been sold, I fear we must survive on ever-dwindling resources."

"Your presence, Miz Hydrangea," LaPoste assured the lady, "is sweetener enough. The lemonade is mighty fine!" As if to prove the point, he glugged down the remaining liquid, smacked his lips, and offered up an enormous smile of very large, very white teeth.

Hydrangea was—as many were—reminded of a rabbit, an unusually peppy, gregarious rabbit.

"It's the least I can do," she said, gazing up from beneath lowered eyelashes, "for all your help with August's pepper plants."

She turned and lifted the netting that shrouded the ramshackle porch, just enough to peek through. Dawn mist from the nearby canal still lingered in the front yard and on the dirt lane beyond. The geometric paths of the old Italian garden were still visible, but the flower beds they encircled were planted not with boxwood and azaleas but with a hundred uniform seedlings.

"You have a green thumb, Mr. LaPoste," observed Hydrangea. "After just a few days in your care, the plants look positively optimistic! Why, I believe I see some tiny peppers hiding beneath the leaves. I may be mistaken; it's hard to see from up here. Could it be so, Mr. LaPoste?"

"Indeed, it is, Miz Hydrangea," said the mailman, pulling his uniform over his sweat-stained undershirt and brushing dirt from his knobby knees. "It appears we have new fruit."

"Oh, my nephew August will be thrilled, Mr. LaPoste. He has been working so hard to revive the DuPont pepper farm.

Why, the child single-handedly collected seeds from the withered plants that clung to life out back. He propagated them in fertile soil dug from the riverbank and planted them after the frosts had passed, for you know how peppers love mild weather.

"In these fragile, tender shoots, Mr. LaPoste, I see a revival—no, a veritable renaissance! August—with no small help from yourself—may realize a pepper harvest this year."

"And if he succeeds," said the mailman, slinging the strap of his bag across his shoulder, "perhaps all is not lost for DuPont's Peppy Pepper Sauce and Locust Hole."

"But as you are aware, sir, Pelican State Bank is preparing to foreclose on the place if we cannot soon make a payment toward our mortgage. Even if our little peppers thrive, Mr. LaPoste, it takes at least two, three years to age the mash sufficiently to produce a quality hot sauce. I do not see how any payments might be made by the last day of June."

"If it could be proven, Miz Hydrangea, that the family business remains a going concern, your creditors might be inclined to hold off. I doubt," said Mr. LaPoste as he glanced around, "that the bank relishes the prospect of acquiring, then trying to *sell,* a property in such a—forgive me—compromised condition."

"You think so?" said Hydrangea as the mailman departed through the swathes of netting. "Oh, that would be wonderful, Mr. LaPoste. Whatever would I do without you?"

"Well now, you don't need to worry yourself about that, Miz Hydrangea," said Mr. LaPoste, pausing on the broken porch steps and flashing an irrepressible smile. "My commitment to the postal service calls me away this morning, but I'll be back tomorrow to check on you and young August's pepper plants. My word," he added, donning his hat, "it is indeed hotter than a polar bear in a Jacuzzi. You stay cool now, Miz Hydrangea."

As the mailman headed toward the gate and Hydrangea flapped her handkerchief in farewell, something unusual caught the lady's eye.

What Hydrangea DuPont saw caused her a shiver of apprehension. Huge, swiftly moving formations of birds—hundreds of them, maybe thousands—were filling up the skies above.

And the huge formations of birds were all moving swiftly in the same direction.

Inland.

Away from the sea.

* * *

Beauregard Malveau usually felt grouchy on first waking up. He resented the unwelcome transition from fuzzy slumber to the sharp waking world, where he was expected to think, to do stuff, and to be charming.

But this particular morning found the boy even grumpier than usual. The day before had been a bad one for Beauregard.

He had fallen some distance from the crow's nest of a pirate ship (or at least a pirate-ship-themed parade float). His descending person had smashed into and destroyed the instrument of the famous xylophonist Yuko Yukiyama. He had been yelled at and bopped on the head with a fuzzy mallet by said xylophonist (not very hard, but still). He had been drenched in soapy, slimy bubble fluid. So had Yuko Yukiyama.

Beauregard had been frightened by the fall, bruised by the impact, and thoroughly humiliated by the entire incident.

And all this was the fault of one person: his cousin August DuPont.

Beauregard had developed a distaste for his owl-faced relative. He was irked by August's unspecified skin condition that attracted butterflies. He was revolted by the decomposing, malodorous zombies with whom August chose to keep company. He was nauseated by August's kind disposition and dogged loyalty to that clinging, dreary creature Claudette.

Beauregard's sister, Belladonna, had recently suggested that beneath this dislike lay her twin's insecurities.

"You're popular," she had observed, "and handsome and enviable, and people do what you say. But is that popular, handsome, enviable person really who you are, Beau? Or is he just a character you play so you can feel good about yourself?

"Our cousin August is awkward, odd-looking, and a bit peculiar—all the things you work hard not to be. I think you're afraid, Beau, that people will like him anyway. And what would that mean for your popularity, your handsomeness, your enviableness?

"It would mean that all the things which make you feel superior are worthless.

"So who would you be then?"

Belladonna had always been sharp-tongued. And smart. Beauregard had told her to shut up, but he suspected his sister was right. It was much easier, however, and more satisfying, to dislike and blame someone else than to examine oneself.

So on this particular morning, Beauregard was busy disliking and blaming August, not examining himself, and feeling grouchy when, scratching his bed-tousled hair, he entered Champagne Fontaine's dining room.

The room, like the lady's home in general, did not possess the smartness of the Malveaus' Funeral Street townhouse or the grandeur of Château Malveau. But the place was spacious and well-to-do, if on the frilly side, with flowery wallpapers and overstuffed seating upholstered in flowery fabrics.

Champagne and her grandson, Langley, were seated at either end of a dining table heavily draped in a flowery cloth. Their crumpled napkins and the debris on their plates suggested that they had already breakfasted.

"Awake at last?" muttered Langley. "You seem rather less

bubbly this morning, Beau." Beauregard shot his friend a scowl, but the lanky boy was engrossed in a thick folio of papers bound in a manila cover.

"Langley!" Champagne chided, setting down her newspaper (Beauregard noticed it was opened to the obituaries). "We do not tease our guests, especially one as welcome as Orchid Malveau's boy, hmm? Your mother is a jewel among women, Beauregard, an invaluable addition to the Guild of Weepy Widows (of which you should know I am the treasurer). Would you like some breakfast, sugar? Of course you would. You like biscuits? Fabian! FABIAN!"

A scrawny, grasshopper-like man appeared at the doorway, wiping his hands on his apron.

"Ah!" said Champagne. "Some sweet-potato biscuits for our guest, Fabian, with pepper jelly. And eggs Sardou, if you don't mind. Thank you, Fabian. My late husband, Henri, was most partial to eggs Sardou, Beauregard, and Fabian's are quite simply the best. How did you sleep, sugar? Take a seat, why don't you? Not too hot in the night? I put you on the third floor for the cross breeze; it's the best in the house. Such peculiar weather, is it not? So warm for March, and humid."

"I slept just fine, Miz Champagne," Beauregard reassured his hostess.

"Oh, good. I hope you'll tell your mother so."

"Thank you again for having me."

"Don't be foolish," simpered Champagne as she poured the boy coffee. "You are Langley's friend. And your mother is a jewel among women."

"I just didn't feel like staying at home last night," explained Beauregard. "Our own house was rather full."

"With your cousin?" suggested Langley. "And his . . . *friends*?" The hint of a smile lurked on his usually solemn mouth, but the boy continued to gaze at the opened folio before him.

Beauregard was irked. He did not appreciate being an object of amusement. He liked his friends to remain in line.

"What's that you've got there, anyway?" he asked casually. "I've never seen you with a book, Langley. In fact, I wasn't aware you could even read."

His heavy-lidded eyes finally rose, a small frown on his face. Langley had awoken the beast, and he knew it. He slid the hand-bound booklet across the table.

"It's the script," he said, a little sullenly. "That fellow Katz, with the cat, introduced me to the assistant director after the parade."

Beauregard placed his hand on the open pages and pulled them close.

"Do we have speaking parts?" he asked, leafing through the document.

"I'm not sure you'd exactly call it speaking," said Langley.

"You will get me home in time, Mimi, won't you? To Pepperville, for the shoot on Friday?"

"My Lord, child, of course!" cried Champagne. "My handsome grandson and his friend are to star in a television show; I am quite beside myself!"

"Just extras, Mimi; we are certainly not the stars."

"Oh, but when they lay eyes on you, sugar, you will be! Beauregard, my Langley has always been a most talented actor. Do you remember, sugar"—she turned to Langley—"when you played the title role in that production of *Chicken Little*?"

"*Chicken Little,* you say?" repeated Beauregard, feigning astonishment and grinning triumphantly at Langley.

"I am not afraid to say, sugar, that Langley eclipsed everyone on that stage, including the teacher! Why, he had everyone in the auditorium quite convinced that the sky actually *was* falling. The *Pepperville Prophet* described his performance as 'decidedly precocious.' Do you remember, Langley? He gets the gift, of course, from his grandfather. My Henri was known to tread the boards back in the day. Shakespeare, no less. He had the voice for it: mellifluous, people called it! Oh, you would make a dazzling Hamlet, sugar, I know you would. You have the range, the pathos!"

"I enjoy dressing up," admitted Langley, succumbing to the flattery. "And applause. Especially applause for me."

"We should go to England!" cried Champagne. "To the home of the Bard himself, William Shakespeare. Would you like that, sugar? London! Perhaps for you to audition at the Royal Academy of Dramatic Art! How could they resist my handsome Langley?"

Beauregard glanced from one Fontaine to the other. He was beginning to think they were both a little nuts. It seemed to him that landing a gig as an extra on a television show hardly qualified a person for some fancy acting school in England.

But Champagne was transported by the sudden notion. She rose and drifted, ruffled black robe billowing, to the open French doors to gaze out over the iron balcony.

"And after London, Paris," she said wistfully. "Shopping. Art. More shopping."

She paused, looking upward, her head tilted with curiosity.

"How peculiar," she said.

"What's peculiar?" asked Beauregard as he suddenly became aware of a great quacking, squawking din.

The boys joined the woman and looked up in the direction of her pointed finger.

What they saw caused them to wrinkle their noses and say "Huh!" Hundreds of birds, possibly thousands, in vast, arrow-shaped flocks, were racing across the skies above.

And the vast, arrow-shaped flocks of birds were all racing in the same direction.

Inland.

Away from the sea.

* * *

Cyril Saint-Cyr, local historian, tour guide, entrepreneur, and general personality, checked his watch for a third time. Dixie Lispings was tardy, and it was most unlike her. Unless Dixie was on location filming an episode of her television show, *Absurdly Opulent Homes of the Very Rich and Even Richer,* she and Cyril *always* met at Café de la Lune, eight-thirty sharp. The pair had been friends since the old days, so it had been this way for years. Whoever arrived first ordered the beignets and café au laits. Normally, by the time the waiter returned with breakfast, the other had turned up.

Dixie Lispings was currently so late, however, that Cyril had eaten an entire plate of soft, warm beignets by himself. So he ordered another.

"My Lord, it's warm for March," thought Cyril, fanning himself with a menu. "In fact, I believe I must remove my coat." The rosy, gnomish little man wriggled awkwardly out of his seersucker suit jacket, then straightened his enormous green bow tie. He would normally never have appeared in public so unbuttoned, but it really was unusually hot.

A sudden startling whistle caused him to look up. Between trees and buildings (the old friends always sat at the same table on the awning-covered patio overlooking Jacques LeSalt Park),

Cyril glimpsed the movement of something very large. The tall, slender smokestacks of a riverboat were passing across his peek-aboo view, hazy in the morning river mist. The *Delta Duchess* was departing on her first tour of the day.

Although he couldn't see it, Cyril could hear the distant thrash of the vessel's drum-shaped paddle, and he immediately remembered the boy who had been struck by one of its mighty blades the previous night.

"Croissant City is not so large a town," mused Cyril. "Still, that the same young man should have crossed my path so many times in two days is most unusual. First, his great-great-aunt's costume (so clever, so gruesome) wins a place on the Weepy Widows' parade float. Then the pair appear at the Sad Celeste House, where their colorful acting troupe from Lapland frightens the tourists half to death.

"Yesterday, they all turn up at Saint-Cyr's Wax Museum in search of an obscure sculpture that had—by wild coincidence—been purchased earlier that day. Hours later, they bring the Grand Parade to a catastrophic end, and shortly after, the boy is being dragged from the river by a great white alligator.

"Dixie always says that Carnival brings the strangest people to town. She's right, I suppose. But now that it's all over, I'm sure things will get back to normal."

But Cyril was wrong.

An expansive chitter-chattering suddenly filled the air.

"Whatever is the source of all that racket?" Cyril muttered, leaning out over the café railing.

What Cyril Saint-Cyr saw when he looked up caused him to gasp aloud. Far above, the skies were disappearing behind hundreds, maybe thousands—definitely thousands—of fleeing birds.

And the thousands of birds were all fleeing in the same direction.

Inland.

Away from the sea.

Simultaneously, the atmosphere of Café de la Lune shifted; a nervous energy rippled through the patio beneath the gaily striped awning. Alerts were chiming. Diners were gasping at their smartphones. Chairs were scraping. People were standing, rushing out without even paying.

Cyril was disconcerted, as anyone might be. But before he had a chance to ask the waitress what was happening, a familiar face appeared, advancing quickly.

"Why aren't you answering your texts?" demanded Dixie Lispings.

"How you feeling, sugar?" Cyril pointed to the sling supporting Dixie's left arm, the result of a ship's mast collapsing onto the balcony from which the pair had been commentating on Croissant City's Grand Parade.

"I've been calling and calling!" cried Dixie, ignoring the question.

"Well, would you look at that," said Cyril, examining his phone. "The thing is muted. When it comes to technology, sugar, I'm about as clever as a rattlesnake trying to knit a sweater!"

He glanced around the patio, where the staff was frantically moving the tables and chairs to the café's interior.

"What on earth is going on? Is the world ending?"

"Not exactly," said Dixie, grabbing Cyril's arm and dragging him from the table.

"There are beignets coming," he protested, quickly snatching up his jacket.

"A hurricane has formed," said Dixie sharply, "in the Pirates' Sea, just off the coast."

"A hurricane?" Cyril scoffed as he was hustled onto the sidewalk. "That's quite ridiculous. Why, it's only March."

"You must have observed the heat, sugar. We've all been talking about it for days. Just last night at the parade, I said it felt like hurricane weather. Did I not say that?"

"You did, Dixie. And yes, surely the weather is unseasonable, but that hardly means—"

"Have you seen *that*?" interrupted Dixie, gazing up at the great squawking feathery migration above the rooftops.

Cyril nodded, suddenly alarmed.

Birds flying inland. Not a good sign.

"I have just gotten off the phone, sugar," explained Dixie, "with Gunther. You know, Gunther Thunder, CCTV's meteorologist?"

"Oh yes, I know Gunther. He's awful good, is he not?"

"Well, whether it's the result of climate change or a freak anomaly, there's a hurricane a hundred-odd miles away. A big one. And it's growing. Fast. The Hurricane Institute has issued the gravest of warnings."

"And it's headed this way?"

"Not directly, but close enough."

"Oh my! Dixie, I need to secure the museum! Then get home to close up the storm shutters. How big *is* this thing?"

They were almost running now, as was everyone in the streets around them.

"It's big, Cyril. They think it might be a monster by the time it makes landfall tomorrow morning."

"Well, Lord help anyone in its path. And where *is* that path, Dixie? Where *will* this monster hurricane make landfall?"

"Let's just say," gasped Dixie, breathless from jogging, "I wouldn't want to be waking up tomorrow morning in Lost Souls' Swamp!"

CHAPTER 3

EMPTY SKIES

The following morning, August DuPont woke up in Lost Souls' Swamp.

He shuffled out of the cabin onto the modest deck, where Marvell waited with his breakfast: a box of Mudd Pies and a chipped mug of chicory coffee. The children shared their chocolate-covered cookie snacks in silence while Claudette sleepily sucked the thumb of her dismembered arm (it had become detached during an encounter with an alligator) and the other zombies looked on passively, still lost to the tranquil state they assumed at nighttime.

The houseboat bobbed gently inside a great yellow-green canopy formed by curtains of Spanish moss suspended from the gnarled branches of a cypress tree. Marvell had elected to spend the night there so the group might remain concealed from the prying eyes of fellow swamp-goers. Back in Croissant City on the night of August's rescue, Orchid Malveau had asked some probing questions about Marvell's guardianship and place of residence. The independent orphan had been spooked by the attention, and was feeling conspicuous.

She had been further unnerved when some uniformed official—perhaps a lock operator—appeared intent on halting the houseboat's progress as it exited Pirates' Pier Lock. He had waved his arms wildly and yelled, but being high above them, at the level of the Continental River, the man had been out of earshot. Marvell had powered up the outboard engine, drowning out his muffled cries entirely, and pretended not to notice him.

But in the end, Madame Marvell need not have worried; the houseboat had not passed another vessel the entire day. The only living creatures the travelers had spied were birds. Lots of birds, high above.

All flying in the same direction.

And after breakfast, the houseboat passed through the tendrils of Spanish moss into a swamp apparently as deserted as the day before. No rhythmic chorus of cicadas. No squirrels scuttling up the trees. No dragonflies skimming the still surface of the channel. Even August's constant escort had been reduced to a meager two or three butterflies.

Once they were outside their leafy overnight haven, the unusual heat was immediately apparent. August found himself missing the shade provided by the ample brim of his beekeeper's helmet. But he certainly didn't miss its netting. Without it, the world was unobscured, clear and vivid. Indeed, despite the heat—or perhaps because of it—the day was a particularly vibrant one, the swamp aglow with color, like an image crafted in stained glass. Holding a rope for support, August leaned out over the water and gazed up.

He realized then, with a puzzled frown, that the skies were completely empty; even the birds were gone now.

"You reckon we truly have a chance of catching up with this Professor Leech and your pirate zombie?" Madame Marvell interrupted the boy's reverie. "They left two whole days ago."

"We will soon have a big advantage," said August, glancing back at the young pilot. "*We* will have a map! Leech does not."

"Would he need a map? Why, he has the pirate himself, the very party who hid away the treasure that he's looking for."

"You don't know Jacques LeSalt yet," said August. "But I promise you, he's about as useful as the rest of them." He indicated Claudette, who had been dragging her severed limb in the water and managed to snare a disgruntled crab, which, much to the zombie's alarm, was advancing up her other arm.

"Would you trust *her* as a navigator?" asked August.

"But you say," Marvell persisted, "that whoever has this so-called Zombie Stone can order the undead around and make them do whatever they want them to."

"Well, I know for sure that my ancestor Orfeo DuPont used the stone to control the zombies in his theatrical act, DuPont's Dance of the Dead. It was some kind of grisly ballet. Not so fun, I reckon, for the zombies."

"So you think the Zombie Stone can bring back Jacques LeSalt's memory?"

"I don't rightly know," admitted August. "Perhaps. But look, even if it did and we are too late, even if Leech has found the treasure before we get to the map, what do you think he might do with the zombie once he has no more use for him?"

"You say this professor person sent you off to some remote place, hoping you'd run into a dangerous gang of smugglers?"

August nodded.

"You say your aunt Orchid calls him a . . . a what . . . an oily charlatan? You say he lied about knowing where your sculpture was at and took a zombie that doesn't belong to him?"

"Yep."

"He doesn't sound like a very honorable person."

"I don't believe him to be an honorable person."

"Then after getting what he wants, he would probably just leave the zombie behind."

"That's what I figured," said August bleakly. "He'll leave the pirate to wander the swamp, lost and alone forever. So even if Leech is long gone, taking the Zombie Stone with him, we have to rescue Jacques LeSalt."

Marvell nodded her agreement, and August turned again to face their direction of travel. Something below him caught his eye. The muddy water was suddenly busy with dark forms.

Fish.

Hundreds of them. No, thousands. All swimming in the same direction.

Then they were leaping from the water, and the channel, which seconds before had been a greenish brown mirror, was splashing and alive.

"Are you seeing this?" August asked Marvell.

Before she could answer, large ripples emerged between the trunks of the swamp trees, rolling across the surface of the waterway, following the same course as the fish beneath them. The surges kept coming, and they grew larger. Soon they were less like ripples and more like small waves. The houseboat began to rock.

And then August saw the clouds.

Above the treetops to the south, a great band of churning cumulus the color of pencil lead was advancing at a dramatic pace.

A violent gust of salty wind smacked the boy in the face and

caused the vessel to lurch sideways. A billion leaves were suddenly thrashing, and after the hot stillness, the sound was loud and aggressive.

August spun, alarmed, to Marvell.

"It's a storm," she confirmed. Her expression was grim.

"Big?"

"Yes."

"How far are we from Locust Hole?"

"It's two hours ahead of us."

"Gardner's Island?"

"Two and a half hours behind us. We better turn on the TV."

There was no reception. The small screen of Marvell's old-fashioned mustard-colored television displayed only hissing gray static. As the girl fiddled hurriedly with the plastic knobs and crooked rabbit-ear antenna, the daylight was abruptly extinguished, and the previously sunny, tranquil swamp outside disappeared beneath torrential rain.

The roar of it on the cabin's corrugated tin roof was almost deafening.

Drenched zombies stumbled into the interior, eyes swiveling in confusion.

A distorted voice momentarily pierced the television's harsh crackle.

"You just had it!" cried August. "Go back!"

Marvell gingerly adjusted the bent telescoping antenna. A fuzzy image appeared and disappeared. The girl persisted.

"Wait! There it is!"

". . . only yesterday," the television presenter was saying, "fully formed over the Pirates' Sea."

The man had a chunky chiseled jaw, thick wavy gray hair, and very dark, serious eyebrows.

"Again, if you're just joining us," he said in an urgent sort of way, "I am meteorologist Gunther Thunder, coming to you from CCTV's studios with the gravest of hurricane warnings. Yes, folks, I said hurricane. Yes, it is only March. Yes, it has formed unbelievably quickly. But, folks, you best believe that the first cyclone of the season is upon us."

Gunther Thunder had a small pointer, which he moved around the digital map superimposed on a wall behind him.

"Hurricane Augusta is right up here as we speak, just off the coast. She's not that large by hurricane standards, only ninety miles wide. But, folks, she is a *monster* in strength, packing powerful sustained winds and pushing a deadly storm surge before her.

"Augusta is headed due north, fast, and will make landfall along the south coast within two or three hours. The Withering Wetlands, Hurricane County, and Lost Souls' Swamp are directly in her path and will sustain a DIRECT HIT!"

Gunther actually yelled these last words.

"If you are anywhere near those areas and can hear me, get to high ground *immediately*. Or at the very least, take shelter. *Immediately!*

"And please, *please,* folks, get off the water!

"*Immediately!*"

CHAPTER 4

THE HURRICANE

Much of the vast forested wetland known as Lost Souls' Swamp was circled by a broad, open stretch of water known as Lost Souls' Lake. This lengthy lagoon was contained by a man-made embankment, which protected the low, flood-prone fields and homes of Hurricane County from capricious tides and storm surges.

By the time Madame Marvell's houseboat emerged from Channel Fifteen B, Lost Souls' Lake was a roiling cauldron, whipped into a frenzy by the fierce, howling gale. Overhead, looming black-purple clouds swirled, although they and everything else were obscured by the dense, driving sheets of rain.

"There's the embankment," Madame Marvell yelled over

the stormy din, pointing to a low gray blur a quarter mile away. "We'll be more protected over there."

But beyond the cypress trees, on the open waters of the lake, there was no protection. The rickety houseboat slammed up and down on wind-whipped waves like an orange crate strapped to a bucking bronco. The furnishings and contents of the cabin—including the zombies—were tossed and thrown around like laundry in a washing machine. And they enjoyed little shelter from the elements, for Marvell required that both front and back doors be open in order to navigate.

August's butterflies had been blown clean away, and the boy himself clung for dear life to the straining ropes that secured the cabin to the pontoon as large pieces of debris—mostly branches—hurtled through the air around him. An entire palm tree—uprooted, perhaps, from some Pepperville yard—smashed directly into the wall beside him with such force that for a second the boy lost his grip and very nearly wound up in the lake.

Twenty minutes of this bone-jarring progress delivered the travelers into the lee of the embankment. The high, grassy mound might have been mistaken for a product of nature had it not been for its uniform shape and size, stretching long and straight as it did for miles and miles like a mighty, thick wall (which, essentially, it was).

The thing blocked some of the wind's violence, and up close

to it, the environment was marginally less hellish. But the structure also served to illustrate how dramatically the water level was rising, for the trees that grew at its base were half submerged, and the dirty waves splashing around their trunks were like a thick soup of objects churned from the lake floor: shoes, patio umbrellas, bicycle wheels, and massive dark, slimy shapes that might represent the remains of some long-ago sunken vessel. A large wooden plaque, the sort of nameplate that might have been attached to such a pleasure craft, bore the ironic words "Lady Luck."

"It's the storm surge!" August yelled back to Madame Marvell.

August had learned all about storm surges from an episode of *Word or Number?,* one of the game shows on his aunt Hydrangea's list of tolerable, butterfly-free television viewing that had furnished much of the boy's education.

"Winds this strong," August loudly explained, "force the ocean beneath them down and out. All that pushed-away water coming onshore is what causes the flooding."

"I've been living on the water," hollered Marvell, a little defensively, "for long as I can remember. I know what a storm surge is. Did *you* know that when the swamp rises to dangerous levels, they close the floodgates at the entrance of Black River to protect Pepperville and New Madrid and the rest of Hurricane County?"

August had *not* known that. It didn't sound good.

"So if the floodgates are closed, how will we get in?"

"We won't. We'll be stuck out here when the worst of the storm hits."

"And . . ."

"And we won't stand a chance!"

"How far now?"

"Not far."

Ahead of them, the seemingly endless embankment was at last interrupted by a broad opening. The houseboat soon swung sharply through it to the right and into a narrow channel clearly designed to permit passage from Lost Souls' Swamp all the way out to the Pirates' Sea.

August was immediately overwhelmed by a sense of his own insignificance.

Two or so miles ahead of them, the arrow-straight outlet disappeared into a vast expanse of angry gray nothingness. It was impossible to tell where the clouds ended and the ocean began, the horizon lost to a watery blur of driving rain and screaming wind.

Toward them out of this thunderous gloom rolled great pale bands that August knew must represent colossal waves overwhelming the normally grassy, bird-filled plains of the Withering Wetlands. At any moment, the first of them might clear the shallow marshes and surge up the channel.

"The gates!" cried Madame Marvell, swinging the vessel to starboard.

August felt a nauseating wave of fear.

Ahead of them lay the high form of the outlet's embankment and, set within it, the floodgates marking the entrance to Black River. They were a modest affair compared to those of Pirates' Pier Lock, but they might as well have been the portal to Mount Olympus . . . for they were closed.

The houseboat's outboard motor screamed, attempting to hold its own against the gale that would have propelled the craft back toward the swamp. The first brine-scented ocean wave coursed up the waterway, causing the houseboat to rise and fall several feet. It was followed by another, and another, each larger than the first, and they battered the small vessel against the rusty barrier to Black River.

Water sloshed across the deck and through the cabin, carrying off blankets and small objects. The rope to which August clung snapped, and the boy swung back helplessly across the aft deck, crashing into Little Prince Itty-Bitty, the smallest of the zombies. One of the surviving oil drums suddenly broke free, shot over the roof, and was lost forever. The balding showgirl, Sad Celeste, let out a wail as her leg was swallowed up by a gap opening between two of the boards forming the craft's deck.

"It's breaking apart!" howled Madame Marvell.

August looked up at the embankment. Could they jump?

Or swim? But the waves were too treacherous. The gale was too powerful. The bank was too steep. They'd never make it.

But suddenly, above him, August noticed a figure. Dimly through the storm he saw a reflective vest—official-looking, like that of an engineer—and long hair almost standing on end in the wind.

"Hey!" yelled August. "Down here!"

But the woman was engrossed in securing some mighty iron gear, the sort of machinery that might represent the controls of a floodgate.

"Hey!" he screamed, this time joined by Marvell. But their voices were small compared to that of Hurricane Augusta.

"She'll never hear us," wailed August.

"If only," he thought, "we could roar like Jacques LeSalt when he spies something he thinks is treasure."

The boy's eyes fell upon his zombies clutching one another in a lurching, slithering unit, loosely braced in the cabin doorway.

He slid across the boards and grabbed at whoever and whatever he could to secure himself to the undead huddle. He pointed at the swirling upright hair on top of the embankment. He lifted his chin and howled at the top of his voice.

Zombie eyes swiveled. Slack jaws drooled.

There was confusion.

"Come on, guys," he urged. "Marvell, you too. Like this."

The living children bellowed again, and Claudette offered up a brief croak.

"Good job, Claudette," cried August encouragingly. "Celeste, Itty-Bitty, other lady, you can do it, I know you can."

The eyes swiveled less. August sensed some comprehension.

Sure enough, the next effort was a joint one, although the result was raspy, dry-throated, and lacking in gusto.

"Again! Louder!"

Another attempt.

"Better. Now louder!"

And then it happened. The zombies, displaying some enthusiasm now, joined their voices to create a truly horrifying sound, the kind of sound that might cause a person to have nightmares. The kind of sound that pierces even the howling of a hurricane.

The engineer heard it.

Clutching her heart in fright and horror, she turned and looked down.

Her eyes bulged at the sight beneath her: a ragtag group of kids and oddballs clinging desperately to some rudimentary roped-together craft on the open waters of the outlet, the whole affair smashing against the floodgates, apparently on the verge of disintegration.

"Oh, my saints!" she bellowed. "What the devil are you doing out there?"

"Open the gates!" yelled August.

The engineer looked down at the channel, then behind her at Black River.

"The water in the outlet is already higher than the river!" she yelled. "You'll have to head back into the swamp."

"We have nowhere to shelter. Our boat is breaking apart. The storm's getting worse."

The engineer studied the horizon. It was a terrifying sight. She glanced back at the houseboat and its unusual and desperate crew.

"Oh, my saints!" she repeated. "All right, all right. Y'all best hang on real tight now, you hear?"

The woman turned a key, jabbed at some buttons, and heaved on the great gearwheel. A muffled metallic grinding from somewhere below produced a space between the iron gates. The houseboat was immediately vacuumed against them as water rushed fiercely beneath the vessel, coursing away from the outlet and through the widening aperture. The oil drums scraped, the ropes groaned, the boards creaked plaintively. August feared the pressure might cause the whole thing to simply implode.

But suddenly the opening widened enough to accommodate the houseboat, and the craft surged violently forward and downward a couple of feet, borne upon a crest of water that carried it a hundred yards up Black River.

By the time August had regained his footing and stood to

wave his thanks, the embankment, the engineer, and the closing gates were scarcely visible shadows in the driving rain.

* * *

Although lower than the waters outside the floodgates and more protected, Black River itself had risen considerably, submerging gardens and flooding structures near the riverbank, thus appearing much wider.

The surrounding vegetation acted as something of a windbreak, but any benefits were countered by the fact that the gale was rapidly worsening. August and Marvell were frequently forced to dodge all manner of airborne debris that on occasion clipped the houseboat (and the less agile zombies): roof tiles, rocking chairs, large sections of ripped-apart fencing.

Marvell steered a wide zigzag, navigating past the great forms of fallen trees that littered the river like drunken giants. Indeed, August almost missed the opening to Locust Hole's canal, obscured as it was by a tortured tangle of roots and branches.

But finally the houseboat scraped and scratched its way to safe harbor.

The canal behind August's home had also deepened and widened, overwhelming the old ruined gazebo so that Marvell was able to use its crooked frame as a mooring to secure the houseboat.

August leaped into knee-high water and urged the zombies

to follow him. The storm was now so powerful that it was difficult to remain upright, and its sound was terrible: the roaring wind, the thrash of leaves, the desperate creak of tree limbs, the crashing and smashing of large things colliding with one another.

The boy shoved and dragged his lurching companions toward the kitchen door of Locust Hole, where a pale face peered out with wide, fearful eyes. As he lifted his hand to greet Hydrangea, August heard an ugly splintering crack, a sound so deafening that it distinguished itself from the surrounding cacophony.

"Look out!" yelled Madame Marvell.

August whipped around, but it was too late.

All the boy saw was something massive and dark and leafy rushing upon him. There was an impact on his front, then another on his back as it met the ground. And then there was a great weight upon him, pinning his limbs, crushing his ribs, forcing the air from his lungs. Twigs were scratching his forehead, oak leaves obscuring his vision.

And there was water, rising around August's ears, and then his chin, and then his cheeks, and it was sloshing into his mouth and filling his nostrils.

CHAPTER 5

THE WALL OF THE EYE

"August!" screamed a voice filled with terror—Hydrangea's voice. *"August!"*

August spit out the water filling his mouth. He snorted and choked as more surged up his nose. He desperately tried to raise his head, but was completely immobilized by the massive branch on top of him.

Cracking, snapping, rustling. Light appeared, and then his aunt's petrified face. Seen from below, her skin looked looser, older. It was drenched with rain or tears or both, strands of vaguely colored hair plastered in snaking clumps across her cheeks.

"Where *is* your helmet, you foolish child?" cried the lady.

August saw her fists now, frantically wrenching twigs and

smaller limbs from the space above him until there was room enough to insert both arms. Surprisingly strong hands lifted August's head from the water. He was sputtering and coughing, but at least he could breathe.

Hydrangea's head turned, and she shrieked orders at the top of her lungs.

"You take the end! No, not you. Great-Aunt Claudette, August says you're uncommonly strong. And you, over there! All together now. HEAVE!"

Instantly, August felt light as a feather, almost as if he were rising into the air, the curious consequence of being relieved of such a heavy weight. And the oak branch was gone, replaced by rain and wind and expressions of concern.

"Ow!" he cried, for suddenly his brain was registering pain in his right shoulder and left knee. But before he could dwell on it, one arm was hoisted over Hydrangea's shoulders, the other over Claudette's, and half walking, half carried, he was stumbling over the broken tiles of Locust Hole's kitchen.

It took the combined weight of Hydrangea, Marvell, and Claudette to close the door. They dragged the kitchen table in front of it, just to be safe.

And suddenly, for the first time in several hours, August was not being battered by wind and rain. The storm howled outside, and the door rattled noisily against the table. But the noise of the typhoon was muffled, the kitchen air still and welcome.

The group stood silent, dripping, stunned, chests heaving.

August stared at his aunt. Her voluminous ball gown was limp and tattered. Her arms bore a pattern of fresh scratches. Her battered pink tiara dangled loosely from a tangled mass of matted hair.

"Aunt Hydrangea," said the boy, with great wonder. "You went outside!"

* * *

August was reclining on the fainting couch in Locust Hole's sparsely furnished parlor.

"You went outside," he said again, "to help *me*!"

With trembling hands, Hydrangea was dabbing the nasty scrape on August's shoulder with a lacy handkerchief soaked in bourbon.

"Oof!" protested August.

"I know, sugar, it stings." The lady placed the boy's hand over the dressing. "You hold that there now."

She turned her nervous attention to the bloody knee revealed by the tear in August's pants.

"You went outside," repeated August.

Hydrangea nodded without looking up.

"You are all I have," she said simply. "You are . . . everything."

The lady glanced at her nephew and smiled weakly.

"You saved my life, ma'am," said August. "I might have drowned."

"Fiddlesticks! Had I not been present, I do not doubt that your most devoted admirer, Great-Aunt Claudette here, would have come to the rescue."

"Perhaps," said August. "But it was you."

"I hope I've prepared everything correctly," said Madame Marvell, placing a laden tray on the overturned fruit crate that served as a table. "There's fresh tea, sugar, hot sauce, and . . ."

"And I have the bourbon right here," said Hydrangea. "Thank you, sugar."

As Marvell poured steaming liquid from the teapot, a screeching gust of wind struck the house like a school bus, jolting the structure to its foundations. Locust Hole's old timbers groaned and creaked in protest. On the other side of the foyer, the plastic bucket chandelier in the dining room swung back and forth. Hurtling debris peppered the exterior walls with a violent sound like machine-gun fire.

"I wonder at Mr. LaPoste's absence," said Hydrangea, shakily dispensing bourbon into her teacup. "He assured me of his return today. I do hope he is unharmed."

"There are fallen trees everywhere, ma'am," August reassured her. "The roads are likely blocked. Who knows if even the iron bridge has survived?"

He pressed his palms to the sides of his head.

"You know, my ears feel strange. Like they're all stuffed with cotton or something."

"It's an effect, sugar, of the changing air pressure," said Hydrangea, standing and pacing, desperately twisting her handkerchief between white-knuckled fists. "The wall of the hurricane's eye must be upon us; it is, I fear, the most ferocious part of the storm."

To prove her point, the double front doors began to bang savagely in their frame, as if a monster were attempting to rip them from their hinges. Outside, Hurricane Augusta's voice rose to a deafening roar. There was a ripping, tearing-off sound from somewhere above, part of the roof, perhaps. A handful of bricks noisily crashed down the chimney and tumbled from the fireplace. Immediately over their heads, in August's garret bedroom, there was a brutal crash.

Hydrangea screamed, then stifled her cries with her hands.

August reached up as she passed, gently grabbed her arm, and pulled her down to sit beside him. Marvell handed her the cup of fortified tea. It rattled in its saucer.

"I don't believe," said August calmly, attempting to redirect his fragile aunt's attention, "you've been formally introduced to my new friends."

Her eyes flitted around skittishly, but Hydrangea—ever the gentlewoman—smiled politely.

"No," she said. "I observe that some of them have much in common with Great-Aunt Claudette."

"In that . . . they are zombies?" suggested August.

"Quite so."

"These are three of Orfeo DuPont's performers from his theater act, DuPont's Dance of the Dead."

"Ah!" said Hydrangea, graciously bowing her head to the little prince, the showgirl, and the half-faced lady in turn. "An interesting line of work," she observed.

The typhoon screeched, and Hydrangea glanced fearfully at the boarded-up windows.

"And *this*," said August quickly, "is Madame Marvell."

"Yes," said Hydrangea, struggling to remain focused. "The unofficial tenant of our canal?"

Madame Marvell flushed.

"Oh, fret not, sugar," Hydrangea assured the girl. "I could hardly demand any rent from a barefoot child. Madame Marvell, you say. Why does that sound so familiar?" Hydrangea bit her lip, musing, momentarily forgetting the cyclone. "Why, I believe my sister and I once had our fortunes read by a Madame Marvell when we were girls. And now I come to think of it, I do believe she lived on a houseboat!"

"That'd be my mawmaw," explained Marvell. "She raised me. I miss her."

Hydrangea's expression became tender.

"Well, from what I recall, sugar, she was a most delightful lady."

"She read your fortune?" Madame Marvell was suddenly and unusually shy. "What did she say?"

"I remember it well," Hydrangea chuckled, "for it was so intriguing. She said that the DuPont family treasure would bring me great fortune." She gazed down at the large black hole in the parlor floor, then up and around at the ruinous interior. "I'm afraid, sugar, that was one prediction that could not have been more wrong."

The woman tensed abruptly.

"My Lord," she said, "do you hear that?"

There was a new, distinctive sound.

It was not the high-pitched squeal of wind, or the complaint of straining joists, or the staccato *pop, pop, pop* of debris striking walls.

It was a deep and ominous rumble. Like that of an earthquake.

Indeed, Locust Hole was trembling in its entirety, as if it rested on the tracks ahead of an approaching freight train.

The earthy, bass-filled boom grew deeper and louder. The tremble grew to a shake. August watched the floorboards bouncing. Displaced dust tumbled from cracks in the ceiling. The hot sauce bottle toppled over, and framed family photographs clattered from the mantel.

"What *is* that?" said August.

Hydrangea shot up, with a stricken expression of realization and horror.

"My God," she whispered. "The embankment!"

All eyes turned sharply toward the foyer, in the direction of Lost Souls' Lake.

But before anyone could make a move, the far dining room wall exploded, and a towering deluge of dense mud engulfed everything.

CHAPTER 6

LADY LUCK

As he awoke, August became aware of the cushion beneath his cheek, threadbare but soft. The other surfaces that cradled him, however, were hard and rigid. He awkwardly pulled himself into a seated position on the spindly wooden settee in Locust Hole's kitchen.

"Ouch!" he mumbled. He was stiff and achy, and there was a dull throbbing in his shoulder and knee, although not painful enough to suggest any serious injury.

Birdsong filled the morning air. Clear golden sunlight streamed through the window of the kitchen door, illuminating the pile of cushions and towels where Hydrangea and Marvell had passed the night. And it was cooler, less oppressive.

The storm was over.

At the boy's feet, Claudette lay on the broken floor tiles, gently sucking the thumb of her detached limb, her eyes upon him, waiting.

As his senses returned, August had a feeling of agitation and unease. But it was not his own. Rather, it crept into his being from somewhere outside. He glanced up to find Little Prince Itty-Bitty, Sad Celeste, and the half-faced lady huddled near the stove, and he knew with certainty that they were the source.

He was picking up on the zombies' vague, blurry emotions, just as he had in the music room on Funeral Street when his cousin Beauregard suggested they be abandoned in the swamp.

Why?

August wasn't sure, but it felt oddly natural.

"Don't you fret now," he said reassuringly to the shabby, swaying creatures. "The hurricane has passed. Why, just look at that beautiful day out there."

But the zombies remained jittery, Claudette included. They shuffled nervously behind him as August made his way into the foyer. His aunt and Madame Marvell were there, helplessly observing the wreckage.

A mountain of stinking mud filled the space, blocking the staircase and any access to the upper floor. The dark avalanche extended into the parlor, where it had smothered the feet of the fainting couch. It rose from there across the foyer and into the dining room, whose ceiling remained but whose northern wall did not. The bedroom that had lain beyond this, Hydrangea's, was gone. In the gaping space above the mudslide, August could see puffy clouds and the breach in the embankment at the end of the lane, terrifying in its scale.

As he watched, a tiny yellow leaf fluttered from the blue skies into the dining room. Hydrangea shrieked, for the leaf was a butterfly.

"We are invaded!" she screamed, fleeing. The kitchen door slammed shut behind her.

"Take a look at this," said Madame Marvell, pointing.

Protruding from the mud was a large carved nameplate. The words on it were partly concealed, but August knew what they said, for he had seen them before.

"Lady Luck."

Why did that name sound familiar?

There were other vaguely identifiable, rotted objects that might represent the sad fragments of a long-ago shipwreck: tremendous splintered planks, a cast-iron pillar, an old-fashioned toilet, half of a scorched life preserver.

August puffed out his cheeks and exhaled. The enormity of the disaster left him speechless. How would they fix all this? How *could* they fix all this? The prospect felt overwhelming. Impossible.

"We best take a look at the state of things outside," he said quietly.

Although the mud mountain was slightly less mountainous by the front door, the entrance would have been unpassable if not for Claudette's powerful assistance. It took her just a few minutes, using her dismembered arm as a shovel, to clear sufficient mud to permit August, Marvell, and the zombies to exit.

The northern end of the porch was lost to the brown mountain. The rest of it was surprisingly intact, although Hurricane Augusta had dispensed—no doubt early on—with the netting that had been installed to proof the place against butterfly invasion.

But beyond that lay catastrophe.

"My seedlings!" whispered August, his spirit crushed by dismay.

"You can always plant more," suggested Marvell weakly.

Claudette hovered close, drooling with an air of sympathy on August's arm.

The boy slowly shook his head.

"I salvaged the seeds," he said, "from the only descendants of my ancestor's plant. They were withering, scarcely hanging on for dear life in the back field, the field that yesterday was lost to the storm surge.

"They won't have survived that.

"Our pepper plants are done for.

"And so, I suppose, is DuPont's Peppy Pepper Sauce."

Observing the boy's bleak expression, Marvell felt her eyes

grow hot and wet. But Marvell never cried. She stared ahead instead.

Before them, where once there had been an Italian garden, pepper seedlings, an old picket fence, and the lane beyond, there now loomed a massive black, slime-coated form, wider than Locust Hole itself. It might once have been taller too, but the structure was slumped, contorted, and ragged. Yet in places one could still discern familiar elements: colonnaded decks, collapsed smokestacks, a large paddle wheel.

This was the vast broken, dilapidated carcass of a riverboat.

"The *Lady Luck*," said August. "Not so lucky now, I reckon."

Marvell whispered something indecipherable in his ear.

"What did you say?"

"I didn't say anything," said Marvell.

Whisper, whisper.

August stiffened.

"Did you hear that?"

"Hear what?" asked Marvell.

But the zombies—who had followed the boy outside—had heard it. They remained restless, shifting and grunting with increasing agitation.

"Shhh!" hissed August. "Listen!"

The zombies quieted down as best they could.

August stood like stone, his senses on alert. He could smell the dank, sweet odor of the shipwreck's rotting timbers. He could hear the tiny *slurp, slurp* of tadpoles wriggling through the great dark puddles that the flood had left behind.

Sunlight penetrated the boy's curly hair to warm his scalp. The splintered porch seemed to press itself against his feet. Or was gravity pressing him into the porch? Could he feel a distant throb, perhaps the very heartbeat of the earth?

Whisper, whisper.

August was visited by a familiar dizziness—a sense of vertigo—and grabbed a post to support himself.

"Are you all right?" asked Marvell.

Whisper, whisper.

August knew those whispers. They tickled his ears, or possibly just his mind, when a Go-Between was close, when a magical object like Professor Leech's Oraculum or the Zombie Stone was used to open a door to a nearby place where restless spirits lingered so they might be heard.

Whisper, whisper.

They were louder now, laced with murmurings verging on the comprehensible, sounds that were almost words. And then, fuzzy and echoing, but unmistakable, August heard it.

"Help me!"

The boy's head swam. What was happening? He knew that the dead were close; he could hear them. But how? The Zombie Stone was miles away, somewhere in Lost Souls' Swamp.

And that voice, no vague whisper but a plaintive, urgent plea for help.

Could someone—a living someone—somehow be trapped in that treacherous, unstable wreckage, a victim of the embankment breach or a refugee from the storm who had sought shelter?

"Help me!" It was loud. Distinct. Desperate.

August cautiously descended the porch steps.

"Where are you?" he cried.

"August," hissed Marvell, "what are you—"

The boy held up a palm to cut her off and listened.

Silence.

"Hello?" called August. "Are you there? I can help you!"

More silence.

But then a movement in the vessel's bow caught August's eye. Was that . . . an elbow?

It was.

A jerking, spindly, nightmarish figure, black with sludge and scum, was clambering from the wreckage. Where its eyes should have been were soulless empty sockets.

August stumbled backward at the alarming sight, colliding with Claudette, who had hurriedly followed him and now growled defensively.

"Oh, no!" he said quietly, his heart sinking. "Not another one."

"August," cried Marvell, "the stern!"

A second skeletal form was emerging.

And a third appeared on the upper deck. A fourth on the lower.

Suddenly the entire muddy, misshapen mass seemed to come alive: a writhing, glistening anthill of scrawny, sharply angled limbs and scores of wasted, bony bodies extricating themselves from the wreckage, all wheezing and hissing and growling in the most unpleasant and unsettling manner.

August, it seemed, had somehow, someway, managed to awaken not one, not two, but an entire horde of zombies.

CHAPTER 7

THE HORDE

The horde stood gathered, swaying placidly and dripping, before the boy with the butterflies.

Having clearly spent many years moldering in the silt of a swampy lake bed, they were, all of them, little more than slime-coated skeletons. They had lost their skin, their faces, and in some cases their hair, and they all wore a coating of weeds and muck, which lent them a somewhat uniform appearance. Yet many were identifiable, at least to some degree, by the tattered remains of their costume.

One sported an important-looking peaked cap and a coat whose brass buttons glinted through the mire: an officer, perhaps, or even the captain. Another wore a flat cap, suspenders, and a shredded bandanna: the humble garb of a laborer. He reminded August of men he'd seen in grainy old-timey pictures shoveling coal into the furnace of a steam engine. Yet another wore the unmistakable (though sadly deflated) mushroom-shaped hat of a chef.

Many others were dressed in the stiff collars, kid gloves, fancy jewels, and general finery of the well-to-do, surely the passengers of this ill-fated craft.

"Twenty-six . . ." August was counting them, slowly moving an extended finger across the motley group. "Twenty-seven, twenty-eight. Twenty-eight zombies!" he cried, grabbing his hair in his fists. "Twenty-eight *more* zombies. With the five I already have, that's thirty-three.

"I don't understand. *How* is this happening? There's not a Go-Between in sight."

"Well, apart from Delfine, of course," observed Madame Marvell.

August looked at the girl sharply.

"That old cloth doll of yours?"

"Remember?" said Marvell. "I told you she helps me talk to my mawmaw in the forever place."

"Delfine?" August frowned. "Has your doll ever made a zombie before?"

Marvell laughed.

"Not even a tiny bit," she said. "I just hold her close and get all sleepy-like and think of my mawmaw, and if I wait long enough, I can hear her voice. Not in the real live world, I reckon, but from somewhere inside of my own self. You know?"

August did know.

"But she *is* a Go-Between," he mused aloud. "That might explain . . . all of them!" He nodded at the unsavory congregation before them.

Marvell followed his gaze with a skeptical look.

But August wore an expression of revelation. Had the answer to his problems perhaps been hiding in plain sight all along?

"I've been so focused on the Zombie Stone," he murmured, "but all this time there's been an alternative right under my nose. Marvell," he said as he turned to the girl in excitement, "if Delfine is a Go-Between, can't she help to *un*make these zombies?"

"Oh, no. No, she can't, I reckon."

"But whyever not? She probably helped to make them!"

"That may be so, or it may not. But in any event, I don't know where Delfine is at."

August looked puzzled.

"But you just said she's someplace nearby."

"She's nearby, all right, I just don't know where exactly. She was surely bouncing around the cabin when we plunged through the floodgates yesterday. But everything was all wind and rain and chaos. When I went looking for her this morning, my old Delfine was gone. She's likely wound up in the canal somewhere, or maybe even Black River."

August abruptly sat his backside on the porch steps with a thud and a loud, frustrated "UGH!"

He slammed the railing with the side of his fist.

"*Whenever* I get close," he lamented fretfully, "everything goes all cattywampus. What, I ask you, am I going to do with thirty-three zombies? Where should I put them? Will I *ever* get to show up to my own life?"

"I'll surely miss conversing with my mawmaw," said Marvell quietly.

August winced with shame.

He had thought only of how the rag doll's loss might affect him, not this strange, untamed, yet unexpectedly helpful child.

"I'm sorry about that, Marvell," he said, looking up at the girl.

She nodded and sighed; she had not held his words against him.

"Don't you fret now, August. We'll find that stone and fix your zombie problem."

He smiled gratefully.

"It was already a mighty challenging situation," he said, glancing resentfully at Orfeo's zombies.

Something was amiss.

The young woman known as Sad Celeste was oddly alert. Her crooked gait was less crooked. Her constant self-pitying sniffle had dried up. Her vague gaze was less vague; indeed, she was peering with a flattened palm above her eyes into the shambling horde of shipwrecked zombies.

"Celeste?" said August.

Suddenly, with a coarse, guttural wail, Celeste lunged past the children on the steps into the static, grimy throng of ship-wrecked zombies. She was shoving them aside with Claudette-like strength, sending them stumbling into one another and falling in every direction.

She came to an abrupt halt.

Celeste was standing before a tall zombie whose garb was that of a dapper gentleman: a broad-brimmed hat and a three-piece suit of some once-light-colored linen, a silk pocket square and the droopy remnants of a flower in his lapel. In his lifetime, he might even have been described as a dandy.

Then Celeste was yelling at him. Well, as much as a zombie *can* yell. She was emitting a frightful racket similar to the sound of a broken vacuum cleaner, but in it was the unmistakable sound of fury. And it was clearly directed at the startled zombie before her.

He responded in kind; his tone, however, was gentler, almost apologetic.

More fast, harsh screeching came out of Celeste.

The dandy held up his skeletal hands in a gesture of explanation.

Celeste promptly swung her arm back and slapped the man across what had once been his cheek. Bone clattered unpleasantly against bone.

"The *Lady Luck*!" cried August in sudden realization. "I knew it sounded familiar. Do you remember, Claudette? Cyril Saint-Cyr told us Celeste's story, that she believed herself abandoned by her sweetheart, but in truth he had perished on a gambling ship that sank: the *Lady Luck*!

"What was the fellow's name? It was a double-'B' kind of thing. Barnard Balloon? Batiste Bagatelle? Batiste something, I reckon. Baguette? That's it! Batiste Baguette.

"That zombie is Batiste Baguette!"

Sad Celeste, wailing piteously, was now battering her fists against the remains of Batiste Baguette's linen vest as the confused zombie attempted ineffectually to defend himself.

"Stop!" cried August, leaping up and splashing across the muddy shallows and through the befuddled crowd. "Celeste, stop! You don't know what happened. It was a terrible misunderstanding."

He grabbed the distraught lady's wrist bones, and as she attempted to break free, he grabbed Batiste Baguette's arm for support.

August was suddenly flooded with emotion, intense and raw. He felt frustration and sorrow and anger. Simultaneously he felt resentment and distress. The rush of conflicting sensations was almost overpowering.

But again the boy recognized that these feelings were not his own; they were the zombies'. He was somehow tapping into

them, experiencing them as one might experience the emotions of characters in a book or a movie—as an outsider.

August rubbed his temples and bowed his head, trying to clear it of these intrusive feelings. And there beneath him, reflected in the black pools of floodwater, was an extraordinary scene. He saw himself, of course, with a bobbing coronet of butterflies and flanked by two figures . . . but the figures were not zombies.

Rather, one was the lovely young woman whose portrait he had seen on his tour of Croissant City's Sad Celeste House. The other was a well-dressed young man with a dashing mustache and lovesick eyes. The garments and hair of both rippled and wafted about them as if they inhabited some breezy place with little gravity.

In the real world, Sad Celeste grunted. In the dreamy, weightless other world, reflection Celeste was more articulate. She murmured sorrowfully, but August heard her words as distinctly as those that had cried out for help.

"Forsaken," she said.

Zombie Batiste Baguette groaned a throaty response. But reflection Batiste spoke quite clearly.

"Love," he said.

This phenomenon was not new to August. It presented exactly as it had before with Claudette's image, in water and glass.

He understood it now.

How it occurred he did not know, but in their reflections, he was seeing the zombies' souls.

August swept his eyes across the sodden, puddled ground around him. Sure enough, reflected there were dozens of people, fully fleshed and lucid and as distinct from one another as the living are.

All appeared to drift on the same floaty, ethereal plane. All were muttering and mumbling, producing a babble similar to the whispering with which August was familiar, but louder and more distinct. Indeed, if he listened closely, August could distinguish words and phrases within the soft cacophony.

"Why me?"

"Must find it."

"Revenge!"

None spoke in full sentences, or at length, but as if in a daze, focused on one important thing.

"Pearls!" And there was the familiar reflection of Claudette. The devoted zombie was, as ever, drooling by his side.

"Forsaken," said Celeste.

"Love," said Batiste.

August focused his attention on the most immediate drama: the quarreling lovers.

"He did not forsake you, Celeste." August was unsure whether to address the flushed woman in the puddle below or the ragged thing before him, so he switched his attention between the two. "The *Lady Luck* ran out of luck," he explained, recounting the vessel's history as it had been told to him by Cyril Saint-Cyr. "Her engine exploded, and she sank with all on board. There were no survivors."

"Forsaken," mumbled reflection Celeste, though with less conviction.

"No," said August, gently squeezing the zombie's brittle wrist. "His ship sank. I swear, it's true. He loves you. Tell her, Batiste." August nudged the zombie's chest.

"Love," said Batiste.

Stiffly, like a jointed marionette manipulated by a puppeteer (more elegantly in his reflection), Batiste Baguette dropped to one knee. He fumbled in his coat pocket (again, less awkwardly in his reflection) and retrieved a small oval box.

The container was presented on an outheld palm, its lid opened to reveal a small mound of putrid sludge. After a little jiggling and scraping, the gleam of a jeweled ring appeared.

"You see?" said August. "He must have been planning to propose on his return. He had the ring and everything."

Reflection Celeste let out a delighted squeal (the zombie, a tortured squawk) and covered her face. Batiste Baguette opened his arms and gathered his sweetheart into them. The couple kissed and embraced as only people in love who have been separated for a century can.

And August sensed something entirely new . . . and strange.

It was a sort of clunking click, like an old brass key turning in a lock, followed by the sensation of rising, like a balloon escaping from a child's fist.

It was a release, and a departure.

August gasped in wonder, for the sorry-looking couple before him had been replaced by vibrant, living forms. No, not exactly replaced. The zombies remained, but only as hollow-eyed shadows flickering somewhere beneath the vivid, shimmering beings.

Sad Celeste held up the fourth finger of her left hand to display her new engagement ring. She held it high and turned around slightly so that all might see.

She and Batiste smiled at August, then at one another, and clasping hands, they rose four or five feet into the air before gently evaporating like swamp mist.

The physical bodies that they left behind, the corpses that had walked the earth as the undead—the zombies—promptly collapsed at August's feet in an unsavory pile of bones, leathery skin, and filthy, tattered rags.

Sad Celeste and Batiste Baguette were gone.

CHAPTER 8

WHERE TO STORE YOUR ZOMBIES

"You say you could see their souls?" asked Madame Marvell. She was high on a precarious-looking ladder, hammering nails into netting to secure it to the lintel above the opening to the dining room.

August looked up and nodded. He was laboring beside Claudette, who was passing him rocks to use as weights to pin the bottom of the mesh fabric to the foothills of the mud mountain.

"Mm-hmm," he confirmed. "They looked, I reckon, like they did the day they died."

"But why can't *I* see them?" asked Marvell, a little resentfully. "That sounds real interesting. Why are you the only one who gets to experience it?"

"I don't rightly know," said August, truthfully.

"And these souls, you say, just dissolve in the air like steam?"

"It sounds peculiar, I know."

"Watching those zombies just collapse into a pile of old bones was peculiar enough. Where do you reckon they went?"

"I'm not sure," admitted August. "But I got the feeling they knew where they were going, like they were headed somewhere in particular."

"*Why* do you think they went?"

August paused, rock in hand, thinking.

"Do you remember our talk with the Admiral at Gardner's Island?"

"Of course I do; it was only a few days ago."

"It was? So much has happened since then, it feels longer. The Admiral reckoned that zombies were the remains of folks whose spirits lingered somewhere near this world. So near, in fact, that a Go-Between could be used to drag them back into it and reanimate their corpses."

"I remember."

"She said that these souls hang around," continued August, "because they die with unfinished business, without finding what they had to find, saying what they had to say, or doing what they had to do.

"So maybe if they wind up finding, saying, or doing whatever they wanted to, if they finally achieve this longed-for thing, maybe they can move on.

"Celeste's soul, the Celeste I could see in reflection, she kept repeating this one word, 'forsaken.' And Batiste, he kept saying 'love,' over and over. And I could feel their emotions. Celeste was so hurt and angry. I reckon she's been hanging around just to deliver that slap. Batiste was crazy mad in love; I think he's been waiting to offer up that ring."

"For a hundred years."

"Unfinished business," said August. "Finally finished. I reckon they had nothing left to keep them here."

"So they left."

August nodded.

"Have you secured the breach, sugars?" Hydrangea's muffled voice came from behind the kitchen door.

August and Marvell exchanged a smile.

"We've replaced the screening around the porch, ma'am," August reassured her, "and installed some in here too. The house is again butterfly-free."

The lady appeared cautiously in the foyer.

"You see," said Marvell from the ladder. She tugged at the netting, testing its relationship to the nails that fastened it to the lintel. "Quite secure."

"Thank you, sugars," said Hydrangea.

But her wan smile faded and her shoulders drooped as she gazed at the ruins of her dining room, bedroom, and beyond, to the ruptured embankment at the end of the lane.

"Oh my, our lovely Locust Hole," she said bleakly.

Her words and manner lacked the shrill melodrama to which Hydrangea was inclined, so August knew that the lady's dismay was deep and real. She pressed a handkerchief to her face and began to sway, as if the will to stand were draining out of her. August scrambled to her assistance (he was sharply reminded of his own bruises as he did so) and guided her across the mud to safety on the parlor fainting couch, where she plopped down beside Little Prince Itty-Bitty and the half-faced lady.

When he gently pried his aunt's fists from her face, he found it grim and haggard.

"We'll fix it, Aunt Hydrangea," said August, his own voice thick. "Not today, perhaps, and not tomorrow. But someday. The DuPonts built this house. It's my inheritance, you've always told me that. And I'll restore it. I'm nearly full-grown, and I'll find a way. I swear I will."

"You are growing up quick," admitted Hydrangea sadly, stroking her nephew's curls. "But not quick enough, I fear, for Pelican State Bank." She chewed her lower lip. "They are call-ing in our debt, August. If we cannot pay at least an installment by the end of June, they will foreclose. In three months, Locust Hole will be lost to the DuPonts forever, and you and I, sugar, will have no roof over our heads."

"You can stay with me," said Marvell, scuttling down the mud into the parlor and wiping her palms on her overalls. "But

I doubt there's room for three in my cabin. And I surely don't have the space for all of *them*."

She nodded at the large black hole in the parlor floor, where from the damp basement below, the riverboat zombies stared (as much as one can stare without eyes) at the boy above them, their skulls swiveling to follow his every move.

"Is there really not," sighed Hydrangea, "somewhere *else* we could store all your new zombies?"

"I can't think of anywhere better," admitted August. "We're lucky, I reckon, to have such a large cellar. They seem quite content down there. I expect it reminds them of their rotting shipwreck."

"We ourselves," muttered Hydrangea, "might soon be sheltering in that rotting shipwreck if we can't pay the bank."

August considered the grisly congregation below.

"The Zombie Stone," he said thoughtfully.

"The DuPont treasure, yes," said Hydrangea. "I know, sugar; you must find it to solve your rapidly growing zombie problem."

"Didn't you say, ma'am, that a specimen of Cadaverite so large was worth a king's ransom?"

"Oh, it must be priceless, sugar."

"So of greater value than our mortgage with Pelican State Bank?"

Hydrangea was silent, absorbing her nephew's train of thought.

"A means," she muttered, "to kill two birds with one stone."

August nodded.

"In this case," he said, "a literal stone. Aunt Orchid wants to get her hands on that thing real bad."

Hydrangea snorted.

"Always has to have the best," she spat. "Always has to have the most expensive. It's always about the money with my sister."

"I'm not so sure," said August. "There's something about Aunt Orchid's interest in that stone that seems almost obsessive, even for a serious collector. But whatever her motive, I bet she'd be willing to pay for it. A king's ransom maybe.

"The Zombie Stone could solve our money problems *and* get rid of all these zombies."

"But are you sure, child," asked Hydrangea, "that you *need* the thing for that? Madame Marvell here tells me that you have already managed to dispatch two of these wretched creatures without this—how do you describe it?—this Go-Between."

August, hands on hips, paced around the basement hole.

"I don't think I did anything," he said. "It seems"—he glanced at Marvell—"there might well be a Go-Between around here someplace, by the name of Delfine. But nowhere I can get at it. The only thing that can help us now is the Zombie Stone."

He faced his aunt.

"Aunt Hydrangea, I have learned that the undertaker, Mr. Goodnight, recently discovered an ancient map, a map that might well reveal the location of Jacques LeSalt's famous treasure."

"Why yes! Yes, he did. I'm surprised that such small-town gossip made it to Croissant City so quickly."

"Well, Jacques LeSalt is a famous figure," observed August. "I reckon he's known of far beyond these parts. I believe, ma'am, that the man who now has the Zombie Stone is headed for that treasure."

"But how would this man know where to look for it, sugar?"

"He has a guide of his own, ma'am. Well, a sort of guide. Perhaps not such a reliable one. But the map will tell us where they are headed. It's our only hope of tracking down the stone. Do you have any idea who has the map now? If I beg them ever so nicely, perhaps they'll let me take a look at it?"

"Why, there's no need for begging, sugar," Hydrangea assured her nephew. "The entire collection of Uranus Goodnight's antique maps is now in the care of the Pepperville Public Library!"

CHAPTER 9

DO ZOMBIES CHEW GUM?

A weary-eyed store clerk approached the glass door of Mont-fort's Mercantile, flipped the sign inside from "Closed" to "Open," and turned the latch. An old-fashioned brass bell jangled as August, Marvell, and Claudette entered the unlit store.

"We're open for emergency supplies only," announced the young man, retreating unhurriedly behind the counter and swiping at some light switches.

"You got any rope?" asked Marvell.

"'Course we got rope," said the youth. "We got thin rope, thick rope, nylon, jute. What you need it for?"

"For repairing my home," said Marvell.

"For fixing a shed to a pontoon," added August, seeing the clerk's blank expression.

"We need some nails too," said Marvell. "Four-inch. And some duct tape."

"And bubbles," added August. "If you have them. I think Hydrangea will have enough for now," he said to Marvell in a lower register. "But with quite so many zombies, we're going to need a lot more."

As the youth gathered the supplies necessary to repair a small, storm-battered houseboat (and bubbles), August asked, "Can you tell me where the Pepperville Public Library is?"

"Continue on up Main Street," said the clerk without looking around, "to Our Lady of Prompt Succor. Just past the church, turn left. The library's a hundred yards or so past the corner. But I doubt Mrs. Motts will have it open yet. Everyone's still cleaning up. Not many people working today, I reckon. Well, aside from those Hollywood folks."

August was intrigued.

"Hollywood folks?"

The clerk glanced up and nodded toward the street outside.

"They're filming some TV show out there. If you're headed for the library, you'll pass them, all right."

* * *

Laden with lumpy grocery bags, the children splashed their way up Pepperville's Main Street, picking their way around massive palm fronds, jagged branches, and slender fluted lampposts, all felled by Hurricane Augusta.

The small town on a sleepy bend of Black River had survived the sudden violent tempest, but not without injury.

The storm surge had not fully retreated, and structures on the riverbank remained flooded. The large window of Jean-Claude's Cafeteria had been shattered by a street sign, most of which remained inside the restaurant. The wooden two-story gallery fronting Black River Tattoo had been crushed by a toppled power pole. The Cinema Athénaïs bore a ragged black gash in its roof, and the only sign of the turquoise shutters that had graced the storefront of Flowers by Fleur was their tortured hinges.

At a point just south of Grosbeak's General Store & Soda Shop, Main Street was blockaded by folding A-frame barriers and signs reading "Closed Set." Beyond the blockade lay a dense, bustling jumble of tents, trailers, and technical-looking apparatus: floodlights on tall stands, articulated arms on wheeled carts, and rumbling generators. People were rushing about in all directions, clearing up storm debris, moving equipment, and barking orders.

The only access to this busy makeshift village (and indeed, to anything beyond it) was guarded by a man dressed much like a police officer, who, judging by his silver mustache, was considerably older than most. His yellow vest was embellished with reflective letters that read "Security."

"Excuse me, Officer," said August, preparing to ask how his party should make their way to the public library.

"Now those," observed the security guard, pointing at the butterflies circling August's head, "are some fine props. Ain't it just amazing what these young tech types can do these days? My grandson, he never goes outside. Can't throw a baseball to save his life. Never climbed a tree, far as I know. But by golly, he knows his way around those robot thingies. He cobbled together some contraption that cracks an egg; ain't that something? And another that pulls up his socks. Though why the kid can't crack his own eggs or pull up his own socks, I can't tell you. Still, impressive stuff, those robots."

"These are not robots," said August quietly.

"And would you look at that?" continued the guard, ignoring the boy and turning his attention to Claudette. "Makeup did a great job with you, sugar. You're real convincing. Real gruesome. Best I've seen all day."

The elderly man waggled his fingers theatrically, extended his tongue, and made a rasping sound in his throat, pantomiming the actions of a monster.

He broke off and, grinning amiably, ushered them through an opening in the roadblock.

"Wardrobe's over there." He pointed into the raucous, milling crowd. "Casting's thataway. Y'all hungry? If so, craft services is by Grosbeak's, up yonder. Got some of that fancy Hollywood stuff, dried seaweed and wasabi-coated peas, whatever wasabi might be. But to each their own, I guess. Don't trip over those branches now."

"He thinks," August whispered to Marvell as they entered the film set, "we belong here."

The television production had so overwhelmed Main Street that it was difficult for August to even see the sidewalk as a guide. But in the near distance, above the commotion, rose the bell tower and steeple of a church: Our Lady of Prompt Succor, August concluded. Some of its clapboard siding had been ripped away by the hurricane, but the structure provided a visible target he could head toward.

It was not easy to maintain a straight course, however, with numerous large obstacles to navigate and scores of busy adults to dodge, each, it seemed, with a decided purpose. One man shouldered a serious and heavy-looking camera, a crackly voice buzzing from the walkie-talkie on his belt. Another adjusted an unusually large white umbrella, which was positioned to capture a bright bluish light. Two young women scurried by, arms brimming with leafy, broken, dripping vegetation.

August's gaze fell upon something that made him gasp in horror.

"No!" he hissed. "No, no, *no*!"

"What?" cried Marvell. "What's wrong?"

August pointed.

Beyond his index finger stood a person about whom something was very much amiss.

His complexion was mottled and gray. His hair was matted and coarse. His head hung limply to one side, and his posture was crooked and awkward, like a leggy foal attempting to stand for the first time. A single strand of spittle drooled from the boy's slack blue lips.

"It's a zombie!" observed Marvell.

August shot the girl a look that said, "I KNOW that!"

"Is it from the *Lady Luck*?" asked the girl.

August shook his head.

"Can't be," he whispered. "The shipwrecked zombies have all decomposed to near skeletons. That one still has his lips and nose and eyeballs, and he's not coated in lake scum. He obviously hasn't spent the last century underwater."

August studied the creature more closely. Was there something oddly familiar about him? Perhaps it was just his expression and gait; they were very similar to Claudette's. Not so remarkable, really, as both were zombies.

"So," pressed Marvell, "where *did* he come from?"

"I don't know. Maybe the storm overturned some old tombs?"

This was a logical hypothesis. You have already learned that in this low, flat place to which both land and sea laid claim, the dead were necessarily interred above the ground, in stone coffins shaped like shoeboxes. Such exposed sarcophagi might easily keel over into waterlogged ground or be smashed open by heavy airborne debris.

"Oh, my Lord!" hissed August. "There's another one!"

It was true. A second snaggletoothed undead face had appeared behind the first. The unsavory pair gazed wordlessly at the hubbub around them. Gazed . . . or peered? Were they searching? Searching for August?

"It's like they're obsessed with you," Belladonna Malveau had once observed. "They follow you around like puppy dogs."

It was clear by now to August (and to those that knew him, and probably to you too) that he was some sort of zombie magnet. He didn't know how or why, but he didn't like it. It's not easy to fit in, to make friends—or even to have some privacy in the bathroom—when you have a grunting, foul-smelling, ever-present entourage of the undead.

"I can't acquire any more zombies," August wailed softly, with a desperate glance at Marvell. "It's becoming unbearable. No more. No more."

"Let's get out of here," whispered Marvell, "before they see you."

August nodded and, dragging Claudette with him, backed away.

"Oof!"

The boy collided with the soft but solid form of a person.

He looked around and emitted a small scream, for staring him in the face was yet another zombie, this one with a cavity in her skull exposing the glistening brains within.

But oddly, she was chewing gum.

"Dude!" snapped the zombie in the clear and testy tones of a teenage girl. "Watch where you're going!"

With a reprimanding scowl, she barreled past him and purposefully strode away, waving at the other zombies . . . who waved back.

"It's me!" cried the gum chewer. "*Me,* Amber-Rose! I know! Isn't this just crazy? I hardly recognize myself."

August and Marvell stared openmouthed.

"Do zombies," asked Marvell, "often chew gum?"

"Actors!" said August, with great relief. "They're actors."

"I suppose," pointed out Marvell, "we *are* in the middle of a TV production."

Claudette swiveled her face from the convincingly costumed performers to August and back again, with a distinctly perplexed expression.

"Why are you dawdling around here?" snapped a harried-looking young woman with one finger pressed to her headset. "We need all the extras over by the soda shop, stat!"

"Oh, no, you're mistaken. We're not—"

But August's protests went unheard, for the distracted woman was barking orders into her mouthpiece as she physically propelled the trio toward the destination she had determined for them.

August suddenly found himself surrounded by zombies.

They were chattering and laughing excitedly, tapping on their mobile phones, offering one another breath-freshening mints. They were of all ages, but a disproportionate number were around his own.

Many of the actors were made up not as zombies but as victims of some gruesome attack, with shredded garments and bloody wounds. One elderly woman seemed entirely unaffected—as she nibbled a cookie—by the large bloody bite mark on her neck. There was even a boy who cradled one dismembered arm in his other (though unlike Claudette's, the severed limb was his left). And of course, he had in reality not lost any arms at all; August could see the faint outline of a protrusion where the boy's real limb was tightly bandaged to his ribs. Costuming can only do so much.

"Oh, Lord!" snarled a haughty voice. "Not you and that revolting monster *again*!"

August turned to see the zombie he had first spotted on the set, the one that had seemed oddly familiar. Now—despite the dark circles around the eyes, the jaundiced complexion and blis-tered lips—the expression of disgust on the boy's face was in-stantly recognizable.

"Beauregard?" said August.

"Are you following us?" asked zombie Beauregard's equally zombified companion, who spoke with Langley's voice.

"No," mumbled August, realizing that this was not an un-reasonable assumption and embarrassed that he might be per-ceived as so . . . desperate.

"Then what," sneered Beauregard, "are you doing here?"

"Going to the library." Said aloud, this seemed a rather weak and unlikely explanation, so August quickly added, "What are *you* doing here?"

"We're extras," announced Langley with unconcealed pride. "Extras," he added, as if he were the world's foremost expert, "are the actors that walk around or dine at a table in the back-ground of a movie or a TV show.

"But Mimi is certain that when the director sees me, I'll surely get a speaking part. She says I have a precocious talent, and that she's taking me to England to study Shakespearean drama."

August didn't know a whole lot about an acting career, but he suspected there were usually more steps between grunting on TV and performing in a very long play by a famous playwright.

He glanced at Beauregard, and the look in his cousin's eye revealed that he was thinking much the same.

"Go on now, get lost! Skedaddle!" snapped Beauregard, perhaps resenting the moment of solidarity. "And take your stupid bugs and your rotting relative with you."

Belladonna had recently suggested that her brother's animosity was rooted in jealousy, that he envied August's connection to a fancy old family name. Beauregard certainly made a point of disparaging the DuPonts at every opportunity.

"He has it all," thought August. "He's popular and rich. All that meanness seems like such a terrible waste of time." Suddenly August felt a little sorry for his cousin and, as a result, rather less afraid of him.

"Insulting a zombie," he said, "seems a strange thing when you are all dressed up . . . like a zombie."

Beauregard shrugged dismissively.

"If we wanted parts on the show, we didn't have much choice; the episode's all about zombies. I think it's titled 'A Very Stella Zombie Problem.' "

August froze. He frowned. He must have misheard that.

"Did you say 'A Very *Stella* Zombie Problem'? Is this . . . is this"—he gestured at their surroundings—"a filming of the *Stella Starz* show?"

"Are your ears stuffed with corn or something?" said Beauregard.

August was stunned, and numbly searched for words.

Marvell grabbed his sleeve and shook it, grinning. She too, after all, was a fan of the show.

"Wha . . . how . . . when?" August could scarcely form words.

"That Katz fellow," explained Langley in an offhand manner, "on the float. In the parade. You know, the one with that cat you were so crazy about."

"Officer Claw."

"Yep, that one. When he heard we were from Pepperville, Katz suggested we sign up as extras. Made it sound like a real big deal, to be on *Stella Starz (in Her Own Life)*."

Langley paused.

"Hey! You still in there?"

He snapped his fingers in the air, for August was staring blankly into space, jaw slightly open.

"Is she here?" he was wondering. "Is Stella actually here?"

"Is she here?" he said suddenly, to no one in particular.

"Is who here?" said Beauregard with irritation. "Stella Starz? Darned if I know. Didn't even know who she was till I saw her interviewed after the parade. Had some nice things to say about you, didn't she?"

August dropped his eyes.

"Didn't she call you—now, how'd she put it?—oh yes, a loser!" Beauregard smiled. "And what was the other one? Wasn't it . . . a monster?"

August felt great conflict.

Oh, how he longed to meet the zany girl whose thrilling, action-packed existence had captivated him ever since he had first observed it on Madame Marvell's old mustard-colored television set!

But what if Stella Starz—or rather Margot Morgan Jordan, the actress who played her—were to recognize him from the well-broadcasted image which, although blurred, had identified him (albeit unjustly) as the primary culprit in the Carnival Grand Parade catastrophe?

Would Stella Starz detest August on sight?

The boy could not decide if the prospect of meeting his heroine filled him with giddy excitement or with dark dread.

"No idea if Stella's here," said Langley. "But that kid is on the show, though, right? Over there, at craft services? He'll probably know if the star is around."

August looked in the direction of Langley's pointed finger.

Beneath a pop-up tent with a black canopy and white legs stood a picnic table piled from edge to edge with edible fare. And beyond the cooler chests, beverage dispensers, pitchers, cartons, and jars was a boy.

He was ripping open a Mudd Pie.

"Is that . . . ?" August whispered to Marvell.

She nodded, beaming foolishly.

"It is."

"That's Kevin?"

"That's Kevin," confirmed Marvell. "Stella Starz's best friend!"

CHAPTER 10

IT'S NOT MY LLAMA

"Zombies, over here!" bellowed an authoritative, in-charge sort of voice. "Near the soda shop window, looking hungry! Victims in the doorway, please, ready to start running and screaming."

Zombies, victims, gaffers, grips, and camera crew scurried around, dodging one another as they proceeded to their prescribed stations. August took advantage of the chaos to discreetly steer Marvell and Claudette toward the snack table.

It was laden with an impressive and comprehensive spread: shiny green apples and photo-worthy bananas, snack-sized bags of (as the security guard had promised) salted seaweed, and—for some reason—a pyramid of fancy canned cat food. But most impressive, at least to August's mind, was a large basket brimming with Mudd Pies, individually wrapped.

The boy August knew as Kevin hovered nearby, absently munching on one such Mudd Pie as he scrolled through his phone with his thumb.

He was taller than August had expected.

"Maybe," thought August, "the television screen makes him seem smaller. Or maybe he's grown since the last season was filmed. Or maybe it's a bit of both."

He could hardly believe it. Was this really Kevin? *The* Kevin, Stella Starz's closest ally and confidant. The Kevin who always counseled Stella with caution but inevitably had her back when her zany misadventures went awry. The Kevin whose palm had high-fived Stella's a million times.

It was so difficult to reconcile the vivid, two-dimensional character that August knew so intimately with this living, breathing physical presence, this *stranger* in front of him.

What should he say? How should he introduce himself? Should he address the boy as "sir"?

"Is she here?" blurted Madame Marvell abruptly.

"Huh?" said Kevin, preoccupied with the screen in his hand.

"Is she here?" repeated Marvell more forcefully. "Stella."

August's heart was pounding.

Did he want the answer to be yes or no? He still wasn't sure.

"Ummm." Kevin remained distracted. "Not yet. Flying in on Monday, I think."

"You're so lucky to be her best friend," said August, scarcely knowing where the confidence to utter the words was coming from. And then, realizing that this might sound a little rude, he added, "And of course, she is so lucky that you are hers. Morning and Hugo too. You are all so lucky to have each other.

"To belong."

For the first time, Kevin looked up, right into August's face.

"To *belong?*" he asked dryly, his eyebrows arched. He studied August for a second with a faint smile, as if waiting for a punch line.

But none came.

"If you say so, dude."

Kevin's gaze drifted upward to the butterflies, then to Marvell, and finally to Claudette.

"I think you guys are supposed to be over there," he said, nodding to where the façade of Grosbeak's General Store & Soda Shop was illuminated by startlingly bright lighting.

"We're not actors," explained August.

"Quiet on set, please!" called a voice. And then again, louder, "I SAID QUIET ON SET! ACTION!"

The muffled but gruesome sounds of thirty-odd actors growling like zombies or screaming like zombie victims filled the air.

"We're not actors," repeated August in a whisper.

Kevin frowned, and again his gaze rose.

"So . . . what's with the butterflies?" he asked, also in a low register.

"It's a medical condition," said August.

"What kind of a condition causes *that*?"

"My skin emits a scent that attracts them. I guess it's a bit like flower nectar."

Kevin did not attempt to conceal his skepticism.

"And what's it called, this butterfly-attracting skin condition?"

"I . . . um . . ." August suddenly realized that he did not know. He had simply accepted the explanation offered by his aunt—his only guardian—so long ago. "I'm not sure," he admitted.

"Well, I've never heard of anything like that," said Kevin. "There's eczema, sure; I have that myself. My cousin gets hives. I even watched a show about something called fish odor syndrome—makes people's skin smell like seafood. But I don't believe there's any skin disease that attracts bugs. Who's your doctor?"

"My doctor?"

"Well, who diagnosed you?"

August felt suddenly out of his depth. The conversation had taken an unexpected turn, and was raising questions that he realized he himself should have asked long ago.

His ignorance of his own unique ailment was embarrassing.

"We're not actors," he repeated meekly, in a flustered attempt to change the topic.

"So"—Kevin aimed his chin at Claudette—"she *always* looks like that?"

August nodded.

"Although she usually has both arms," explained August. "You see, there's this alligat . . ."

He trailed off suddenly, for he had spied two flat, familiar faces approaching the craft services tent, faces that instantly explained the presence of so much cat food.

"Oh, no!" he hissed. "I don't think Officer Claw will be at all pleased to see us. There was an incident."

"Claw," responded Kevin, glancing over his shoulder to follow August's gaze, "*is* an incident! He's rarely glad to see anyone. He's just about the worst-tempered animal ever. I tried to pet him a couple of times early on, but he wasn't very . . . receptive."

Kevin paused, studying the singular group of children before him . . . who were not actors.

"Let's get out of here," he suggested, "before the cat arrives. There's someone I'd like you to meet."

* * *

Skirting a grumbling generator, August and his companions followed Kevin up the fold-down metal steps of a long trailer, its side emblazoned with a large logo that read "Celebrity Wagons."

Inside, they found a space not unlike a beauty salon.

Two large swivel chairs faced wall-mounted mirrors surrounded by exposed lightbulbs, and a counter equipped with combs, hair dryers, trays of false eyelashes, and plug-in devices that contained something that looked like bubbling melted wax.

In one of the chairs sat a doe-eyed girl with loose golden braids. A tall, lean man with shiny dark hair that fell to his waist and at least twenty bangles and bracelets on his wrists was applying powder to the girl's cheeks with a large, soft brush.

"Hey, Abigail," said Kevin, hurling himself into a third chair, this one with its back to a sink, intended—August concluded— for the washing of hair. "Hey, Estefan."

"Hey, Griffin," said Abigail and Estefan.

"That girl is Stella's friend Morning," Marvell whispered into August's ear.

August nodded. He recalled from the credits of *Stella Starz (in Her Own Life)* that Kevin and Morning were played by actors whose real names were Griffin and Abigail. He could not for the life of him, however, remember their last names.

"Say hey to some fans," said Kevin (or Griffin) as August's trio filed inside. "The boy has a skin condition that attracts butterflies. But more amazingly, the zombie one does her own makeup."

Estefan and Morning (or Abigail) were observing the newcomers in the mirror before them. August suspected they did not see there the floaty, fresh-faced Claudette that he did, for their jaws dropped and the man spun around instantly, his hair swirling.

"Shut *up!*" he cried, brandishing his makeup brush at Claudette, bangles and bracelets jangling. "Your look is *on point,* girl. This is *waaay* beyond extra."

Claudette emitted a sound somewhere between a gurgle and a giggle: a girgle, you might call it.

"Griffin, honey," continued Estefan, "you need to get this one over to special effects. They'll be straight-up shook, you know it."

As the makeup artist effused, Abigail caught August's eye in the mirror and smiled.

"So you are fans of the show?" she asked kindly.

August glanced at Madame Marvell before both nodded enthusiastically.

"How is your llama?" asked Marvell. "It's a real spitter, ain't it?"

"It *is* a spitter," laughed Abigail. "But thank goodness it's not mine in real life, just on the show."

"So the llama's an actor too?"

"Sure. I think it's part of a special union and everything."

"I have a clown named Kevin," blurted August abruptly, caught up in the gushy giddiness of the moment; he still couldn't quite believe he was conversing with the *Stella Starz* gang.

"A *clown*?" said Griffin.

"Not a real one, of course," said August. "It's a model I made. A skeleton clown. I named him after you. Well, after Kevin, your character."

Griffin swiveled his chair to face Abigail.

"Hey, Abby," he said, grinning broadly. "This kid here— What's your name, anyway? August? Like the month? August here thinks we're all so, *so* lucky to be friends with Stella Starz."

Abigail shot her co-star a sharp glance.

"Leave him alone, Griffin," she warned gently.

"What did that mean?" August wondered. There was some unspoken element to the exchange that lay beyond his understanding.

"*Estefan!*" A flustered-looking young man popped his head through the trailer door. "Are you finished with Abigail yet? They need her for the next take. Oh!" He stopped short on noticing August, Marvell, and Claudette. "What are *you* doing here? You should be out by the soda shop."

"They're not actors!" announced Griffin, Abigail, and Estefan simultaneously.

"The owlish one," said Griffin, "has a bug-attracting skin complaint."

"The dirty one," added Estefan, "well, the *dirtiest* one, applies her own cosmetic effects. Can you believe it?"

The incoming young man's urgency seemed momentarily quelled. He stepped fully into the space to examine the one-armed girl.

He was neither tall nor short, but wiry, with a cropped, sparse beard. Frameless glasses sat atop a rather shiny, rather pointy nose, and his mousy hair was scraped into a small tight knot on the top of his scalp.

"Wow!" he said frankly. "Just . . . *wow!*"

He turned to Estefan, who shrugged with an "I *know,* right?" sort of expression.

"Better than any of that lot out there," observed the new-comer. "No offense, Estefan."

"Oh, none taken," said Estefan. "Seriously, honey," he addressed Claudette, "you need to give me some pointers, because you're a straight-up genius. I'd give my right arm to achieve that effect. But then, I guess you *did!*"

Estefan shrieked with laughter at his own humor.

And again, Claudette girgled.

August had observed on several occasions that his undead great-great-aunt appeared to enjoy this sort of admiring atten-tion.

But to be fair, who doesn't?

"You know what I'm thinking?" said the bespectacled man, hands on hips, biting his lower lip in concentration. He glanced over at the young actors and their makeup artist. "The final scene?"

"When it seems like the zombies are all dead," said Griffin, "and Stella has saved the town?"

"But there's that unexpected ending when that last one just erupts from the grave and grabs Stella by the ankle?" said Abigail.

"Oh, she's *perfect*!" said Estefan.

"We need to get you over to casting," said the other man. "Stat!"

"But," gasped August, "I don't think that will . . ."

"Oh! I'm sorry," said the man, addressing Claudette. "I'm Leaf, by the way, the production assistant. You do *want* to be on a TV show, don't you?"

"I don't think we really have time— Ow!"

Claudette had clubbed August quite deliberately with her spare arm. She seemed to think that they *did* have time.

"Look," said Leaf. "What's your name, kid?"

"It's Claudette," said August.

Leaf seemed to scarcely notice that August was speaking on behalf of the little zombie girl.

"Look, Claudette. Margot's arriving on set Monday. She is literally going to flip over you. *Flip!* Can you come back then? She *has* to get a look at you. Honestly, you're about the most repulsive thing I've ever seen."

"You mean Margot Morgan Jordan?" asked August quietly. "Stella Starz herself? We would meet her?"

"Well, if Claudette here is in the show, of course you'll meet her."

Could it be, wondered August, that Claudette might finally prove to be an asset rather than a liability? Could she actually be the reason that he, a nobody from Locust Hole, might meet the world-famous Stella Starz face to face?

It was an unnerving prospect.

Of course he longed to meet the girl who had shown him that a world of excitement and adventure lay beyond sleepy Locust Hole. The girl who had introduced him to the concept of showing up to one's own life. The girl whose close and familiar group of friends had revealed what it was like to not be lonely.

What it was like to belong.

But as Beauregard had so kindly reminded him, that girl had called August a loser. No, a monster.

But then, the image on the news had been rather blurry. Had he really been so recognizable? Besides, Stella Starz did not know the real August. She didn't know that he would never frighten a cat—or anyone. At least not deliberately.

Might this not be a chance to redeem himself? Maybe if she got to know him, Stella would like him. Maybe she would even high-five him.

August breathed in deeply, put his arm around Claudette's shoulder, and gave her an encouraging jiggle.

"She'll do it!" he declared.

CHAPTER 11

A MAGICAL PLACE

In order to pass Our Lady of Prompt Succor, August, Marvell, and Claudette were forced to circumvent a yellow-taped construction zone, where city workers were toiling to restore a hurricane-felled traffic light.

August walked in a slight daze.

In only three days, he would actually meet Stella Starz. *The* Stella Starz. In three days.

"Can we get to the center of the swamp and back," the boy asked Marvell, "in three days?"

"Well, I've never been there," admitted the girl, "but I reckon so. First things first, though; let's see if the library is even still there."

"And if it's open," added August.

A hundred yards or so farther on, and their first concern was dispelled.

The Pepperville Public Library, although its roof and landscaping were strewn with crape myrtle branches, still stood.

The second concern, however, was realized when the children promptly discovered that the library was indeed closed.

The building was a solid, handsome one, newish but built in an old-fashioned style, with walls of red brick, tall arched windows with tall arched shutters, and a deep portico supported by fat white Greek columns. The entrance was a wide double-door affair with narrow sidelights, in one of which the "Closed" notice was displayed.

August cupped his hands around his face and pressed them to the glass pane above the sign, blocking out any reflections so he might see inside. The space was dark, the only light originating from a single lamp on the reception desk. It had the air of a public place slumbering in the absence of any public.

August was about to turn away when a slight movement caught his eye. A human silhouette passed in front of the reception desk lamp.

Someone was in there.

August knocked on the sidelight. The shadowy figure seemed to be receding. He knocked again, harder, more urgently. The shadowy figure seemed to reverse and advance.

The shadowy figure became a woman, who stopped several feet from the front door. She flapped a hand in August's direction.

"We're closed!" she said, voice muffled by the structure between them but still discernible.

August knocked again.

"We'll be open again Monday, like as not!"

Marvell joined August's side, and they knocked persistently together.

The woman approached the glass and stood close enough that they could all observe each other quite clearly.

She was around Hydrangea's age, guessed August, but big and vivacious rather than limp and harried. She was dressed not in shapeless cardigans and tweeds (like the librarians at Stella Starz's high school, who had turned out to be, successively, a spy and a smuggler) but in a plum-colored velour tracksuit and turquoise sneakers. Her hair was escaping from the curly cloud on top of her head as if it had been styled hastily by someone who had just emerged after a hurricane.

Although August had certainly never met her before, the woman seemed vaguely familiar.

"Are you the librarian, Mrs. Motts?" said August loudly.

"I am Mrs. Motts," confirmed the woman, sweeping a tendril of hair from her face, which promptly fell back into it. "But the library is closed." She tapped the back of the sign below August's nose.

"We were hoping," August persisted, "to see the antique maps that Mr. Goodnight found recently. I heard they were in your care."

"I am sorry," said Mrs. Motts, "but there is still a whole lot of mess up in here, and the staff members are naturally tending to their own repairs and so forth. As I say, we'll be open again next week."

She turned away.

"Mrs. Motts," cried August urgently. "I must tell you how important it is that I see those maps today. Well, just one of them, at any rate: Jacques LeSalt's."

"What could possibly be so important, child, that this can't wait until Monday?"

"I have a small problem, ma'am," explained August, "that is getting larger by the day. My only hope of solving it is to find a runaway professor, and only the map can help me do that."

"A *runaway professor?*"

Octavia Motts's gaze traveled across the three young people with more purpose, as if she were seeing them for the first time, or rather, scrutinizing them. She saw a boy with an owlish head circled by several butterflies. She saw an awkward, crooked girl in a ghoulish Halloween costume, and another with wild hair, a squirrely demeanor, and startlingly naked feet.

"Well, ain't you all stranger than a pig on a bicycle!" she muttered.

The librarian disappeared behind the door. August heard the metallic sound of an opening latch, and suddenly he was inside.

"Get along with you now!" muttered Mrs. Motts, hurriedly shooing butterflies out the door before closing it. "I won't be having any moths eating holes in my books, no sir!"

Although the tall, arched windows had been securely shuttered against the hurricane, the reception desk lamp and a distant "Exit" sign rendered the interior dimly visible. August could see that it was more modern than the building's traditional exterior might suggest, with an office-style dropped ceiling, fluorescent light panels, and a floor of royal blue carpet squares.

Long, freestanding bookcases of blond wood were arranged like ranks of soldiers on either side of the expansive hall, every shelf crammed with books, surely totaling tens of thousands. A glimpse down the little corridors created by the shelving units revealed more books lining the outer walls. A wide, airy central aisle accommodated inviting groups of low seats and rectangular tables furnished with wooden desk chairs and computer monitors.

Not that August had ever owned, or even used, a computer. But Stella Starz did and had, so he knew what they were. He had even seen a couple at large in the world since he had ventured forth from Locust Hole the previous summer.

He understood that the devices might be used to access almost any information one could imagine. Stella and her friends habitually conducted "internet searches," and whatever those were exactly, they usually supplied the knowledge desired almost instantly.

It suddenly dawned on the boy how limited his exposure to the universe had been. The interesting tidbits gleaned from a handful of television game shows—no matter how "educational"—were a drop in the ocean compared to all the information contained in this one room. August itched to scurry off and hunt down a volume about Jacques LeSalt's life, with sumptuous, colorful pictures of pirate ships. He eyed the computer monitors—little portals to the entire sum of human knowledge—eager to search for "butterfly skin conditions" and "how to get rid of unwanted zombies."

The place had a bookish odor and a distinctive atmosphere that was entirely new to August. It was hushed and still, but unlike Locust Hole, it left him feeling not lonely and sad but rather tranquil and welcomed.

He loved it.

He turned to Octavia Motts to tell her so, and found her staring at Madame Marvell's bare feet.

"You are very fortunate, Mrs. Motts," said August, "to spend so much of your time in such a magical place."

The librarian lifted her eyes to his and chuckled.

"Magical, is it? Well, perhaps you should spend more of your own time here, hmm?"

"I would like that. Would I be allowed to read the books?"

"Lord, child, it's a public library," laughed Mrs. Motts. "That's the whole point. You know, if you become a member, you can even take them home. As long as you bring them back, of course."

"Oh, I don't think I could afford any fancy memberships, Mrs. Motts."

"Why, it doesn't cost a nickel, young man."

"You don't say!" The boy beamed.

So did Mrs. Motts, and August felt certain she could not possibly be the sort of person who engaged in espionage or smuggling in her spare time.

"We always love to see a new face around the library," said Mrs. Motts, clearly delighted by August's enthusiasm. "I tell you what, child," she added kindly, "I'll get you a copy of that map you are so eager to see, *if* you fill out an application. Why, then you can spend just about as much time as you've got to spare in this . . . *magical* place. It's a deal? Excellent. I'll fetch a form from the office."

The librarian retreated into the building, pausing at a supporting post to flip a switch. Beyond the farthest bookcases, the top of a doorway was suddenly illuminated by a light in the room beyond (the office, August assumed). Simultaneously, a handful of ceiling lights flickered to life along with those inside a shallow display cabinet near the entry, all presumably wired to the same circuit.

The newly lit glass-fronted case in the nearby foyer was typical of small-town post offices or general stores, with sides of scratched-up wood and mounted on the wall. Predictably, one side was devoted to a collection of local bulletins: handwritten advertisements for help wanted or offered, photocopied flyers promoting school plays and church fêtes, notices of lawnmowers and kittens for sale.

The other side contained a tidier, more deliberate arrangement of objects, images, and uniformly printed information cards, an exhibition of sorts, albeit a very modest one.

August would likely have paid it little attention if something had not caught his eye, an object that he immediately recognized.

"Hey!" he exclaimed. "Will you look at that!"

He drifted toward the cabinet, head tilted, followed by his companions. There, vertically displayed on a little ledge, was a book.

"I own a copy of that book," said August. He spoke with a measure of surprise, for he had very few books, and so it was quite a coincidence that one of them should be featured in an exhibition. The volume was clearly antique, of the hardback variety printed before the invention of dust jackets. Its elaborate embossed and gilded title read *The Capsicum Compendium: A Practical Pocket Guide for the Professional Pepper Planter.*

In the upper regions of the cabinet, a sign identified the subject of this small exhibition as "LouLou Bouquet, Pepperville's Own Premier Pepper Expert."

"Hydrangea," said August, glancing back at Claudette and Marvell, "says that no one has produced a more learned or reliable manual on pepper farming. She says LouLou Bouquet's authority on the subject is absolute. I didn't know she was from Pepperville. But then, I guess we do grow peppers here, so . . ."

August bent forward, peering at the other elements of the exhibition, his curiosity fueled by some small knowledge of its subject matter.

There was a single very smart eggplant-colored glove with tiny buttons that was claimed to have belonged to the local author.

There was a hand-painted botanical illustration, age-stained but beautifully executed, of a pepper plant. The corresponding label identified this as "the specimen brought to these shores from his mother's garden by LouLou Bouquet's father. The unique variety of chili pepper—unknown elsewhere—formed the foundation of a family hot sauce empire, but has been lost to the mists of time."

"Hmm!" grunted August. "My ancestor came to this country with a pepper plant from his mother's garden and founded a hot sauce empire with it."

There was also a marriage certificate.

And when he examined it, August gasped, but not loudly, for he had already guessed there were too many coincidences here for them to be coincidental at all.

Bouquet was the surname of LouLou's husband. The lady had taken it as her own, for she had lived a long time ago, when such things were the norm.

Her maiden name—the surname with which she was born—was DuPont.

"She's your ancestor," observed Madame Marvell.

"I reckon so," said August. "Her father must have been Pierre DuPont. He created DuPont's Peppy Pepper Sauce. I guess his daughter *would* be a pepper expert."

The boy's gaze drifted downward to the final contents of the display case. There was an old photograph, even older and grainier than that of Claudette and her brother Orfeo on the parlor mantel at Locust Hole. The portrait was of LouLou Bouquet.

And August was sure he knew her. He covered the lower half of her face with two fingers. What was left, the upper part, was all too familiar.

If he imagined all the flesh below the lady's nose having decomposed to expose her lower skull and jawbone, if he imagined her teeth chattering excitedly and her eyes bulging and blinking, it was immediately clear that LouLou Bouquet was the only unidentified member of Orfeo's zombie act: the well-dressed half-faced lady currently in the care of August's aunt back at Locust Hole.

CHAPTER 12

THE INCIDENT

"It's not much of an exhibition, I know," said Octavia Motts apologetically, handing August an application form. "But ours is a small-town library; our budget for nonessentials is pretty meager. Most of what you see displayed is on loan from the Bouquet family, descendants of the local personality featured here."

August accepted the form without looking at it.

"It seems, Mrs. Motts," he said with an air of wonder, "that LouLou Bouquet is also an ancestor of mine!"

"You, child, are a Bouquet? As in the Bouquets of New Madrid? Why, my late husband was a distant cousin of theirs, and I don't recall seeing you at any of the family gatherings; I would certainly have remembered that."

August pointed at the mildew-spotted marriage certificate.

"I am a DuPont, ma'am, as was Miz LouLou before her marriage. I think she must be my great-great-great aunt. Or something like that."

The librarian's eyebrows arched, and an "aha!" expression transformed her face.

"*You* are the so-called ghost of Locust Hole," she said, nodding as if to confirm the fact to herself. "The boy long rumored to lurk in the attic of that old place. I had heard that Mr. LaPoste, the mailman, had laid eyes upon you at last. August, is it not?"

August nodded, and the librarian studied him for a moment with gentle curiosity.

"You're Lily's boy, they say. I can see her in you."

"You knew my mother?"

"Not really, child. Not well. She was younger than me. But her older sister was a girlhood friend of mine."

"Orchid?"

"Lord, no!" Octavia Motts rolled her eyes. "She was a handful, that one, I can tell you. No, your aunt *Hydrangea* and I were in the same grade. We were quite close at one time."

The woman paused, her expression part sympathy, part curiosity.

"How is she?" she asked cautiously. "Hydrangea. Is she still . . . so fearful? Has she ventured beyond the walls of Locust Hole?"

August shook his head. The librarian tutted in a sympathetic way.

"Your aunt was never quite the same," she sighed, "after The Incident."

August blinked with a blank expression.

"What incident?"

Octavia Motts glanced at the boy sharply, with a little frown of disbelief.

"You don't *know*?" she said, clearly stunned. "Hydrangea has never shared with you the details of The Incident? Why, everyone was there. Everyone saw it."

"Um, no. I know nothing about . . . *it*."

August suddenly felt very conscious of his ignorance, given that *everyone* else had seen *it*, whatever *it* was.

"The Goodnights were there; why, young Jupiter had just started working at the family funeral parlor. The LaPostes were there too, so proud that their youngest had been accepted into the mail carrier training program. Old Mr. Grosbeak was still alive at the time; he was there.

"The Juneaus and Moreaus were there, the Fontaines and the Fontenettes, the Landrys and the Lacys. Why, I don't think there was a family in Pepperville who didn't attend the pageant that year."

"Pageant?"

August immediately recalled the newspaper clipping he'd

stumbled upon in the carriage house of the Malveaus' Croissant City dwelling and the revelation it contained.

"You mean the Chili Pepper Princess pageant? The one my aunt"—he hesitated—"*Orchid* won?"

Octavia Motts nodded with a heavy sigh.

"And you were there too?" said August. "Like everyone?"

"Well, naturally *I* was there," said Mrs. Motts, "being the prior year's winner."

"Of course!" thought August. "That's why Mrs. Motts looks familiar."

Although older and rather rounder, the woman was still recognizable from her likeness in that yellowed clipping, where she was pictured placing Hydrangea's tiara (which wasn't really Hydrangea's at all) on Orchid's head, as she would have, being the previous title holder.

"But I don't mind telling you," said the librarian in a half whisper, "that it was all I could do not to snatch that bouquet out of Orchid's arms and smash it over her diabolical head. What she did to her sister that night was nothing short of a betrayal!"

"Betrayal?" said August quickly. It was a word of which his aunt Hydrangea was fond, especially in connection with the Malveaus.

Mrs. Motts nodded.

"Hydrangea was robbed of that title, and worse, of the man she loved."

"Loved?"

August was astounded. It can be startling for a young person to be presented with evidence that their elders were once young persons themselves.

"Aunt Hydrangea was in love?"

"Oh, like she'd been shot through the heart by Cupid himself. Although, given the family rivalry and how her father felt about the Malveaus, she shared her feelings for René with no one. Except me." The librarian paused, frowning. "And Orchid."

August scratched his head, struggling to accommodate this glut of astonishing information.

"Aunt Hydrangea," he repeated carefully, to ensure that he had it all straight, "was in love with the man who later married Aunt Orchid, René *Malveau?*"

August was transported to a dusty not-so-long-ago afternoon in the parlor of Locust Hole when his aunt had energetically denounced her sister for marrying into the rival family.

"But Aunt Hydrangea," he confided to Mrs. Motts, "said the Malveaus were the source of all our family's misfortunes. She said their wealth was built on treachery and betrayal. How could she spend so long blaming Aunt Orchid for doing the exact same thing she planned to do herself?"

"I will tell you," said Mrs. Motts simply. "When she discovered that René was home from college and had been invited to be a pageant judge, Hydrangea immediately entered the competition. It was her girlish notion, you see, that this was an opportunity to catch the young man's eye."

"You mean he didn't *know* how she felt?"

"As I said, Hydrangea had told no one but myself and Orchid. And Orchid, it transpired, had an agenda of her own. Even at that young age, Orchid had airs, you know. It was no secret that she had grown, oh, *disenchanted* with her own (admittedly quite eccentric) family.

"The DuPont fortunes were in decline, Locust Hole too. The Malveaus, grand and wealthy, had everything, *were* everything that Orchid wanted to have and be. So . . . she entered the pageant also." The light from the lamp on the reception desk gleamed in Mrs. Motts's bulging eyes. "With sabotage in mind!"

"Sabotage?" interjected Madame Marvell, as enraptured by the strange history as August. "That sounds sinister."

"It was, child, and worse," said Mrs. Motts. "Catastrophe struck during the pageant's talent section. It was supposed to be a simple, charming magic trick, with a wand and a conjurer's top hat—you know, the kind with a secret compartment from where one might withdraw a white rabbit or, in Hydrangea's case, release a handful of butterflies."

"But," protested August, "she's terrified of butterflies."

"It was not *always* so, child. Young René was a student of entomology—that is the branch of zoology devoted to insects;

the library has a nice little section on it. This, I'm sure, inspired the theme of Hydrangea's intended performance.

"She even had her costume trimmed with milkweed so the butterflies—attracted by the nectar-rich flower—might alight upon it, decorating her gown like living jewels. It was a pretty idea to grab René's attention."

The librarian puffed out her cheeks and let out a breath.

"But?" said August and Marvell together. Even Claudette was staring at Mrs. Motts with a sort of glazed fascination.

"But! When Hydrangea waved that wand and proclaimed 'Abracadabra!' it was more than a *handful* of butterflies that erupted forth. Rather, it was a number closer to thirty. And the thirty were followed by fifty. And the fifty by one hundred and fifty.

"Lord, children, within moments the little creatures had swarmed that poor fragrant girl until not one bit of her was visible. And as you know, four or five butterflies make for a lovely thing. Even ten or fifteen or twenty-five are quite tolerable. But one, two hundred bugs (for that is, after all, what they are) with those spidery legs and twitching antennae all over your hair and arms and *face,* well, that is an altogether different matter.

"She panicked, of course. In such circumstances, who would not? Screaming and flapping her arms in distress and terror, Hydrangea staggered around, a whirling, flailing figure lost entirely beneath fluttering wings.

"The horror ended only when (blinded as she was) Hydrangea tripped over the footlights, plunged off the stage, and crashed into the judges' table below. There she lay, a weeping, crumpled pile of taffeta and crushed butterflies . . . at the feet of the dashing René Malveau."

"How mortifying!" said Madame Marvell.

"Poor Aunt Hydrangea," said August.

Claudette made a wet but sympathetic sound.

"After The Incident," continued Mrs. Motts, sighing, "several townsfolk reported having seen Orchid earlier that morning flitting about Black River with a *butterfly* net. But frankly, sugars, it was Orchid's expression in that moment—an expression of pure triumph—that convinced me that she, Hydrangea's own sister, had orchestrated the disaster."

The librarian scoffed bitterly.

"And indeed, her demonic ploy was a success. At least for her. René Malveau cast the deciding vote that secured Orchid's victory that day. She was crowned Miss Chili Pepper Princess, and the two were married faster than two rabbits in a three-legged race."

August nodded wisely.

Suddenly it all made sense.

Hydrangea's resentment of her sister. Her retreat behind the boarded-up windows of Locust Hole, where no butterflies or

betrayals might seek her out. Her distorted attempts to save her nephew from the same anguish.

The boy felt for his fragile guardian as never before, for now he understood her. Hydrangea was broken.

He saw the loneliness in her now.

He had thought he was the only one.

Not that she would be lonely at that very moment, with all those zombies to entertain. August hoped his aunt had not yet exhausted the bottle of bubbles that Claudette had carried in her pocket from Croissant City.

The troubling idea of what might happen if she had run out turned his attention back to the matter at hand.

"Did you manage," he asked Mrs. Motts politely, "to get a copy of Jacques LeSalt's treasure map?"

Octavia Motts produced a piece of paper folded in three, accordion-style.

"Mr. Goodnight's maps are very old and delicate," she explained, "and far too valuable to remain here at a small regional branch. They are to be permanently housed at the Pelican State Library in the capital."

She handed August the folded paper.

"Which is a blow to us, of course. However," she said, inclining slightly and beaming with pride, "I have been assigned the honor of designing a pamphlet to promote the exhibition in which the maps will be the star attraction.

"This is just a copy of my mock-up. But if you unfold it—that's right, turn it over, on the back there—you'll find a facsimile of LeSalt's map.

"You are a lucky young fellow, August, to get a look at this before every amateur treasure hunter in the nation decides to brave the depths of Lost Souls' Swamp in search of that fabled treasure."

August expressed his heartfelt thanks.

"Now!" said Octavia Motts briskly. "A deal's a deal. I'd like a library membership application from you, young man."

August obediently followed the woman to the reception desk.

"Here's a pen," said Mrs. Motts. "You fill out that form while I make a quick phone call."

With a final frowning glance at Marvell's bare feet, the woman headed toward the warmly lit room at the back of the library. August pressed the crusty tip of the ballpoint harder and harder into the paper, attempting to produce a mark. But no ink emerged; the pen had run dry (isn't that always the way?).

The boy headed behind the reception desk to find another.

"I wonder why she had to make a phone call so suddenly," said Madame Marvell. "August? What's the matter?"

"I know who she's calling," said August, lifting a grave face and holding up a printed sheet of paper for his companions to see.

"What is this?" said Marvell, leaning in to study the type by the light of the reception desk lamp.

"'Missing child,'" she read aloud. "'Female. Age between ten and twelve. Small frame. Dark eyes. Light hair. Hates shoes. Find likeness below and report any sightings to the State Department of Child Services.'"

Marvell's gaze dropped to the image beneath the text.

"Oh my!" she gasped quietly.

For, although a little younger and less unkempt, the girl in the picture was clearly Madame Marvell.

PART II

CHAPTER 13

THE LAST ISLAND

"And this, you claim," asked Mr. LaPoste, studying the bottle of bubbles in his hand, "is a means of controlling your . . . guests?"

"Not controlling," explained August, "so much as distracting. In Croissant City, I discovered that bubbles fascinate them. Maybe the drifting, transparent things remind them of the floaty spirit world they come from. Honestly, I don't know why, but they're the only thing I've found that keeps them occupied enough to forget about *me*."

"And you are certain we have enough of these to keep them busy until your return? That is a rather *large* number of zombies in your basement."

"I am *not* certain," admitted August, wincing. "But it was all that Montfort's had. I bought the entire stock. I'm sure you'll be just fine," he added, with forced optimism.

Mr. LaPoste looked skeptical.

"You see," he said, pink nose twitching, "I have devoted my entire career to the science of mail delivery and have had very little experience with the undead. And by 'very little' I mean almost none. And by 'almost none' I mean none."

"One can hardly," protested Hydrangea from the safety of the kitchen doorway, "regard *that* as a personal failing, Mr. La-Poste. Indeed, your presence here is what some might call heroic, rushing as you have to my deliverance."

Mr. LaPoste shot the lady an immensely enthusiastic toothy grin.

"I wish I could have gotten here sooner than this morning, Miz Hydrangea. Came as soon as the roads were cleared, first thing this morning. But I am surely no one's hero."

"Well, sir, you are *my* hero!" Hydrangea flapped her handkerchief at the rabbity man, who blushed. "I don't know how I would manage all those creatures alone, what with August headed into the swamp for Lord knows how long."

"You ready, August?" asked Madame Marvell impatiently. She had been in a "let's get out of here" mood since they had fled the library the previous afternoon.

"I'll be there in a second," said August. "Here, take this and put it somewhere safe. It's a little fragile."

He handed the girl a large blue shoebox, and with a nod, she headed toward the canal, where her houseboat awaited.

August turned to the mailman.

"Thank you for this, Mr. LaPoste," he said sincerely. "Please take care of my aunt."

"Are you certain, sugar," said the lady through the cracked door, "that this expedition is wise after sustaining such injuries as you have?"

"Injuries?" scoffed August. "I have a grazed shoulder, ma'am. And a cut on my knee. And you have bandaged both expertly, thank you."

"Well, won't you at least wear a helmet, sugar? We have another somewhere, I am certain."

"The butterflies don't bother me, ma'am."

The exchange caused August to pause and think.

"What *is* the name of my skin condition, Aunt? Who diagnosed it?"

"Oh, there hasn't been a doctor in this house since you were born, sugar. But you were still in diapers when those things began to drift through open windows to hover around your crib. I drew my own conclusions; what other explanation could there be?"

Hydrangea's expression grew fretful.

"I swear, sugar, it was as if those tiny-winged monsters were coming to claim you. I had to shut them out, I just had to."

August sighed.

"Butterflies are not betrayals, ma'am," he said gently.

Hydrangea, distracted, shifted her dark, watery eyes about.

"Don't fret, ma'am. With Jacques LeSalt's map, I can find the Zombie Stone. And then we'll send these zombies away and save our home.

"And I guess I can see a doctor about the butterflies.

"I promise, Aunt Hydrangea: I'm going to make sure that you never have to be afraid of anything ever again."

* * *

"How's that old pepper barrel working out?" August yelled from the stern.

"Well, it's heavier than an oil drum," Marvell yelled back. She was leaning over the bow, conducting inspections. "And less buoyant. But in a way, it works out better. I did a fine job, I reckon."

It was a self-congratulatory statement but a true one. Marvell had devoted the previous evening to her repairs, and they had resulted in an improved craft.

Although there was one flotation device fewer, the girl had redistributed the remainder to create a vessel more even-keeled than the perilously pitched vessel August had first spied from his garret bedroom. Indeed, it floated practically parallel to the water's surface (although, admittedly, rather closer to it).

The ropes securing the cabin to the platform were new and

taut, the boards that formed the deck abutted tightly, and the roof was neatly patched with bits of bark and rugged canvas.

For his part, August was becoming quite adept at steering the houseboat to compensate for the off-center engine, its position resulting from the partial loss of the rear deck and transom to the jaws of an alligator.

The course August was forced to set, however, was a circuitous one, for the local waterways had been reduced to a tangled obstacle course of wind-tossed branches, fallen trees, and bits of large things ripped up or off or out and tossed around by Hurricane Augusta.

Nonetheless, the travelers had made good progress and after several hours were well inside the swamp.

"Starboard bow, Claudette!" called out August. "Looks like a chicken coop."

With a combination of breaking, kicking, and hurling, the small zombie obediently dispensed with the unpassable obstruction. She was certainly an effective—if unusual—sort of debris-deflecting fender.

Having reviewed and approved her improvements, Madame Marvell rejoined August at the tiller. She was oddly quiet.

"You all right?" asked August.

The girl shrugged.

"Well as can be expected," she replied, "for a wanted fugitive."

August opened his mouth to contradict her, but realized he could not: a wanted fugitive is exactly what she was. He opened it again to say something comforting, but again realized he could not. There was no silver lining to this particular situation.

"It's getting late," he said instead, glancing at the sun. "Are you certain this is Channel Fifteen B? I can hardly tell one place from another with all this storm damage."

"I'm certain," said Marvell. "I've been up and down this way a thousand times. I reckon the entrance to Gardner's Island must be hereabouts."

She stepped to the starboard side of the cabin and, holding on to a rope for support, leaned out to search the riverbank.

"There!" she said, pointing with her free hand.

And in moments, the indicated object slid into August's sight.

Scarcely visible in the reeds and undergrowth, lying now on its side, languished an abandoned "No Entry" sign.

* * *

The hamlet August knew as Gardner's Island was in a shocking state.

The unusual dwellings, constructed primarily of nautical salvage, were gravely battered. Many of the steel hull roofs had been mangled or pried away altogether, exposing pot-bellied stoves, splintered furniture, and tattered draperies within.

The large hand-painted "Gardner's Island" sign that had arched across the jetty hung limp from a single nail.

But despite the extensive damage, the place had an air of optimistic industry, for its mostly ginger-haired, mostly silent residents were busy gathering, sloshing, hammering, and fixing. As one by one they noticed the putter of Marvell's houseboat, they paused in their toil, stood, and turned their freckled faces.

They did not smile. But many tugged at their hat brims or lifted a hand in salutation. It was certainly a warmer welcome than the travelers had received on their first visit. One small girl even came splashing down the partly submerged pier to meet them.

"Gabrielle!" cried August.

She was followed shortly by two indistinguishable boys.

"Gaspard! Gilbert!"

As they seemed always to be together, August was not sure if he would ever need to identify which boy belonged to which name.

"Is the Admiral here?" he asked as Marvell threw a rope to the children. "I have a trade to make that might interest her."

* * *

"You made this yourself?" said the Admiral, peering into August's large blue shoebox.

The loose skin around her wrists jiggled as she reached inside, cast aside some wrapping tissue, and removed an object: a model skeleton.

It stood about sixteen inches tall, its skull crafted from clay molded over a Ping-Pong ball, its bones from coat-hanger wire, all painstakingly wrapped in papier-mâché and sanded to a finish smooth as ivory.

It wore a festive costume fashioned from the satin lining of an old waistcoat and studded with tarnished sequins. Its hat was a solid silver thimble. Its face was painted with particular care.

It was the second-best model that August had ever made.

The Admiral examined the juggling clown through a small magnifying device that she lodged in her eye socket, not unlike a miniature telescope. Simultaneously, a bright pink bubble of gum formed at her bright red lips and popped smartly.

While he waited, August glanced around.

Gabrielle, Gaspard, and Gilbert had delivered the visitors to a rusty structure that had once been the pilot's tower of a working vessel—perhaps a tugboat—but now served as a compact dwelling. It stood upon a shallow rise, the only patch of dry land in sight, the last remaining island of Gardner's Island.

The Admiral's parlor was on the upper deck, in the wheelhouse, which was fitted with windows on all sides, affording it an airy and impressive view.

"Repurposing," announced the Admiral, removing the jeweler's loupe, "is a shamefully underrated talent." She looked up at August with shrewd little eyes. "A talent, sugar, you clearly possess. I admire that."

She smiled and chewed at the same time.

"All right," she said, "there is a deal here to be struck. But I fear you may be disappointed, for the first of your requests I cannot grant. The young zombie's black pearls lie somewhere down there."

August turned in the direction of the woman's plump finger. Beyond a cluster of slender tupelo trunks, protruding from the still, dark water of the lagoon, was the pointy bow of an old sailing. It was fitted with a crooked metal chimney and had once formed the rooftop of the Admiral's handsome office.

August glanced at Claudette and winced in a combination of sympathy and apology.

"Sorry, Claudette," he said. "I realize those pearls must mean a great deal to you; why, you never stop talking about them. But we needed an engine to get the houseboat to Croissant City, and they were all we had to trade."

He turned to the Admiral.

"I'm sorry too about your sunken office, ma'am," he said. "And about the whole village. Do you think things round here can ever get back to normal?"

The Admiral rose from the small table at which she'd been sitting and joined August near the window, swatting butterflies out of the way. Her vivid red lips formed a small, sad smile as she gazed at nothing in particular.

"This time," she said quietly, "I reckon they can. The storm surge is still receding." She brightened and gave the boy a hearty nudge. "Don't you worry about us Gardners. We're resilient folks. Just keep bouncing back. Might as well try to keep a beach ball underwater."

She returned to the table, pineapple earrings dancing merrily.

"How about we get back to our little bargain? You mentioned there were two things you wanted in exchange for this charming fellow here (the thimble really is a clever touch). We have established that I no longer have access to the first of those things. What is the second? Are you in search of a new bee-keeper's helmet?"

"No, ma'am."

August produced the copy of Octavia Motts's pamphlet mock-up, unfolding and smoothing it so the facsimile of Jacques LeSalt's map was visible in full.

"I must find my way, ma'am, to this 'X' marked here."

"The last time we met, sugar, you were on a mission to track down a so-called Go-Between, that you might return this poor creature's restless soul"—she glanced at Claudette—"to where

it belongs. Is your intended journey into Lost Souls' Swamp related to that search?"

August nodded.

"I have reason to believe I can intercept it there, yes," he
said. "Can you tell us how to reach the place indicated? I don't
see any recognizable routes on here."

"Well," said the Admiral, "if this truly is a document created
by Jacques LeSalt, it is two hundred years old, and was drawn
long before the embankments were built and the rivers redi-
rected, and long, *long* before the oil channels were dredged."

She dragged a fingertip across the paper, frowning in thought.

"But what routes are and are not included on the map, sugar,
is of little consequence. This 'X' lies in the densest, remotest, least
traveled part of Lost Souls' Swamp. No man-made canal has *ever*
penetrated so far into the wilderness, and they likely never will."

She tapped the "X" with a fingernail.

"There is only one party," she mused, "that I know of who
has the knowledge necessary to identify this location, a person
who knows the swamp as a child knows their own mother."

"Who is it?" asked August, intrigued.

"A root wizard," said the Admiral, "who goes by the name
of Papa Shadows."

"A wizard," said August, wide eyes even wider, "who per-
forms magic spells and so forth?"

"Some say as much."

"Well," said August. "Can you at least tell us how to find this . . . *root* wizard?"

"Oh my, sugar, for those who dwell beyond Lost Souls' Swamp—dry-landers such as yourself—the way to Papa Shadows is in itself a treacherous journey, one that could easily see a searcher wind up lost for days."

August scratched his head, looking crestfallen.

"However," continued the Admiral, "I find myself unusually attached to your little clown, and a deal is, after all, a deal. I cannot return the pearls, and I can hardly send you off with directions that might put you in danger's way." She paused. "But I can offer you guidance there."

August blinked. He looked at the solidly built woman in the bicorne naval hat, searching for the diplomatic response.

"Um . . . our vessel is not large, ma'am. And I don't reckon you'd find it very comfortable."

"Good Lord, child," laughed the Admiral. "I am hardly proposing that I *myself* should accompany you."

She leaned over toward a large tarnished ship's bell mounted on the wall, grabbed the rope dangling from the clapper, and jerked it back and forth for several seconds to produce a strident, hollow, metallic sound.

"No," continued the Admiral. "I shall furnish you with a guide in the form of one of my young relatives, who is currently obligated to do just as I say."

August heard heavy footsteps on the metal exterior staircase.

"Ah!" said the Admiral. "Here he is. This, sugar, will be your chaperone."

As the door to the wheelhouse opened, August turned to see a familiar face.

It was Beauregard's friend Gaston.

CHAPTER 14

LOST SOULS' SWAMP

August had thought that on his journeys to and from Crois-sant City he had seen Lost Souls' Swamp.

He hadn't. Not really.

Yes, he had skirted its edges on broad, open rivers and lakes. And through narrow, leafy passages branching off the oil channels, he had glimpsed the swamp's gloomy interior. But the impressions with which he was left were similar to those you might have of a village or a lake spotted from a speeding car or train.

But now, as the houseboat ventured down one of those narrow, leafy passages, leaving the sunny Channel Fifteen B behind, August found himself enveloped by a foreign world that was possessed of a terrible, haunting beauty.

The seemingly endless cypress forest that formed Lost Souls' Swamp rose from glassy waters of jade, a color so vivid that it was worthy of Orchid's gemstone collection. Many of the trees were so ancient and mighty, the diameter of their gnarled, moss-smothered trunks might have accommodated Locust Hole's kitchen. They towered upward into a dim, sky-obscuring canopy, and from twisted branches drifted vast swathes of Spanish moss, each the width of theater draperies and so long that their feathery tendrils tickled the water's surface.

The ghostly forms of ibis flitted silently through the distant gloom. Shadowy forms—catfish the size of reef sharks—snaked beneath the houseboat's pontoon. The vessel plowed through undulating rafts of water hyacinth so thick with leaves and purple blooms that the crew was frequently obliged to clear the engine's propeller.

Apart from the occasional splintered tree limb dangling from above, the mysterious watery place showed little sign of Hurricane Augusta's wrath. August guessed that the forest here was so dense that it provided its own protection and had survived nearly unscathed.

The surrounding stillness had an almost sacred quality that did not invite conversation. But after the tumultuous nature of the previous several days, August found it more tranquil than spooky, more soothing than unsettling.

It was Gaston Gardner who, after three wordless hours, finally broke the silence. The boy was sitting on the bow, his bare heels skimming the water as it passed beneath him. He turned his blunt, freckled nose over his sturdy shoulder.

"Hard to port, miz!" he called. "By this here broken trunk."

Madame Marvell, who at that moment was manning the tiller, obediently steered the houseboat into a waterway that was only a foot or so wider than the deck and so overgrown that August might never have spotted it.

"How do you find your way?" he asked. He was perched on the generator, leaning against the cabin and observing Gaston's mass of ginger curls. "How do you even know where we are?"

Gaston pointed at the broken trunk as it glided by on their left, marking the watery junction. Within the woody contours and peeling bark, certainly invisible to anyone who was not looking for it, there was nailed a strange little figure. The poppet was crafted of sticks and coarse fabric, with a tuft of Spanish moss for its hair. It was faceless, however, and strange, and more than a little eerie.

"They mark the way to Papa Shadows's place," said Gaston gravely.

August joined the young Gardner, taking a seat beside him on the front of the craft.

"Who *is* Papa Shadows?" he asked.

"Depends on who you ask," said Gaston, staring straight ahead. "I've come this way with my folks before, but never

actually seen him. I reckon he must be real old, though; been around since before anyone can remember. There's some say that despite that, he looks young and fit. There's some say he's tall. Some say he's short. Some say he's not a he at all but a she. Or both. Or neither. The Admiral says Papa Shadows might be not just one person but more of a position . . . like a job. You know?"

Gaston again directed his voice to the stern.

"Swing to starboard, miz!" he yelled.

And so it was they proceeded, Gaston scanning the surrounding undergrowth for the crude, sinister-looking dolls and their unspoken instructions to turn this way or that, guiding the travelers ever deeper into the swamp.

August occasionally sneaked a curious glance at the boy beside him.

He recalled a look of gratitude on that freckled face, the product of an incident merely five days before, when August had—during some rowdy youthful jousting—helped Gaston thwart Beauregard's overbearing dominance. August and Gaston had shared a brief moment of understanding, an unspoken acknowledgment of what Beauregard was.

August had encountered Gaston only in the role of Beauregard's minion, as part of a seemingly inseparable trio. But now, alone with him for the first time, he found himself considering the boy as a distinct individual. It seemed odd, given his eager participation in the Grand Parade, that Gaston would be missing out on all the Hollywood action involving his cohorts.

"Beauregard and Langley," ventured August, "are extras in the *Stella Starz* show. They're filming an episode in Pepperville. Did you know?"

Gaston nodded without looking at him.

"Uh-huh."

"You wouldn't want to play a zombie on TV?"

"Sounds about all right."

Gaston was not exactly talkative. August sensed that further inquiry might be intrusive, but curiosity got the better of him.

"So why aren't you there," he asked a little shyly, "with your friends?"

Gaston shrugged.

"The Admiral."

"The Admiral?"

"The Admiral. She says to me, 'Gaston, you used to be a nice kind of boy, always bringing me a big ole bass you caught, singing those silly songs of yours, picking water hyacinth for your mama. But lately, son, I see a different boy: always pushing young Gaspard and Gilbert around, saying ugly things to Gabrielle. It ain't her fault that her teeth are taking so long to come in. How come you're not such a nice boy anymore, Gaston? I'm disappointed in you.'"

Gaston twisted around again.

"Port now, miz!" he yelled to Marvell. "See where I'm pointing?"

As the houseboat turned, he reached out, snapped off a passing reed, and popped it in his mouth, where it bounced around as he chewed on it.

"The Admiral's words," he continued, "they made me feel real bad." And then, more quietly, "Because she was right."

"How are you and the Admiral related?" asked August.

"I don't know," admitted Gaston. "I'm not sure we are. But everyone knows she's the boss of Gardner's Island. Tough but fair, that's her. No one wants to disappoint the Admiral."

Gaston snatched the reed from his mouth and cast it away, frowning.

"And now I have."

"Did you really change," asked August, "like the Admiral said?"

Gaston shot August a glance.

"Yes," he sighed. "Yes, I did. And we both know why, I reckon."

"Beauregard?"

Gaston nodded.

"He was cool and all at the beginning. He lives in that big old house and has all this great stuff. You can get kind of overlooked in a place like Gardner's Island when you got a heap of kinfolk. But Beauregard made me feel special, like I belonged."

August nodded, remembering all too well how charming and welcoming his cousin could seem.

"But sometimes he could be mean," continued Gaston. "Not so much early on. But the longer I knew him, the more often he was that way. And sometimes he wanted me to be that way too—never to him, of course, but to other folks. And so sometimes I was, in part so's Beauregard didn't pick on *me*. But in part so's he'd keep on liking me."

Gaston shook his head and stared at his lap.

"I tricked you into coming out of your house," he said regretfully. "I really did think you were a ghost. But then . . . I played catch with her eyeball."

He glanced over at Claudette, who hovered nearby with an attentive expression.

"That wasn't right, and I'm real sorry about it now, miz." He turned to August. "And I reckon I owe you an apology too."

August nodded and reached out an open hand. Gaston took it. They locked eyes and exchanged a small smile.

But the handshake ended abruptly when Gaston snatched his hand away and used it to point.

"Look!" he hissed.

August turned to discover another of the rudely formed twig-and-moss figures, this one rather larger than the others and garbed in trailing sackcloth stained with dark red paint. Or blood.

"We have arrived," said Gaston in hushed tones.

August looked around, mystified.

There was absolutely nothing to distinguish this wild, unin-habited part of the swamp from any other: reeds and moldering tree stumps, thousands of soaring cypress trunks, a muddy bank indicating the presence of some solid ground concealed beneath the tangled undergrowth of ferns and shrubs.

But suddenly August's neck and arms prickled with horror.

There was movement.

One of the cypress trees was slowly and silently splitting in two. Or rather, a smaller section of its trunk was uncurling and fluidly detaching itself from the main, like an octopus emerging from the lair in which it had been camouflaged.

Except it was not an octopus. Or part of a tree.

As it took on a more distinct form, that form was human.

And the great sinuous protrusions spreading from its head were not tentacles or branches.

They were horns.

CHAPTER 15

THE ROOT WIZARD

The creature advanced less by walking or even running than by flickering through the shadowy foliage, disappearing for a millisecond only to materialize again, noiselessly, marginally closer than before.

At least that's the way it appeared.

"Is that . . . ?" said August.

"Papa Shadows." Gaston nodded. "I reckon so. Don't you?"

August did.

He scrambled to his feet and stepped to the edge of the deck. A deep, gravelly growl rumbled near his elbow. Claudette, ever protective, was clearly unsettled by the sinister apparition.

So was August.

"Are you the root wizard," he called out, heart pounding, "Papa Shadows?"

The figure arrived at the water's edge, merely feet away, so suddenly that August stepped backward into Claudette, who grunted reproachfully.

The person was tall and slender and draped in flowing, shapeless robes woven from a coarse stuff that looked much like the Spanish moss that bedecked the swamp around them.

At such close proximity, August could see that the elegantly sinuous horns were formed not of bone but of vegetation: twisted vines, *living* vines, to judge by the leaves sprouting from them. This was a curious thing, given that they could hardly be rooted in the ground.

Slender tendrils from this weird headdress snaked around the head and face of its wearer, and so integrated were they, it was impossible to tell what was plant and what was human, what was vine and what was vein.

All of the creature—horns, robes, face, hands—was of the same color, a drab greenish brown that rendered it virtually in-distinguishable from the surroundings.

Except the eyes.

The eyes were of the same vivid hue as the swamp's green waters, and they glowed within the wizard's muddy complexion with an intensity that made August increasingly uneasy.

"Are you," repeated August, his voice little more than a whisper, "Papa Shadows?"

"I am the possessor of that title," said the figure.

Its thin, moving lips revealed a startlingly pink tongue, and its voice was breathy and rustling, like the breezes that drifted from the swamp through August's garret window on summer nights.

"Who is it," asked Papa Shadows, "that seeks me out?"

"August DuPont," said August simply. "Me."

"You travel with the undead." Papa Shadows lifted a long finger toward Claudette. "It would appear she is in need of repair."

Claudette drew close to August, tightly hugging her dismembered arm with a defensive air.

"You have come with a request," rustled the root wizard. "Only those with a petition ever venture here."

August nodded cautiously.

"Then you best come in."

With a great sweep of his sleeve, Papa Shadows extended a welcoming arm.

August glanced around at the uninhabited wilderness, puzzled.

"Come in . . . where?"

The root wizard retreated, flickering, a few feet and drew back a sheet of Spanish moss to reveal the vast, deeply ridged trunk of a colossal tree. The knotted, tortured bark was cleaved by a narrow vertical opening no more than two feet wide and four feet tall, a natural doorway.

And the portal was illuminated by a greenish light that originated within.

* * *

The cavity inside the tree was large enough to accommodate the whole party.

Madame Marvell and Gaston perched upon a bed-like platform of tangled roots blanketed with thick, soft moss. Both chose to cross their legs rather than leave their feet on the ground, where a five-foot snake—olive green and marked in a pretty diamond pattern—was slithering curiously around.

August and Claudette also eyed the serpent, from stool-sized boulders so ancient that centuries of buttocks had worn their tops into shallow, saddle-shaped curves. The DuPonts were seated near the fire at the center of the room. If one could call it a fire. More accurately, it was a chartreuse flame that danced upon the dirt, produced by no visible fuel and creating no heat.

Despite his (or her) obtrusive headdress (if that's what it was), Papa Shadows moved about the compact space with surprising ease and grace, although everyone else was forced to occasionally duck or dodge to avoid the long, twisted horns.

He (or she) crouched beside a modest arrangement of pots

and cauldrons on the floor, above which a series of shelves had been carved into the dwelling's walls. These were crammed with containers, some formed from glass so mottled as to be virtually opaque, others from dusty organic materials: gourds, animal hides, fish skins.

The wizard's slender, twig-like fingers selected a handful of the vessels and removed their corks and stoppers.

"Let us," said Papa Shadows, "first attend to your damaged companion. You would prefer, I assume, to have *both* arms attached to your torso?" The wizard addressed Claudette, who nodded slowly, cautiously, while spittle oozed from her skewed blue lips.

"Pfsst!" The wizard shooed away the snake, who, while inspecting the proceedings, had upset an open bottle of reddish brown powder.

"Bloodroot," explained Papa Shadows, scooping the spilled contents into a crudely hewn stone bowl, "because the undead have no blood of their own."

He or she glanced at Claudette.

A small, cloudy vial was lifted and emptied.

"Red Fast Luck Oil," the wizard explained. "This is more commonly used to stir a romantic attraction, so let us hope that the little girl's arm and shoulder remain fond of one another. And here a scoop of graveyard dirt to act as cement. And lastly, the most powerful of healing agents"—the wizard paused as a few drops of brilliant, sparkling fluid fell from an upturned bottle—"Dragon Tears!"

The concoction was slowly pulverized with a large bone— perhaps the femur of a cow or wild boar—that had, over years of such use, been smoothed and rounded to a pestle-like form.

"Sir?" said August hesitantly.

Was this person a sir? He wasn't sure, but as Papa Shadows offered no objection to the label, August proceeded as if he was.

"Mr. Shadows, sir? Are you a magician?"

"Some do claim," said the man, with a voice like dried leaves, "that root wizards are workers of magic. Others dismiss us as peddlers of trickery or charlatans. There are even some who condemn us, calling us agents of evil."

Papa Shadows cast a viridian eye briefly upon August.

"But we root wizards call ourselves servants."

"Servants?" August was puzzled. "Who do you serve?"

With long, pointed fingernails, the man gently caressed the deeply grained wall of his dwelling.

"We serve the trees," he whispered. He lifted his eyes. "We serve the skies." He ran his fingertips across the compacted dirt beneath him. "We serve the Earth. We love her like a mother. We respect her and protect her, at least as best we can. And in return, she shares with us her secrets."

The wizard fetched an old cigar box from the uppermost shelf.

"That knowledge—of the universe's hidden wisdom—is what some might call magic."

A creamy, crudely made candle was lifted from the box.

"White," muttered Papa Shadows, "for mending."

A large, intimidating knife appeared from the flowing robes of Spanish moss, and its viciously sharp tip was oh-so-delicately applied to the candle. August leaned in to get a better look at the unfamiliar symbols being carved deep into the wax, and was shortly forced to lean back again when the wizard reached over to light the candle from the yellow-green flame at the center of the room.

After it sputtered to life, the wizard held the burning candle an inch or so below his open palm. August wondered if perhaps because of its source the candle's fire also burned with no heat.

"No soot," announced Shadows, holding up his hand so they all might observe his unmarked palm. "A clean-burning flame is vital to the process."

He tilted the candle so that it might drip into the stone bowl, then tilted the vessel to swirl its contents together. Then, quickly, before the melted wax had time to harden, the wizard dragged a three-foot length of thread through the liquid brew. Thus coated, the fragile fiber was held up to the wizard's eye and passed through a tiny hole in a long, pale fish bone.

Brandishing this alarmingly large fishy needle, Papa Shadows turned to Claudette and held out his other, open hand.

"Come now," he said. "Hand it over." And then, perhaps with the tiniest hint of humor in his voice: "At least you won't require any anesthetic."

Claudette's eyes swiveled wildly toward August.

The boy patted the zombie's shoulder kindly, with an encouraging smile.

"Give him your arm," said August. "Everything will be just fine." Although he had no idea if it would.

With a snap of the wizard's fingers, the olive-green snake slithered into place, coiling itself around Claudette's upper body and cleverly fixing her dismembered arm where the wizard had returned it to its socket.

"That's right, chérie," the wizard addressed the snake as he commenced stitching. "Keep it still like a corpse. My, you do make an excellent clamp."

The serpent flicked its little tongue in appreciation of the praise.

"Tell me," muttered Papa Shadows as the needle swung upward and then downward, "how did this limb come to be disunited from its owner?"

"I don't think," said August, "it was very securely attached in the first place. There were stitches there before, you see. Claudette's arm may have been severed somehow when she died. She fell off our gazebo roof. Into the canal."

"An old propeller, perhaps," suggested Papa Shadows, without looking up from his mending. "Submerged and concealed."

"Possibly," agreed August. "Probably."

"And the more recent cause of separation?"

"You see the tooth marks? There was an incident with an enormous alligator."

Papa Shadows paused.

"Was this alligator," he asked, "by any chance some forty feet long and pure white?"

"It was, sir."

Papa Shadows nodded.

"For many decades," he said, resuming his needlework, "that same beast has lurked in the dark waters of this region. I have sensed a complexity in the creature, and have wondered if it is not, perhaps, possessed by a restless spirit."

"Possessed?" August was not sure what the wizard could mean.

"Those who die before they are ready," explained Papa Shadows, "with unfinished business, are sometimes reluctant to quit this place. They linger in some shadowy place between this realm and the next."

"Restless spirits," said August, recalling Admiral Gardner's theory. "Vulnerable to those who might force them to return to their moldy corpses." He smiled sympathetically at Claudette, who was too absorbed by the snake and the sewing and the wizard to notice.

"But what if," proposed Papa Shadows, "there was no moldy corpse to which such a spirit might return? Flesh and even bone, after all, must someday return to dust. What then?"

August did not know, and said so.

"Such souls, consumed still by the living world and without remains of their own to linger near, might settle themselves in some other creature, simple beasts with limited mental defenses against such invasion. And so they exist together, the human spirit thrilled to revisit the physical sensations of living but subject to the natural instincts and habits of its host."

"And alligators," asked August, "are often, as you called it, *possessed* in this way?"

"Why no, not at all," scoffed the wizard. "Alligators are rather large, unwieldy beings for a gossamer, bodiless ghost to manage. More often the accommodations are provided by feeble, fragile things with little will of their own: minnows, chickadees, deer mice."

Papa Shadows's gaze lifted slowly and deliberately to the space above August's head.

"Butterflies."

"I have a skin condition," muttered August, with less certainty than he had in the past.

The wizard sat back with a quiet air of achievement, and smiled strangely as he wiped off his fish-bone needle.

"How does that feel?" he asked Claudette, dismissing the reptile assistant with a flutter of his fingers.

The zombie lifted her freshly restored arm and dropped it. She extended it forward and then backward. She rotated her shoulder. She wiggled her fingers, then used them to pick her nose.

Overall, she seemed satisfied with the restoration, and August was impressed.

"Have you had much experience, sir," he asked, "with this sort of repair? You see, sir, I have a rather larger zombie problem back home. You seem to know a great deal about restless spirits and where they wind up."

The wizard was cleaning up and putting away the tools of his craft.

"I have," he admitted, "over the years had some dealings with the undead. It would be most curious, after all, to live in Lost Souls' Swamp without encountering the occasional lost soul. But root wizards, child, concern themselves mainly with Earth, and all her children. We attend to the living. For assistance with the *un*dead, one best seek out a specialist in the field—a necromancer."

Papa Shadows suddenly tilted his head quizzically.

"I am realizing," he said thoughtfully, "it can be no coincidence that such a magician should have recently passed this way, mere hours before the storm struck."

August felt the sudden thrill of satisfied expectations.

"A necromancer?" he asked eagerly.

The root wizard nodded.

"So the man described himself. He was a sweaty, bulbous-eyed person, in a hat so flowery that it resembled an azalea bush. He was traveling with an undead vassal: a large, drooling pirate. The so-called necromancer was in possession of an extraordinary stone of uncommon beauty, an amber sphere with a swirl of black at its center.

"It looked for all the world like an alligator's eye."

CHAPTER 16

LITTLE GREEN JOHNNIES

"*That* is the Zombie Stone!" cried August, standing in excitement. "Professor Leech—the man you describe—is using it to compel Jacques LeSalt to reveal the location of his famous treasure."

The root wizard also rose, fluidly, as if attached to a string.

"This professor," he said skeptically, "struck me as an amateur and a fool, with just enough talent to get himself into trouble. Certainly the man I met was not in the business of effectively compelling anyone or anything; the pirate was far from cooperative."

"He has been taken against his will," explained August. "Zombie-napped, you could say."

"And this talisman, this magical object whose very mention lights up your face: You say it is known as the Zombie Stone?"

"That is one of its names, yes, sir. It has been a possession of my family for many years, so we call it the DuPont treasure. Technically, though, it is a specimen of the mineral Cadaverite, which most people know as alligator's eye.

"But besides that, sir, the stone is a Go-Between, a sort of bridge between this world and the spirit world that can be used to communicate with the dead."

"Or," said Papa Shadows quietly, "by a skilled necromancer, to control them. Even to force them back into their physical remains and create . . ."

He made a small, long-fingered gesture toward Claudette.

"Zombies," said August, nodding.

"And your DuPont treasure is responsible for the presence of this young lady?"

"Yes, sir. And others. Quite a few others. A great many, actually. Which is why I must get it back, so I may return Claudette here to where she belongs, and the rest of them too. They have become . . . a problem!"

"I sense," said the root wizard, "you are closing in on the request that brought you here. As I observed, only those with a petition ever venture to my door."

August quickly produced Octavia Motts's pamphlet and knelt on the floor to spread it flat.

"Can you tell us," he said, "how to travel to this 'X' here? Everyone thinks it marks the resting place of Jacques LeSalt's treasure, and they are probably right, as he seems to be leading Professor Leech in that direction. You say they came through here the day before yesterday and have not returned. Maybe we will pass them on their way back."

"And if you do?" asked Papa Shadows.

"I am not sure," admitted August. "But if Professor Leech has located his treasure, he has no more use for the stone or the pirate. Perhaps I can convince him to return them both to me."

"You are," said the root wizard, gazing around the party gravely, "a daring band of searchers. Or perhaps"—he caught August's eye—"merely foolhardy."

He inclined slightly to briefly study the map, nodded, and beckoned the group to follow him outside. Beyond the curtain of Spanish moss that concealed his doorway, thigh-deep in ferns and shrubbery, Papa Shadows raised a twiggy finger and pointed into the dark recesses of the swamp.

"That way," he said simply.

August glanced at Marvell and Gaston with a doubtful expression, then turned back to the root wizard.

"But there is no channel, sir," he protested.

"There is always a channel, child," said Papa Shadows, "if you look closely enough."

The man bent, lifted a thin branch from the ground, and used it to push aside a nearby cluster of palmetto leaves, revealing a dark, glinting ribbon of water beneath. The waterway was scarcely large enough to accommodate Marvell's houseboat, and was visible for merely a couple of yards before disappearing into the gloomy green tangle of vegetation.

That this might represent the entrance to the lair of some mighty reptilian predator was not hard to imagine. And navigating it was not an appealing prospect.

"How will we know the way?" asked Marvell, not unreasonably.

"Just wait!" said the wizard.

Obediently, the young travelers stared silently in the direction of the wizard's open hand.

Suddenly the inky nothingness was brilliantly but briefly pierced by a tiny flicker of light, a light of the same greenish color as the flame that illuminated the wizard's tree dwelling. Moments later there was another, several yards to the left of the first, but slightly longer in duration. The next did not appear for almost a minute, but the *next* just a second or two after that.

"What are those?" asked August.

"Little Green Johnnies," answered Gaston from behind him. "Swamp sprites. It's told they mark a path to hidden riches, but only a dang fool is like to follow them, for they are treacherous critters; they only aim to get you all turned around and so lost in the swamp, you can never find your way out. Then they claim you for their own. They are the whole reason the place is called Lost Souls' Swamp."

August looked to Papa Shadows for confirmation. The wizard nodded.

"In some parts of the world they are known as will-o'-the-wisps. But the stories surrounding them are the stuff of superstition. The Little Green Johnnies have no intentions, good or bad."

Gaston scoffed.

"And they are truly fairies?" asked August, incredulous.

Papa Shadows gave a mossy shrug.

"If it is easier for you to believe, think of the phenomenon as swamp gas."

"Gas?" August was not sure if this *was* more believable. "How can gas lead anyone anywhere?"

"There are those who suggest the stuff conforms to prevailing currents, thus revealing a pattern that might be read. But whether it be gas, swamp sprites, or gas manipulated by swamp sprites, there is no doubt that pirates and fugitives once navigated the deepest regions of the swamp using routes marked by these fickle phantasms. Your Jacques LeSalt was likely no different. Follow the Little Green Johnnies. I do not doubt that they will lead you to your precious 'X.' "

August stared silently into the darkness, waiting for the green flashes, searching for some sequence or order but finding none.

"They seem totally unpredictable," observed August.

"It would take years," agreed Papa Shadows, "to learn their

language. But the levelheaded searcher who proceeds with caution, who observes their route and overcomes the impulse to panic, may safely return."

"Have there been others," asked August, "who have gone this way before? Apart from Professor Leech?"

"A few have braved the journey during my time here."

"And how many of them made it back?"

Papa Shadows looked the boy in the eye.

"None."

* * *

"Got it!" hissed Madame Marvell triumphantly, lassoing a broken cypress trunk with a strand of purple Carnival beads.

At regular intervals, the Little Green Johnnies would become shy, leaving the houseboat to idle and its crew to patiently await the next flickering appearance. To indicate their route and aid their return, Marvell was marking each such juncture with a glittering necklace. ("I have tons of them," she had announced earlier. "They kept falling through the boards of the Croissant City pier when I was moored beneath it.")

It was becoming more difficult, however, to aim the things (a couple had already been lost to the water), for the trees were now so thick that the travelers progressed in near darkness. The only natural light was scattered overhead where gaps in the black forest canopy revealed a dim sunset sky.

Because the swamp was otherwise so very still, the cease-less high-pitched chorus of cicadas and tree frogs was almost deafening. The only other sound was the bubbling putter of the outboard engine, waiting.

"Do you see anything?" whispered Gaston. "It's been three minutes at least."

August did not.

"There!" cried Marvell.

"Where?"

"Two o'clock."

The engine growled, and suddenly the craft was headed toward the latest dancing apparition.

There was no longer any channel or canal to speak of. Rather, the houseboat was proceeding through a swampy wilderness, a boundless maze of water, trunks, and jungled islets, its route determined solely by the Little Green Johnnies.

The patches of orange sky dimmed to rose and purple, then disappeared altogether. The cypresses grew so large and densely packed, it was scarcely possible for the houseboat to pass between them.

August sat at the bow with a small flashlight. It was not so bright that the swamp sprites might go unnoticed. But it provided illumination enough to spot any obstacles with which the vessel might collide.

Here and there the sweeping beam fell upon ominous wreckage, the jagged bony remnants of ill-fated watercraft from long ago. Although the edges were softened by moss and slime, it was clear the vessels had met with brutally violent ends, all splintered and smashed as if crushed between giant jaws.

But suddenly there was something that gave off a dull reflection. The something was not old and mossy, formed of ancient rotting wood, but hard and new and metallic. As it collided gently with the corner of the houseboat's pontoon, August identified the twisted, tortured stern of a small aluminum fishing boat. It was similar to the one in which Professor Leech had made his escape from Croissant City.

Of the bow and cabin there was no sign, but lodged in the wreck's hull was an enormous yellowing tooth, the size of an ice-cream cone.

August tried to grab it, but the thing was too heavy and slipped away. Before he could react, a faint yet distinctive sound silenced him. His ears were suddenly on high alert, listening for any noise beyond the sputtering engine.

He went to where Marvell—in the stern—could see him, and waved his flattened palm across his throat.

"Quiet!" he hissed.

The girl cut the engine to a gentle burble, and the houseboat slowed.

"Listen!" said August quietly. "I heard something."

"Help!"

August's heart sank.

"Not again," he thought. "Surely not more zombies; I just can't . . ."

"Help me!"

"Who *is* that?" said Gaston.

"*You* heard it too?" asked August, greatly relieved.

"Me too," said Marvell. "It came from somewhere up ahead."

"Please, help me!"

The voice was louder, closer, not in the least ghostly, but very human and shrill and filled with a pathetic level of desperation.

"Help! Who goes there? I can hear your engine."

August swiveled the flashlight from left to right, but all it revealed was swamp life and more nautical wreckage.

"There's the cabin," muttered August. "Or at least what's left of it."

"Help me. Up here!"

Marvell killed the engine, and the flashlight's beam swung abruptly upward, illuminating leaves and tree limbs . . . and, perched on a branch, two muddy figures whose shredded clothing and stricken expressions identified them as survivors of a brutal attack.

One of them was an undead pirate.

The other was a baby-faced man in a flowery hat that resembled a sorry-looking azalea bush.

CHAPTER 17

SPANISH GOLD

August lowered the flashlight slightly, and the men above lowered the hands that were shielding their eyes.

"Is that . . . August DuPont?" asked Professor Leech incredulously, his bulbous, pug-like eyes wide with fear and fatigue. "The boy with the butterflies? I thought you . . . I saw the . . . I . . ."

"You thought I'd perished in the wheel of a riverboat," said August flatly.

"Why yes," admitted the professor, who then added placatingly, "which caused me the greatest anguish, I can assure you, that someone so young . . . and all because of our little disagreement."

"You seemed less than concerned about my well-being when

you directed us to Pelican Wharf," observed August, "knowing well that we might run into a dangerous gang of smugglers."

"Phfttt!" Professor Leech flapped away the accusation. "How dangerous, I ask of you, can smugglers of chocolate doubloons be? I hoped they might slow you down a little, is all. I can assure you—August, is it not?—that I am mighty glad of your survival right about now. We were attacked, you must understand, by a great white monster. Came out of nowhere. Enormous it was. Teeth the size of ice-cream cones. And so, so many of them."

The professor paused to swallow and wipe the sweat from his neck.

"Half the boat was gone before we even knew it. I scarcely had time to leap to safety before it came for the rest. I've been stranded here for two days. Two whole days. There was a hurricane, a *hurricane,* I tell you! It is an earthly wonder I still survive. Do you happen to have any water? Perhaps a beignet? Thank the Lord, I am rescued at last."

The babbling, wild-eyed man shifted forward and braced himself, clearly preparing to drop from the branch.

"Not quite so fast, sir," said August, gesturing to Marvell, who, discerning the boy's intention, quickly put the outboard motor into reverse so the deck slipped away from the region below the professor's feet.

"I know, Professor Leech," said August, "that you bought it

fair and square from Galerie Macabre, but I need you to hand over the Zombie Stone. You used it to take an entire zombie that does not belong to you, and I can't risk your doing the same again. Or worse. I will pay you back the price of the sculpture when I can. But in the meantime, the stone and the pirate in return for your rescue. Do we have a deal?"

Somewhere in the back of his mind, August wondered if Admiral Gardner would have been impressed by this negotiation.

The professor's bulbous eyes narrowed, just for a second.

"Now, August," he simpered, with an oily smile, "be reasonable. Without the stone, I lose the pirate. Without the pirate, I lose the treasure. Come now, you're a sensible young man. We'll share the booty, how's that? Who couldn't use a little Spanish gold in their pocket, hmm?"

Spanish gold.

Gleaming. Tantalizing. Priceless.

August thought of the look on Hydrangea's face when she first surveyed the wreckage of Locust Hole after the hurricane. He thought of the guilt and misery in her eyes when she revealed the bank's plans to repossess their home and turn them out.

He thought of the apologies for gumbos without sausage, for étouffées without crawfish, for banana puddings without bananas.

He thought of a tired-looking woman counting the remaining bottles of DuPont's Peppy Pepper Sauce that might be sold and wearily calculating how long the proceeds might support the two surviving DuPonts.

August looked at Madame Marvell.

She shrugged.

He looked at Gaston.

"It's up to you, August."

August looked at Claudette.

The zombie's tongue lolled out of her mouth, and she petted the boy's cheek with dank, dead fingers.

"All right," said August, frowning uncertainly at the flowery-hatted man in the tree. "Everyone gets a share." He indicated his companions. "But I still need the stone."

August did not trust the professor as far as he could throw an undead pirate.

"It is safer, I reckon, if it is in my care." The little smile remained fixed on the professor's soft, round, shiny face. It was the quiet, bitter smile of a cornered viper. "The thing has, in any case," he said steadily, "proved to be less effective since we left Croissant City. Controlling this thick-headed beast"—he nodded at an offended-looking Jacques LeSalt—"was far from easy, a fact that cost us precious time and landed us in that storm."

August said nothing, but pursed his lips, tossed the flashlight to Gaston, and thrust forth his open palms.

Ten feet above, a gloved hand slipped into a boxy purse, and a familiar object was removed.

August's model had not weathered its travels well. The wire stand still survived, twisted and painted to resemble a string dangling from the sphere of Cadaverite that served as a balloon. But of the skeleton boy that had clung to it, only a bony fist and arm remained.

And as the thing sailed through the air toward the house-boat, the mounting glue finally gave out, and the Zombie Stone broke away, its greater heft propelling it toward August as the remains of what had been his finest sculpture dropped into the water.

And suddenly, after so many months, so much drama, so many zombies, the thing for which he had been longing, searching, rested in August's hands.

Orfeo's Cadaverite.

The jaw-dropping sphere of alligator's eye.

The DuPont treasure.

The Zombie Stone.

A surge of relief and joy coursed through the young DuPont. Finally, August had recovered the key to his happiness. With the ancient Go-Between, he could dispatch his undead horde, which in turn would permit him to show up to—no, to *star* in—his own life, just like Stella Starz.

As a boy without zombies, he might even make friends.

Belong.

It was months since he'd seen the thing this close up, when

he'd gifted it to his aunt Orchid, believing it at the time no more than an impressively large marble. But not since he had completed the sculpture in which he'd employed it had he contemplated the stone this consciously.

It was stunning.

The soft beam of the flashlight penetrated the lustrous, vivid sphere to its core, so that it seemed almost illuminated from within and cast an amber reflection on August's wide-eyed face. The feature that rendered the gemstone so like an alligator's eye—the swirl of compressed carbon at the center—was the dense, velvety black of night, but on close inspection, it sparkled with a million minuscule stars.

So entranced was the boy by the object's beauty, he scarcely noticed the houseboat edging forward or the jolt caused by Professor Leech dropping to the deck.

"How do you use it?" August wondered. "How does it work? Perhaps Papa Shadows can help me figure it out."

"Look out!" cried Marvell.

August's gaze shot upward to catch sight of a large undead pirate launching himself gracelessly out of a cypress.

Devoid of coordination, balance, or common sense, the zombie plummeted like an enormous scarecrow stuffed with potatoes, and landed, limbs akimbo, facedown on the houseboat's deck. The impact caused the vessel to lurch violently; suddenly

August was on all fours, and the lustrous marble sphere was rolling toward the water.

"Nooooo!" he screamed, scrambling over the timbers with no
care for his hands or knees.

Just before it disappeared over the edge of the deck, August
felt the dense, cool smoothness beneath his palm.

The stone was safe.

"Well rescued," said that oily voice, with a curious hint of
triumph in it.

As the houseboat's rocking quieted, August picked himself
up, turned, and gasped.

"I forgot about *that,*" he said with a regretful grimace.

Professor Leech was wielding Jacques LeSalt's cutlass. And
its rusty yet formidable point hovered inches from Gaston Gardner's temple.

"Let's go," hissed the professor with a look of maniacal glee,
"find *me* some treasure!"

* * *

"There's another one." August pointed. "Turn left here!"

The houseboat turned toward the chartreuse light that
danced flirtatiously between distant tree trunks.

August, from his lookout position at the bow, glanced over
his shoulder.

Jacques LeSalt and Claudette clung awkwardly to the ropes tethering the shed to the deck, watching August with anxious eyes.

Marvell was at the tiller.

Leech sat on the generator, with Gaston in front of him cross-legged on the floor. The professor was posed almost like a monarch on a throne, the Zombie Stone resting in the upturned palm of his left hand, his right holding the cutlass like a down-turned scepter, its point piercing the fibrous wood of the deck uncomfortably close to Gaston's thigh.

August's thoughts raced.

With the weapon so close to the Gardner boy, the situation was far too dangerous to make a grab for stone or sword.

But perhaps, if they ever located Jacques LeSalt's "X," the covetous professor might become so preoccupied with the pirate's treasure, August and his companions could find an opportunity to make a getaway. No one, after all, can swing a cutlass while hungrily running gold doubloons through their open fingers (which is how August imagined the professor reacting to such a find).

"That's strange," said Marvell from the stern, pointing.

The most recently spotted swamp sprite had not promptly and frustratingly disappeared. In fact, as they watched, it was joined by a second shimmering beacon, and then, more distantly, a third.

The change in the swamp sprites' behavior felt significant.

"Papa Shadows said," murmured August, "that the Little Green Johnnies would lead us to the 'X.'"

And indeed, an entire string of them was now visible, clearly marking a distinct route. It felt like an entrance.

In the distant green lights August sometimes imagined he could see tiny outstretched fingers, wizened little faces, and the jig and jerk of skinny limbs. Sometimes he could detect only the flicker of flames. Whatever they were, the things disappeared before one could get close enough to confirm their nature, leaving the voyager to seek out the next of their kind.

The swamp sprites guided the houseboat through a great swath of Spanish moss, then another and another, all closely stacked like the gauzy layers of a ghostly cake. But finally the wispy tendrils parted to discharge the houseboat into a clearing about the size of a large duck pond in a public park.

It was the airiest, most generous space the travelers had encountered since entering the swamp. The glassy surface of the pool and the leafy canopy above reflected the mercurial light of thirty Little Green Johnnies who capered silently near the water's edge.

At the middle of the mini lagoon lay a mini island scarcely thirty feet long—an islet, you might say. Judging by its muddy, slime-smothered appearance, the low, oval-shaped rise spent as much time beneath the water's surface as it did above it.

And at its center rose another, smaller lump.

And while this too was swaddled in a heavy blanket of swampy vegetation that softened its edges and obscured its shape, it was still possible to discern that the form beneath had straight sides and a slightly curved top.

The slime-smothered lump was a chest.

CHAPTER 18

VILLAIN IN A FLOWERY HAT

The islet's surface was so slippery that it was difficult to remain upright. Standing beside Claudette and Marvell at the water's edge, August found himself sliding into the shallows.

Leech had placed himself and the pirate on the opposite side of the trunk-shaped protrusion. The professor held the cutlass extended so that its tip indented Gaston's ample cheek.

"You two, the living ones." The professor's voice remained calm and low and smarmy. He briefly swung the sword toward August and Marvell, then toward the chest. "Open it!"

Exchanging glances, the young people slipped and slithered their way toward the coffer. It sat at an angle, having had two hundred years to settle into the waterlogged ground beneath it.

"Hurry yourselves now!" Leech licked his lips with a thin lizard tongue.

Attempting to penetrate two hundred years' worth of swamp slime is never an agreeable task. There was much grimacing, and even some retching, as August and Madame Marvell used their bare hands to scrape away sufficient sludge to identify the chest's fittings.

"Oh, come," said Leech with a sneer. "It can't be that bad for those who keep company with rotting corpses."

"There's a padlock," said August, straightening and wiping his hands on his pants. "It's locked."

"You!" The cutlass was directed at Jacques LeSalt. "Where's the key?"

The great zombie shuffled backward, looking uncomfortable and glancing at the professor apprehensively.

"The key, you lumbering, dim-witted brute."

Jacques began to twitch in alarm.

Suddenly the Zombie Stone was held aloft.

"Po-na-fantom," called Professor Leech, although with less confidence than he had in Croissant City, as if he had been experiencing less consistent results. "Ancient talisman. Bridge of Ghosts. Go-Between. I call upon thee."

The professor seemed surprised and delighted when the stone was instantly illuminated by and surrounded with crackling fibrils of brilliant electric light.

Whisper, whisper.

August was visited by a tidal wave of dizziness and ghostly mutterings far louder than ever before. The butterflies seemed to circle him more quickly, in something close to frenzy. The boy was overwhelmed and stumbled, falling to his knees as Madame Marvell rushed to his side.

If Leech was surprised by, or even aware of, August's reaction, he didn't show it.

"Spirit who calls itself Jacques LeSalt," he said, leveling his gaze, "reveal the key!"

August, supporting himself between the chest and Marvell's arm, turned to see the zombies as he had feared—entranced as they had been on the evening of Leech's escape, their postures untwisted and neutral, their eyes empty and glazed, glowing with milky light.

"The key!" repeated Leech, thrusting the stone at Jacques as if that might improve its efficiency.

The large undead pirate, without his usual awkwardness, placidly searched through the pockets of his greatcoat. And then the pockets of his pants. He patted his ribs. He ran a finger beneath the cuff of his boots. He removed his hat and examined its interior. He peeped down his shirt.

Finally he simply held forth his empty palms.

Leech was losing his patience.

The viperous smile beneath the flowery hat was fading. His

knuckles were whitening as his grip on stone and sword tightened. A bead of sweat trickled from his scalp down his temple. The dimple in Gaston's cheek created by the tip of the cutlass was growing deeper.

Gaston whimpered.

August's heart was pounding, his head swimming. He glanced at Marvell and saw fear in her eyes. He felt it too. Who knew what this smarmy, unscrupulous man would do if his greedy quest was frustrated?

"Claudette!" yelled August, scarcely knowing what he was doing or saying. "Break the padlock!"

"The little girl?" scoffed Leech. "Why not the pirate? How can *she* possibly . . ."

August shot Leech a scowl as Claudette, blank-eyed, obediently approached the chest.

The small zombie reached out her pasty little hand, gripped the padlock, and with one swift movement ripped it—screws, fittings, and all—from the face of the chest, taking a generous amount of wood as well (which, to be fair, was softened with rot, so the achievement was not quite as impressive as it appeared).

Leech's face lit up. His smile returned. He looked at August.

"Let's see what we have here, shall we?"

Marvell helped August to his feet.

He shook his head, trying to hold the chorus of papery whisperings at bay. He found that by concentrating intently on his surroundings, he could keep the voices at a level that would not drive him insane.

He nodded at Marvell.

They lifted the lid.

Because the chest was sitting askew, one corner rather lower than the others, its contents immediately spewed forth with a great slithering, clinking sound.

Professor Leech could not resist. He abandoned his hostage, rushed around the mossy lump, ushering August and Marvell away with several prods of the cutlass, then grew very still, staring in wonder.

He lifted a coin from the pile. It was not especially impressive, coated as it was with centuries of goopy silt. But as the professor's thumb wiped away the thick grime, it revealed the gleam of gold.

Held merely inches from the professor's face, the luminous coin cast an eerie reflection in his bulbous eyes.

"At last," whispered the man, "an end to this lean, penny-pinching existence. At last, an end to the twittering of dim-witted widows, to the peddling of potions and cure-alls and five-dollar charms. At last, an end to saccharine smiles and small talk and low ceilings and backroom ball readings."

Leech dropped to one knee, but August's expectations were disappointed when the professor did not lay aside his weapon. Rather, he pocketed the Zombie Stone and used his free hand to stir the doubloons around while using the other to keep the sword pointed rigidly outward: impassable.

"With a fortune such as this," he muttered, "I can open my own theater!"

"Theater?" August's fear was surpassed by his surprise. "You intend to be an actor?"

Buying a whole theater seemed an elaborate and expensive way of achieving such an ambition. Unless, of course, the professor was a very bad actor, and it was his only means of getting on the stage.

The professor did not look up from the treasure, but scoffed quietly.

"I will produce a theatrical spectacle of grotesquerie," he said with quiet conviction, "that will shock the world. I will direct my own Dance of the Dead, a ballet so beautiful in its grim horror that it will eclipse the name Orfeo DuPont, condemning it to obscurity. My gifts will finally be recognized and applauded."

His smile widened just a little to reveal small, babyish teeth.

"I will be celebrated as the greatest necromancer on earth!"

"Necromancer?" said August. "Fame? That's what you wanted all along, not just the money?"

Professor Leech finally raised his eyes to meet August's.

"You see me as a villain, August, don't you? No doubt many would. But you should know, boy, that for any villain, it is rarely *just* about the money; it is what the money can buy."

Leech stood, and again the Zombie Stone was crackling and sparkling in the air, and again the voices of the dead were muttering and prattling in August's ears.

"Jacques LeSalt!" commanded the professor. "Spirit known as Claudette! Remove this coffer to the watercraft!"

The chest was so decayed, its timbers so softened, August thought its handles might rip off in the fists of the obedient, empty-eyed zombies who lifted it. But they held out long enough for the treasure to be deposited on the deck of Madame Marvell's houseboat.

The weight of seven hundred Spanish doubloons, two zombies, and an evil professor—in combination with its reduced buoyancy—caused the vessel to pitch so steeply that the port corner of the deck dipped below the water's surface.

The oil drum beneath it was forced into the mud, causing the professor some difficulty in pushing off from the islet with his foot.

"What are you doing?" cried August. "You can't just leave. We have no boat. We cannot just walk home."

"Well," said the professor, waving the cutlass around the lagoon, "you certainly won't die of thirst. And perhaps, if you develop a taste for raw catfish and slugs, you might even survive. For a while."

He made a phony sad face.

"Not for long, though, I suspect. Not long enough to

complicate my plans any further than you have. Lost Souls' Swamp has just, I fear, acquired three more lost souls."

The houseboat was clear of the mud and drifting away.

Leech had his foot on the transom, clearly enjoying his moment of victory before starting up the engine.

Claudette and Jacques lingered behind him, still subject to the power of the Zombie Stone. But August could feel the alarm within them, the fear that, because of their entranced condition, they were unable to express by the usual means of shuffling and grunting and eye swiveling.

And suddenly August was very frightened for them.

"You can't do this *again*!" he cried, scrambling and slipping to the water's edge. "You can't take them. You can't *have* them. Leave them with people who care about them."

"*Leave* them?" laughed Leech in disbelief. "What? Do you imagine that I, Professor Tiberius Leech, should perform in my own Dance of the Dead, when I am very much alive? That would be a deception, August. I'm surprised at the unscrupulousness of your suggestion."

The professor was glaring at the boy across the water with a hateful smirk.

"No, August. This pair will be perfect. I believe the big one has experience in the performing arts. They will make a good start, at least until I can determine how to create more."

"No," August whispered as the full extent of Leech's motives dawned on him. "There are people in there!" he yelled angrily, pointing at the zombies. "You can't just . . . just steal ghosts and force them back into a world where they don't belong, just to entertain, to make you feel like you're good at something, like you're important."

"You mean," simpered Leech, "like Orfeo DuPont, your own ancestor, did?"

August clenched his jaw.

Leech was right, of course.

It was clear to August now what exactly about Orfeo's poster was so unsettling, even disturbing. What was depicted there behind the theatrical font, in full, fun color promising diversion and delight, was not a ballet. It was not a performance.

It was a puppet show.

With hapless, unwilling participants as the puppets.

It was revolting.

"Orfeo was wrong," he cried passionately. "That is *not* what the Zombie Stone is for. It can't be."

"Well," sneered the professor, placing the cutlass on the deck and firing up the engine, "when you have a Zombie Stone of your own, August DuPont, you can use it however you like."

"That," hissed August DuPont, "*is* my Zombie Stone."

There was a small rocky protrusion near his foot. Without it he would not have had a solid surface from which to leap. The houseboat was already yards from shore, but August had gained sufficient leverage to grab a thick hank of Spanish moss droop-ing over the water. He could only hope that it would support his weight as he swung.

It did.

The boy hit the deck at its lowest point, and while he was a wiry fellow and a little small for his age, his weight was enough to pitch the houseboat to the point of disaster.

As the heavy chest of coins slid toward him, the boy scarcely had time to dive out of its path. In doing so, he collided with the calves of Professor Leech, who tumbled over him, landing face-first, arms extended in a desperate attempt to rescue the slithering box.

There was a ghastly, bone-chilling, inhuman scream—it came from the professor—as the great slimy lump-that-was-a-chest quietly slid overboard and the houseboat's pontoon accordingly bounced upward, as if relieved to shed the extra burden.

August grabbed the transom and peered over to see an ex-plosion of bubbles. As they cleared, he caught a last glimpse of the coffer and the glimmer of spiraling doubloons before they were swallowed up entirely by the darkness below.

There was sudden stillness.

Leech was on his belly, fingers gripping the edge of the deck, his breath heavy and ragged as he stared at the rippling water.

When he turned, his baby face was the ominous color of a thundercloud at sunset. Before August could recover his footing, Leech was looming over him . . . with the cutlass. The man's lower lip trembled like that of an infant on the verge of a violent tantrum.

"You," he said, attempting to recover a quivering smile, "have proved to be less easily dispatched than I imagined." He glanced down at the water with a scowl. "Fear not, boy, it may take some time, but I will have your beloved zombies recover that gold. They will not, after all, require any breathing device."

The smile finally disappeared altogether.

"*You,* however, and your meddling I must be rid of. I *will* be rid of."

The cutlass swung high into the air.

Its rusty but formidable blade flashed with the light of the Little Green Johnnies as it descended upon August DuPont.

But suddenly, before the boy had even fully appreciated what was happening, there was an ugly, terrifying, bestial roar.

August was instantly enveloped in hot, rank, fishy air.

Everything around him was screaming, splintering, crashing, razor-sharp teeth the size of ice-cream cones, the shockingly pink interior of massive jaws, and a vast, flexing black gullet.

CHAPTER 19

THE TREASURE IN THE TREASURE

August scrambled backward onto the islet's slippery bank.

Claudette and Jacques LeSalt staggered from the water nearby, like sparrows concussed after colliding with a window.

In the lagoon, still sloshing and choppy, there bobbed a soup of wreckage: splintered timbers, a door, some roofing, two mangled oil drums, and a pepper barrel.

August rubbed his temples; the whisperings and giddiness had receded. He looked around to see Madame Marvell and Gaston staring at the scene before them with stunned, openmouthed expressions.

The houseboat was gone.

So was Professor Leech.

"It ate him," said Marvell simply. "The alligator ate the professor."

"Just swallowed him whole," agreed Gaston. "And most of the houseboat."

"And the Zombie Stone?" asked August, dreading the answer.

Marvell shook her head with an expression of sympathy.

"No! NO!" August wailed, gripping his hair in desperate fists. "Every time I get near the thing, something goes wrong. It is always ripped away from me."

He was so consumed by frustration, it was all he could do to keep from crying. He had been searching for so long. Gone through so much. The key to his good fortunes, to his aunt's, had been in his *hands* only hours before. How could it be gone after *all this*?

He stared at the lagoon. Could he search for it in there?

But the waters of the swamp were not clear like a mountain river or a sheltered coastal bay. They were muddied with nutrient-rich silt borne by the Continental River, which left them virtually opaque.

Besides . . . the alligator.

Who knows: maybe the stone was even in the beast's stomach.

"This was my last hope," said August bleakly.

"At least," noted Gaston, "the alligator didn't eat *you*."

"Or your house," added Madame Marvell.

The expressions on their faces caused August a pang of guilt. His first thought had been for himself.

A girl had lost her home.

An evil professor had lost his life.

He tried not to be selfish about the situation, but it was difficult to dismiss his sense of injury.

August was doing his best to hide it, at least, when suddenly an ear-splitting howl erupted from Jacques LeSalt, who, freed from his spellbound servitude, had spied something that caused him to plunge, grunting and wheezing with excitement, back into the undulating raft of flotsam.

After several moments of frenzied splashing, groaning, and scooping, the pirate slowly returned, cradling a prize in his great hands with something close to tenderness: a small dripping, greasy leather bag. He made a fumbling attempt to loosen the drawstring, but he was, after all, a zombie, with little coordination and fingers like sausages.

August came to his assistance.

"May I?" he said, stepping into the shallows and holding out his hand.

Jacques LeSalt turned his face to August, and for a moment, one might have imagined he was smiling.

Inside the oilskin purse was a parcel of waxed paper. Despite their age, both bag and parcel had been waterproofed sufficiently to perform their task of protecting the contents inside.

A document.

The thing was spotted and edged with mildew, crumpled by the weight of seven hundred Spanish doubloons, and so brittle and fragile that August had to unfold it with great care so it would not rip.

The single sheet of paper was rather larger than that on which Octavia Motts had printed her pamphlet mock-up or the notebooks that Hydrangea purchased from Grosbeak's for her accounting. Its dimensions were closer to those of the *Pepperville Prophet.*

It boasted a large, important-looking wax seal and was decorated with elaborate scrolls and heraldry. But the primary body of the document was handwritten in large script with impressive loops and flourishes. It took a moment to interpret what it said.

" 'Let it be known that I,' " read August hesitantly, squinting to decipher the antique penmanship, " 'the duly elected president of these united dominions, do hereby grant to commissioned privateer Jacques LeSalt a full, entire pardon from all charges of piracy, buccaneering, and general nautical skulduggery.' "

August paused, digesting the communication.

"This is a presidential pardon," he said, looking up at Jacques.

August had learned all about presidential pardons on an episode of *Win It or Lick It,* from which he had come to understand that while they might be valuable, historical documents did not necessarily taste good.

"This was in your chest," said August, putting two and two together. "It wasn't the gold you sought at all but this pardon? The plaque on your statue in Jacques LeSalt Park states you were tried and hanged as a criminal. But all the time, you were an innocent man."

The pirate shrugged and made a dubious "not exactly" sort of expression.

"All right, you were pardoned, at least. I reckon that means the history books have got you all wrong." August turned the document to face the zombie. "*This* was the true treasure all along, wasn't it?"

Jacques LeSalt heaved a ragged sigh and his huge shoulders slumped, as if the weight of seven hundred doubloons had slipped from them.

"Everyone will know the truth now, Jacques," promised August. "I'll make sure of it. Librarian Octavia Motts will know what to do with an important thing like this."

A great uplifting wave of relief surged through the boy. And he instantly knew it was not his own but Jacques's. He felt something feathery and light emerging and rising, like a dove released from a cage.

It was a release—and a departure.

And suddenly the hollow eyes, gravestone teeth, and

parchment skin of the pirate zombie were scarcely-there shadows beneath the floaty, shimmering form of a hearty sunburned fellow with a big gold earring and a flashing white smile.

The gossamer, hologram-like figure raised his great hand in salute, then, with a last devilish grin, rose into the air and dissipated like salty spray rising from the ocean's waves.

The pirate's physical remains crumpled into a gruesome heap of moldy cloth and skeletal bits and pieces in the mud.

Jacques LeSalt was gone.

"Just like Celeste," said August, looking at Marvell.

"And Batiste," agreed the girl.

"What in tarnation?" cried Gaston with a revolted expression. "That was just plain nasty!"

"It is a little unpleasant," admitted August. "But I reckon it must be best for them. They look so happy as they leave."

"He sees their souls," Marvell explained to Gaston.

"Like ghosts?" said Gaston.

"I suppose so," said August. "I feel them too. There's this sensation, like a release. Like something detaching and rising. And a bushel load of relief."

The boy bent and lifted the pirate's crumbling hat from the sad little pile.

"He was executed unjustly. That was the unfinished business that kept Jacques from passing along: he just wanted everyone to know the truth before he left this place."

August glanced out to the lagoon.

"I guess the Zombie Stone is close enough that it opened the portal for him somehow." He shook his head. "I've still got thirty more zombies to get through that door between worlds. But I don't know how I can accomplish that, what with the Zombie Stone in there somewhere."

"You don't need the stone," said a voice.

"Huh?" said August.

"We didn't say anything," said Marvell, speaking for all present.

"You didn't hear a voice, a man's voice?"

"Professor Leech?"

"No, no. A different man. Less creepy."

"I didn't hear anything," said Marvell.

"Me neither," said Gaston.

August looked at Claudette.

She nodded. She had heard it. That could mean only one thing.

"I'm right behind you," said the voice.

August turned around. But what he found was not another freshly hatched zombie.

What he found, not twenty feet away, was a monster.

Its mammoth head and front feet rested on the opposite end of the islet. The rest of the behemoth snaked away, disappearing into the brown depths of the swamp.

Its jaws were the length of a truck bed. Its teeth were the size of ice-cream cones. Its eyes were yellow and reptilian, with thin almond-shaped pupils, and August had stared into those eyes before.

They were the eyes of a forty-foot, pure white alligator.

Let it be known that I,

the duly elected president of these united dominions,

do hereby grant to commissioned privateer Jacques Le Salt

a full, entire pardon from all charges of piracy,

buccaneering, and general nautical skulduggery.

Luisa Livingston, President

CHAPTER 20

CONVERSING WITH A MONSTER

Gaston straight-out screamed. You could hardly blame him. Madame Marvell covered her eyes. This is not, admittedly, the most effective way to deal with imminent danger, but it is a surprisingly common one.

Claudette lumbered to August's side with a protective air while defensively (and understandably) shielding the stitches of her recently restored limb.

"Come closer," said the man's voice.

August looked around wildly, searching for the speaker. It had sounded almost as if the voice had come from inside the alligator.

Could Professor Leech be in there . . . *alive*?

"It is *I* who speaks."

The voice was certainly not Leech's. But it did certainly originate in the mighty gator, despite the fact that its jaws had not moved an inch.

"You know it is I, August. Come closer, boy. I have saved your life now more than once. I have had every opportunity to eat you. Come closer. Please."

"What are you *doing*?" hissed Gaston.

"It's conversing with me," explained August, cautiously edging across the slimy knoll.

"Tell me he's not going over there," whispered Marvell, palms still pressed against her face.

"He says it's conversing with him," responded Gaston.

"Closer, August, closer," said the voice. "Closer still."

August was now merely feet from the reptile's snout and its two flaring nostrils, each large enough to accommodate a boy's head. The creature's scales were thick and gnarled, those on its back ridged and pointy, almost like those of a dinosaur. Its breath, which came in wheezy gusts, was ancient and foul, its odor not dissimilar to that of a bag of old crawfish shells and rancid bacon fat that has been left in the trash for two whole weeks.

"Down here," said the voice. "No, here."

August looked down.

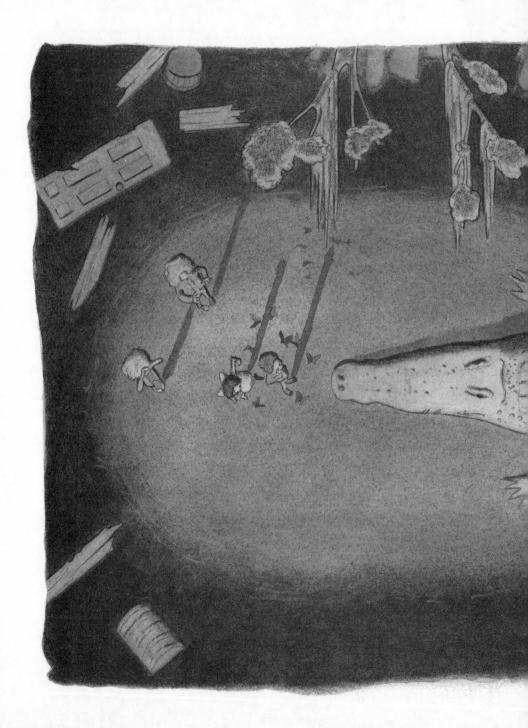

There, in the dark puddles of the muddy bank where the monster's reflection should have rippled beside his own, was, instead, that of a man.

His piercing, marsh-grass-colored eyes were unusually large and round and rendered even larger and rounder by large, round eyeglasses. His nose and mouth were, by comparison, quite small.

He reminded August of nothing more than a baby owl.

With a mustache.

"Orfeo DuPont?" August recalled that the two were related. "I mean, Great-Great-Uncle Orfeo?"

The inexplicable apparition gave August a little wave.

Stunned, August waved back.

"Orfeo DuPont?" cried Madame Marvell, curiosity causing her to uncover her face.

"Who is Orfeo DuPont?" asked Gaston.

"What is happening?" August demanded of his great-great-uncle's reflection.

Orfeo's hair and garments floated gently around, as if he existed weightless in some unearthly vacuum.

"August," he said. "At last you are here. We have much to discuss. You must have many questions."

"Why, I just asked you one," said August. "What is happening, precisely?"

Orfeo chuckled.

"I am guessing, August, that this is not your first out-of-the-ordinary experience with a reflection. Am I correct?"

August nodded.

"You have deduced, then, that in the nebulous world of mirror, you, August, see the soul trapped inside an undead corpse or, in cases such as mine, trapped inside a living host.

"Yes, it is true. I, Orfeo DuPont, reside in this great beast before you. My spirit is, for want of a better explanation, an uninvited guest. The monster's frame may be large, but her mind is simple and small; there is plenty of room for my psyche in here."

"A root wizard," said August, "told me he believed the alligator to be possessed. Is your own body, um . . ." The boy was unsure how to ask the question tactfully.

"My once-handsome anatomy is no more," confirmed Orfeo DuPont, "having been consumed by this very alligator. It was supposed to be a simple fishing trip, you see. I had my rod and a packed lunch ready for a brief respite from the hectic life of a renowned necromancer. I was about to bite into my crawfish sandwich when *this* thing comes out of nowhere, all teeth and gullet. Whoosh, smash, splash, munch, munch, and that was that."

"How awful for you," said August. "Did it hurt?"

"The beginning was most unpleasant," admitted Orfeo. "But it didn't last long. Afterward, however, there was not much of me left to return to, so it seemed only fair that the responsible party should house my spirit. Although I confess I did not expect the arrangement to be so long-term. It is fortunate that my amphibious host has had such an extraordinarily long life."

"On the TV show *Are You a Dummy?*," said August, "they said that some alligators can survive for more than a hundred years."

"I have no idea," said Orfeo, "what a TV might be." (The necromancer *had* been eaten a very long time ago.) "But this show you speak of sounds like an informative kind of entertainment. Oh my!" Orfeo's face suddenly brightened with a smile. "Is that my little sister, Claudette DuPont?"

August felt the dank, lifeless form of a curious Claudette pressing against his arm, and simultaneously her shiny-haired, clear-eyed reflection appeared beside his own and Orfeo's.

Puddle Orfeo bent and smiled at puddle Claudette.

"Well, ain't you prettier than a picnic basket full of rainbows!"

Confusion lightly creased Claudette's brow.

"It's me, sugar, your big brother, Orfeo; I'm just a little older than you remember. See, I had to grow up without you, sugar. My Lord, Locust Hole felt empty after you . . . well, left us. I recall that day so clearly; it wasn't long after your kitty-cat died, and my, you were melancholy. I had picked you a bunch of wild iris and came looking for you on the gazebo roof. I knew you'd be there, right under your sweet kitty's favorite oak tree."

Puddle Orfeo paused and sadly brushed a rebellious ringlet from his puddle sister's cheek.

"But I was too late," he said. "My poor little Claudette."

Both Claudettes stared at Orfeo, then turned to stare at August with puzzlement.

"I think she thinks that I am you," explained August. "I have been told we look alike. Claudette follows me everywhere."

Orfeo DuPont gazed out from his puddle, studying his great-great-nephew with the large, round eyes the color of marsh grass.

"I am afraid," he said, shrugging, "I don't see the resemblance. But even if there is one, I do not believe that is why young Claudette is so drawn to you."

"Well," said August, "whatever the reason, I am most anxious to be rid of her. Nothing personal," he added quickly, glancing at the small zombie. "And of course, the others too."

"There are . . . others?" said Orfeo slowly.

"Thirty."

"Thirty?" Orfeo was shocked.

"Thirty, sir. And they are not at all helpful when it comes to making friends and being a normal boy. I need to get rid of them, sir. I need to send their souls back to where they belong, and I need your famous Zombie Stone to do it.

"Might you possibly have your alligator friend look for it in the swamp? You must have some influence over her. You remember what the stone looks like, now, don't you, Great-

Great-Uncle? You had a perfect sphere cut from the hunk of Cadaverite you used in your act, the Go-Between you used to reanimate the deceased for diversion and delight."

Puddle Orfeo placed his arm around puddle Claudette's shoulders and smiled at August sympathetically.

"As I said upon opening this conversation," he said gently, "you, August, do not need the Zombie Stone to control the undead. Why, the Cadaverite is merely a talisman."

"What *is* a talisman, exactly?"

"Such objects have no real power of their own. They are, you might say, special *tools* that help a necromancer to focus and direct their sorcery. Think of a talisman as a lightning rod: by itself a lifeless pole, but employed with wisdom and skill, it can capture and direct the very power of nature itself.

"The more skilled the coppersmith, the more conductive the lightning rod.

"The more powerful the necromancer, the more effective the talisman."

"So . . ." August paused, digesting this information. "You mean the Zombie Stone would never have been of any use without a necromancer to operate it?"

"The necromancer, not the talisman, is the source of the magic, August, as the thundercloud, not the rod, is the source of the lightning."

"But then I am doomed," said August, "to life as a zombie

keeper. The only living necromancer I knew was just eaten by, well . . . by *you*! I doubt Professor Leech would have been anxious to assist me, but perhaps . . . if I had paid him . . . if I had promised him . . ."

August placed his face in his hands, engulfed by weariness and defeat.

"It doesn't matter now. Nothing matters. I have no way to control the zombies: no necromancer, no Go-Between."

"August, child, look up. Look at me."

Orfeo shook his head fondly, smiling out of some unshared wisdom.

"Do you really not see it yet?" he asked. "The butterflies. The sudden appearance of the undead. Their obstinate attachment to you. The inexplicable reflections that only you can see.

"August, my dear boy, the Zombie Stone is not the Go-Between.

"It is not the DuPont treasure.

"*You* are!"

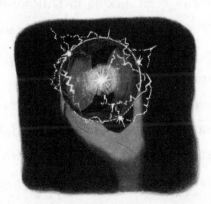

CHAPTER 21

THE BRIDGE KEEPER

"Or more precisely," continued Orfeo, "your *gift* is the family treasure."

"My *gift*?" August could not keep the frustration out of his voice. What was this puddle person talking about?

"The DuPont treasure is a family trait, a genetic anomaly, that has for centuries been lurking in DuPont veins, to reveal itself every generation or two (or even three) in some unsuspecting young person."

"For *centuries*?"

"Since before our ancestors were even known as DuPonts. Why, it was this unique gift that earned us our family name. Do you know, August, what 'DuPont' actually means?"

August had asked this of Hydrangea once. He repeated what she had told him.

"It's French," he said, "for 'of the bridge.'"

"The bridge," confirmed Orfeo, "that connects the land of the living to that of the dead. You, August, are the latest recipient of the ancestral gift. You are the new bridge keeper. A Go-Between."

"But, but . . ." August felt panic rising in him. "But I thought a Go-Between was a thing, not a person. I don't want to be a Go-Between, I don't want to be a bridge keeper. I want friends! Living ones. I don't want to belong to the dead."

August turned to Marvell and Gaston. They saw the fear in his face, but hearing only half of the conversation, they had no idea how to help him.

"No, not *belong,* August," insisted Orfeo. "Not belong. But . . . you cannot escape your true nature, child. Whether you like it or not, you have a connection to the world of spirits.

"You are a born necromancer."

"A *necromancer*! *I* am a necromancer?"

"Between the land of the living," explained Orfeo, "and the forever place lies a netherworld, where restless souls—those who cannot leave their mortal existence behind—linger. It is a murky, gray domain of confusion and swirling fog.

"You, August, are like a beacon in that fog, something bright glimpsed through a keyhole. You are the only point of reference in their blurred, vague existence. You are all they see.

"Why, child, do you think you are constantly surrounded by butterflies?"

"It's a skin condition."

"I think you have known for some time now that that is not true. The creatures circling your head at this very moment are possessed by spirits whose corpses are no more.

"Such fragile beings are easy prey for those like me. No real intellect to resist our entry. A sweet and pleasant diet. Their lives, of course, are rather short, rarely longer than a month or so. Constantly hopping from one to the next can prove tiresome (I tried it myself before settling down in here).

"August, those lost, fluttering souls are attracted to you as a bug is drawn to a porch light. And, oh my, but your light is a bright one, far brighter than my own at your age, your power far greater.

"I made zombies very rarely, with enormous effort and—frankly—mixed results. And now you tell me that before the age of thirteen you have made over thirty. *Thirty!*" The necromancer repeated the number with the same amazement as before.

"I did no such thing!" protested August. "I never made a zombie in my life."

"Not on purpose, perhaps," admitted Orfeo.

"How, then?" snapped August defensively. "*How* did I make these zombies?"

"You've heard voices of late? Whispers in the shadows, in quiet corners? Perhaps in your head?"

August nodded reluctantly.

"And moments of heightened awareness of the smells and sounds and sensations around you?"

"Yes," said August cautiously. "Yes, I have. And underneath all that I can feel a kind of throb, like a heartbeat. What is it?"

"It is your gift, August. It is you, plugging into the universe.

"It is you, the bridge keeper, opening the bridge.

"Afterward you hear the voices of the dead more clearly, don't you? You see their reflections more vividly. They seem closer, more insistent.

"Tell me, did the voices ever ask for help? Did you offer it?"

Casting his mind back, August realized that before the appearance of every fresh zombie, he had indeed offered his assistance.

"You did not mean it as such, but that was an invitation, child, a welcome mat to those who would cross that bridge. And when they did . . ."

"Zombies."

"Yes. Zombies."

"I made them."

"You did. But by accident. Unlike me."

August paused.

"Orfeo DuPont's Dance of the Dead," he said gravely, picturing the poster which he now found so sickening. "*You* made your zombies on purpose, just so you could put on a show!"

"I did," sighed Orfeo. "Although it was not as easy for me as it appears to be for you. But yes, I sought out the graves of Jacques LeSalt and Sad Celeste and Little Prince Itty-Bitty and LouLou Bouquet. Even in death, all four enjoyed a level of celebrity; this is a region, after all, that loves its ghosts and macabre legends. I suspected that they would draw larger crowds than perhaps less famous corpses."

"You were no better than Professor Leech," said August, this chapter of his family history filling the boy with shame.

"Not as heartless," said Orfeo quietly. "Or as greedy. I did it more for the showmanship, the applause. It is true, though, that I permitted my ego to eclipse my humanity.

"But, August, I can assure you that I was justly punished for my crime. For a hundred years now I have resided in this foul-smelling lizard, coming to understand just how terrible it is to be trapped in a place you do not belong.

"I have never acquired a taste for raw catfish. Or raw professor, for that matter."

"You *ate* Professor Leech!" cried August, suddenly realizing the implications. "You killed him."

"I was saving your life," said Orfeo impassively, studying his fingernails. "And remember," he added, "there are two beings inside this monster. I share this vessel with a wild animal—a large one, with a healthy appetite. When she spots an appetizing morsel, there is only so much I can do."

August looked at the alligator's dripping teeth and took a quick step backward.

"Oh, no need for alarm!" chuckled Orfeo. "She'll be digesting for a couple of days. When her stomach's not grumbling with hunger, she is surprisingly open to my . . . let's call them suggestions."

"Why, then," said August thoughtfully, "have you not spoken to me sooner? You've been following me, haven't you? You've been sighted—well, your alligator has—many times in Black River. You were there in Croissant City; you rescued me from the river."

Orfeo nodded as if he had been anticipating this question.

"I have been awaiting my successor for a century now. Imagine, then, how thrilling it was for me to sense a tiny ripple in the universe, a reverberation that could derive only from the reappearance of the DuPont treasure at Locust Hole.

"I knew immediately that a young DuPont would soon be receiving the gift; it always emerges at the end of childhood.

"But it takes some time to develop.

"I tried to approach you several times, once when you were

having some trouble with your little canoe; do you remember? I confess the gator got a little away from me on that occasion. I should probably have fed her first.

"But in any event, the talent had not fully bloomed in you yet. You could not see or hear me, only the monster."

"I wish I could see only the monster," grumbled August petulantly. "I just want to be normal."

"A normal DuPont," laughed Orfeo. "Now there's a strange idea. Do not yearn to be something less than you are, August. You are special."

"I don't want to be special. I don't want to be the bridge keeper for zombies, a porch light for lost souls."

"You don't want to help people?" asked Orfeo gently. "Help the wanderers find their way? Help poor lost things like our dear Claudette?"

"Why can't *you* help her? *You're* a necromancer. She's *your* sister."

"*I* am but a shadow, August, a flimsy reflection of something that used to be. I have no power or influence in your world.

"But *you* do."

August glanced resentfully at Claudette.

"All she says is 'pearls,'" he grumbled. "Over and over. Her necklace is gone. I don't know how to help her. I don't know how to help any of them."

"Listen to them, August. Necromancers are, by and large, simply listeners."

"How will listening achieve anything?"

"Listen not with your ears, August, but with your heart. Listen not to a spirit's words but to its feelings. Then all will be well."

"How can you listen with your heart . . . to a feeling? What does that even mean? What if I can't do it? What if they won't leave?"

"You might indeed find that a disquieted spirit may be reluctant to depart. But in such cases, August, a necromancer with skill such as mine, such as yours, may *command*.

"There are words, ancient words, that spoken by the right mouth can enchant, can compel! Believe me, DuPont's Dance of the Dead relied upon such incantations."

"I have heard the words," admitted August. "I have seen the zombies' empty, glowing eyes, their"—he gulped, feeling nauseous—"obedience. Professor Leech has used—"

"*Leech?* Ha! Why, that amateur could never harness such power. No, August, if you have witnessed your zombies so bewitched, the state has resulted from your very own presence. Without *your* proximity, Leech could have achieved little with the Zombie Stone, certainly nothing so ambitious as an entrancement of the undead."

"You make it sound," said August meekly, "as if I am entirely unique. Is there really no one else who could take my place?"

"There is only you. And there will be only you. Until, of course, the treasure is passed along to someone else."

"Someone else?" August brightened. "When will that be?"

"No one can know for sure when the gift will reappear in another young DuPont. Fifty years? A hundred? Two hundred?"

"*Two hundred years?* I won't live to be two hundred years old!"

"You most certainly will not," chuckled Orfeo. "But if necessary, you will wait patiently, as I have, in this ghost world for the exquisite cosmic tremor that announces the arrival of your successor.

"Perhaps your spirit will linger in your own lifeless bones. Or perhaps you will find a biddable host, as I have. I would urge you, however, to settle in something other than an alligator. They do, on the whole, make for the most revolting form of accommodation."

"And what should I do then, when I am some . . . some reflection living inside a . . . whatever?"

"You will do as I am doing now. You will explain to a confused child that they are uniquely gifted. You will tell them what they are. And when you have welcomed them to their own destiny, you too will be free to leave this place forever."

The reflection of Orfeo DuPont began to dim, and the dark mass of an alligator became increasingly visible in his place.

"Wait!" cried August. "Great-Great-Uncle Orfeo, are you leaving?"

"I have passed the torch, August." Orfeo's voice was fading too. "I have secured the DuPont treasure. My unfinished business is finished. Farewell, my dear, dear Claudette."

The nearly gone image of Orfeo DuPont took his sister by the shoulders and delivered a feathery peck to each of her cheeks.

"I suspect we shall be seeing each other real soon, sugar."

August felt something lift and vaporize, like tiny bubbles rising through champagne and bursting into the air.

What was left of Orfeo DuPont pressed the tips of his fingers to his mouth, then threw them outward, releasing air kisses. He crossed his hands over his heart and took a great bow, as if bidding a final adieu to the audience of the Théâtre Français.

Then he was gone.

The forty-foot, pure white alligator grunted with surprise.

She heaved a hot, fishy sigh, and her great scaly frame relaxed into the mud, belly distending like a giant plastic bag of groceries being placed on the floor.

And the alligator began to snore, loudly, as if she hadn't had a good night's sleep in a hundred years.

PART III

PART III

CHAPTER 22

DEMISE OF A HOUSEBOAT

"August," ordered Gaston, "that plank is coming loose; tighten the knot! How's that starboard oil drum holding up, Marvell?"

It was perhaps not surprising that Gaston, a son of Gardner's Island, where salvage and recycling were revered, had taken charge of building the raft.

The thing was cobbled together from the remnants of Marvell's houseboat: one of the cabin doors, several splintered timbers, the pepper barrel and surviving oil drums. The three flotation devices had necessarily been arranged like the wheels of a tricycle, with one center front and one at each back corner.

Distributing weight on such an unevenly supported platform was precarious business, and it was soon discovered that all aboard must be informed before any significant movement was made.

With no hammer or nails available, the whole thing was held together instead by ropes crudely fashioned from twisted strands of Spanish moss. They were feathery and fragile and difficult to tie.

It was not the sturdiest of vessels, and it had taken much of the night to complete. But it remained afloat, which was the most important thing expected of it.

The houseboat's outboard motor was somewhere at the bottom of a lagoon, so power was supplied by a small zombie. Claudette lay facedown in the swamp (as Professor Leech had pointed out, it wasn't as if her kind required any type of breathing apparatus), her hands braced against the raft before her, water churning around her kicking feet.

The Little Green Johnnies had been more elusive and even less helpful on the outbound route than on the inbound. Although they had not disappeared entirely, there was a petulant resentment to the infrequency and briefness of their appearances, as if they were piqued that anyone should have the nerve to find their way *out* of Lost Souls' Swamp.

Marvell's trail of Carnival beads had in the end proved to be a far more predictable and reliable sort of guide, glittering in the beam of the flashlight exactly where they had been left. Gaston, classifying them as a form of litter, had insisted on collecting every one. And because unlike the swamp sprites, the rainbow-colored necklaces did not materialize only on a whim, the travelers had gone from one marker to the next far more swiftly.

By the time morning light pierced the canopy above, the makeshift raft had already passed the home of Papa Shadows (although he had made no appearance), and Gaston was once again in territory known to him, navigating by means of the eerie, faceless stick poppets.

August glanced at Madame Marvell. She had been unusually quiet.

"I fear it is my fault, Marvell, that you lost your home," said the boy quietly. "If we hadn't gone searching for the Zombie Stone . . ."

"I lived in that houseboat," Marvell said, her voice thin and hesitant, "my whole life. With mawmaw. I already lost Delfine, the only way I had to talk to her. Now I've lost her posters, those hard candies she liked so much, and her colored candles too. It's all gone. There's nothing left of mawmaw now."

"I'm sorry," said August, feeling horrible for the barefoot, squirrel-eyed orphan with the mass of unkempt hair.

There was a moment of silence. August focused on securing the knot of Spanish moss rope as instructed by Gaston.

"It wasn't your fault," said Marvell suddenly. "Why, it was that big old foul-breathing gator. I hope trying to digest Professor Leech gives it a bellyache. Did it really converse with you?"

She looked at August curiously. "Did it really tell you you're a necromancer?"

"Well, it wasn't exactly the alligator that told me. But . . . yes."

"And you don't need the Zombie Stone," asked Gaston, glancing over his shoulder from the bow, "to control the undead? You can do it all by yourself?"

"According to my great-great-uncle," sighed August wearily. "Although I have no idea how. He said something about listening, but I don't see how *that* will get anything done. The only souls that have quit their bodies so far have found whatever it is they were looking for. Aw, shoot!"

The Spanish moss knot in August's fingers had become a waterlogged tangle and suddenly disintegrated into a mess of broken fibers. The rest of the handcrafted rope was also loosening and breaking apart.

Suddenly August's knees were separating, one on the cabin door, the other on the board to which the oil drum was fixed. He struggled to close his thighs, but the forward momentum created by Claudette's thrashing legs was forcing them apart.

"Stop!" cried August. "Claudette, stop!"

But it was too late.

The plank and drum broke away. Without their support, the rest of the raft collapsed sideways, the abrupt torque on its remaining elements causing the second oil drum to pop free.

Suddenly everyone was in the water, clinging to something that was no longer a craft but merely an angled door buoyed by one old pepper barrel.

"August," sputtered Gaston, spitting out water, "you go fetch that oil drum. I'll fetch the other."

"But . . . I can't swim," replied August, tightening his grip on whatever he could.

"Say what now?" Gaston was astounded. "How can anyone grow up in Hurricane County—a place that's more water than dirt—without learning to swim?"

"I'm the ghost of Locust Hole, remember?"

Gaston reddened.

"*You* were the one who flushed me out for the very first time. Not much opportunity for swimming in an attic."

"You might have mentioned this before," protested Marvell. "We've spent a heap of time on the water—would have been a good thing to know."

"All right," said Gaston. "August, you sit tight. Marvell, you swim, yes? Okay, you go."

Marvell hesitated, gazing at the wreckage slowly drifting away.

"I wonder," she muttered, "if that alligator has digested Professor Leech yet."

"Orfeo," responded August, "said it would take a couple of days."

Marvell nodded but did not smile.

"But it's not," she observed, "the only alligator in the swamp. Is it?"

All eyes immediately peered anxiously into the water below.

Gaston splashed hurriedly away to rescue one drum, and Marvell the other.

The voyagers used their elbows to push upward off the door to grab at the lowest-hanging strands of Spanish moss. But snatched at the ends, the tendrils broke away easily, rarely in strands long enough to be of any use. Besides, attempting to weave them into something resembling rope while remaining partly supported by the half-submerged door was impossible.

Eventually it became clear that the raft was beyond repair.

They were stranded.

All four children floated in silence, each trying to form a plan (apart from Claudette, who was perfectly content to hang around aimlessly in cold, damp places).

Occasionally something moving through the water disturbed the nearby reeds or appeared briefly, darkly, and ominously above the surface.

"If I am eaten by an alligator," thought August, "I will make a better choice than Uncle Orfeo and settle my spirit in a less gruesome creature—possibly a raccoon, or an osprey—until my replacement comes along. I wonder how Aunt Hydrangea will manage with all those zombies in the meantime."

The boy's musings were interrupted by a sudden hiss from Gaston.

"Do you hear that?" he whispered.

August did.

It was the *putt-putt-putt* of an outboard engine in low gear. And it was growing slowly louder.

The view of the channel was obstructed by jungle-like foliage and Spanish moss, but this soon parted to reveal a small open fishing boat with a single occupant.

"Cousin Grizel?" cried Gaston in surprise.

"Y'all look like rats in a vat of sarsaparilla," said the teenage girl with long braids of ginger hair.

"You out fishing?" said Gaston conversationally, as if he were not in the water, clinging desperately to the splintered ruins of his vessel.

"Nah," said Grizel with equal indifference. "Admiral sent me looking for you. She said, 'Grizel, you take my runabout and go find your cousin Gaston. Like as not, you'll find him down Papa Shadows's way. He didn't come home by sunup, so I reckon he's run into some trouble.'"

Gaston gave August's backside a healthy shove, propelling him into the skiff as Grizel surveyed the sorry remains of the raft that was itself the remains of a houseboat.

"Looks mighty like the Admiral was right. What was it, gators?"

"You could say that," chuckled Gaston, the last of the castaways to scramble aboard and wrap himself in one of the towels supplied.

"Let's get you home," said Grizel, maneuvering the small boat in the narrow space to return the way it had come.

"Actually, Grizel," said Gaston, glancing at August, "mind if we get these three back to Pepperville? I know it's a ways off, but August here has just had some important news.

"I reckon he has a small problem needs some taking care of."

* * *

The warm weather that preceded the hurricane had been replaced by cooler, more seasonal conditions. It had taken several hours to reach Locust Hole, but when the DuPont party was deposited by the Gardners on the banks of the canal, August and Marvell were still damp and chilled (Claudette, of course, was perfectly comfortable).

After August had shaken off his butterflies, Hydrangea had urged the young adventurers into clean, dry clothes, although Marvell had firmly (and not especially politely) refused to wear one of the lady's old pageant gowns, opting instead for a shirt and pants that August had outgrown.

"*Necromancy!*" cried Hydrangea, pacing the parlor where they were now gathered. "*That* is the DuPont treasure?"

"Why, that sounds like a dandy thing," said Mr. LaPoste

with a huge rabbity smile. "Just dandy. Congratulations on your gift, August."

"So . . . it was *you*," continued Hydrangea, "not the Zombie Stone, who were responsible for creating *them*?" She flicked her lace handkerchief sharply toward Little Prince Itty-Bitty and LouLou Bouquet, who lingered, uncertain, nearby. "And *them*!"

All eyes turned downward to the horde of skeletal faces gazing up through the hole in the floor.

The bedraggled, weed-strewn zombies who had emerged from the sunken riverboat swayed and shifted, making small wet noises, enraptured by the little stream of bubbles blown by the mailman.

"And the Cadaverite is gone?" continued Hydrangea. "Really gone this time?"

"I am afraid so, ma'am," said August with a sigh.

"So we have nothing, then. Nothing to sell Orchid. Nothing, indeed, to sell anyone. No means to pay the bank. No way to save Locust Hole!"

The lady promptly burst into tears and hid her face in her hands.

"What would your mother think," she sobbed, "to know that I have failed to keep a roof over her dear son's head? What will become of us . . . of you? And whatever will become of *them*?" She limply indicated the entire assembly of undead persons.

August slipped to her side and patted her arm.

"We may not need the Cadaverite, ma'am," he said consolingly. "I have recently come across a certain something that might solve our money troubles."

"But I thought, sugar, you were unable to salvage any of Jacques LeSalt's gold."

"It is not the gold, ma'am, that I have acquired. I am not entirely sure if this other thing will help us just yet. But I will explain it all when I am certain.

"And as for the zombies, I was trying to explain that I do not require the amulet to get rid of them. Great-Great-Uncle Orfeo said that just as I can make them, so I can *un*make them. I just have to release the spirits from their corpses."

"And how exactly does one go about that?"

August made a grimace, expressing his uncertainty.

"Apparently I just have to listen, not with my ears but with my heart. Listen not to their words but to their feelings. If I listen, all will be well."

"Why, son, can you hear anything now?" asked Mr. LaPoste, grinning enthusiastically.

"Well, I . . . I haven't really had the time to . . ."

"Why not give it a try?" suggested Madame Marvell.

August nodded. It was time to get started.

The boy filled his lungs with air and exhaled slowly. He closed his eyes. Time slowed.

He focused on the smell of decomposing flesh rising from

the basement. He heard the scaly sound of Claudette scratching her dead little legs (clearly irritated by the netting of Hydrangea's frothy pageant gown) and the gentle *rat-a-tat* of a woodpecker somewhere on the exterior wall.

The parlor's rough old floorboards seemed to press against his feet. Or was gravity pressing him into the floorboards? All the smells, the sounds, the sensations seemed connected to each other, to him, all swimming around together in a great cosmic soup. He felt that dull, distant throb: the heartbeat of . . . everything?

August opened the bridge.

And the dead came to him immediately.

Whisper, whisper.

Although his heart rate increased and his breath grew more rapid, this time the boy did not shy away from the voices. He could have closed his mind to them. He could easily have opened his eyes, flooding his senses with his physical surroundings. He could have pushed them aside as he had before.

But he didn't.

The whispering grew in volume. It began to sound more like the buzzing chatter of a crowd in a large room, a rustling cacophony of voices talking over one another. Now and then the audible fuzz tossed out an identifiable word or phrase.

"Regret!"

"I am sorry!"

"Where is she?"

They were powerful words. Words swollen and heavy with emotion.

"Loss!"

"Sadness!"

And then August heard a different sort of word, singular, in fact, in its subject matter. The voice that said it was louder too, as if it originated from somewhere nearby.

It said the strangest thing.

"Fingers!"

CHAPTER 23

FINGERS!

"Fingers?" August repeated it aloud, so surprising was the word's mundane nature in stark contrast to the grave, solemn statements that surrounded it.

He heard it again.

"Fingers!"

The voice had decisively elbowed its way to the fore now. Indeed, it was so distinct that it might have been spoken by someone in the parlor of Locust Hole. August opened his eyes to find out if it had been.

"Fingers!"

August cast his gaze across his companions.

The living were looking at him blankly; they had heard nothing.

Little Prince Itty-Bitty, however, was staring at August intently, with the faintest hint of a sparkle in his undead, unfixed eyes. His entire silk-garbed frame was trembling slightly, as if he were choking.

"Prince Itty-Bitty?" said August. "Is that *your* voice I'm hearing? Are you saying . . . *fingers?*"

"Fingers!" There it was again.

"Aunt Hydrangea!" August turned quickly with an outstretched hand. "Do you have a mirror?"

"Well, I did have one in there." Hydrangea pointed through the butterfly-proof netting toward the great pile of mud that had been the dining room and her bedchamber beyond it.

"Something shiny, then," said August, "that would show a reflection."

Hydrangea held up a finger.

"In the kitchen, perhaps."

She returned moments later with a copper frying pan, vigorously polishing its underside with a dish towel. When August gripped the handle, it was the strangest thing, but he sensed some sort of familiarity, as if he were taking the hand of an old friend.

Though once a handsome utensil crafted of solid copper, the pan was now warped and scratched. But Hydrangea's efforts had produced a surface that was impressively reflective. Reflective enough, in fact, that when he held it up before the little prince, August was immediately introduced to the likeness of a robust, spirited young boy, grinning eagerly from ear to ear.

His garments and jewels billowed and shifted as if he were standing over a subway grate.

"Fingers!" said the frying-pan prince, and the word was unmistakable.

The boy, like his three-dimensional counterpart, was gripped with tremors. But in the world of mirror, it was clear to August that rather than choking, Itty-Bitty was *laughing*!

"Fingers?" said August. "I don't understand, Your Highness. Help me understand."

The prince's mouth was forming words, but his voice was fuzzy, fading in a little, then out to nothing at all, like the sound on Marvell's television when reception was poor. August could not decipher any meaning in the odd syllable or two that made it through.

"Just listen," thought August, recalling Orfeo's advice, "not to the words but to the feelings."

"Come!" He guided the zombie to the fainting couch and, after evicting Marvell, settled in and patted the seat beside him.

He took a deep breath and gazed at the prince in the frying pan. He listened with his heart.

What was it like to be that boy? Why did he linger? What did he still have to achieve? Was he frightened? Was he lonely? How did he *feel*?

"Where are you?" asked August quietly.

"I don't know," said Itty-Bitty, and suddenly his words were clear as day. "It's a funny, vague sort of place. I'm not sure it's a place at all. But I'm awful glad you found me, August DuPont. I've been waiting ever so long for someone to talk to."

"I'm listening, Your Highness," said August, thinking, "With my heart, I guess." "You have been trying to tell me something, I believe . . . about *fingers?*"

The little prince promptly covered his mouth, smothering a fit of giggles. They were infectious, and August found himself smiling. The small royal was so overcome with mirth, it was difficult for him to get his words out.

"Do zombies," he finally managed to sputter, "eat pralines with their fingers?"

"Huh?" August was completely confused. "Zombies? Pralines? Oh! Wait!" The pattern of speech was suddenly familiar. "Is this . . . a *joke?* Why yes, that makes sense. The display at Saint-Cyr's Wax Museum said that you died from laughing at your own joke before you could finish the punch line. Is this . . . is this the joke you've been waiting to tell?"

Itty-Bitty spluttered and guffawed, nodding frantically.

"All right. All right, then. Please, begin again."

"Do zombies," chortled the prince, "eat pralines with their fingers?"

"I don't know," said August good-humoredly. "*Do* zombies eat pralines with their fingers?"

"No!" guffawed Itty-Bitty loudly. "They eat their fingers separately!"

The young boy burst into body-racking laughter, doubling over and clutching his stomach. His fit of hilarity was so forceful, August feared he might collapse.

"Is that not the funniest joke you ever heard?" choked Itty-Bitty.

"I reckon my sides are about to split," said August. In fact, it was not the funniest joke he had ever heard, and his sides were perfectly fine. But it was a small lie and well intentioned; August did not have the heart to disappoint the jovial little prince.

"Oh, my goodness gracious!" giggled the prince, recovering slightly and wiping his eyes. "At last someone got to hear the funniest joke I ever wrote. I am glad it was you, August. I am glad you found my joke funny. Will you tell it to other people? Will you tell them all it was my joke?"

"I will, Your Highness," said August sincerely. "I promise."

The small prince looked up with shining eyes and an endearing grin.

"Thank you, August," he said, "for listening."

August felt a sensation that was growing familiar, a liberation and a lift, like a dragonfly released from a jelly jar. He lowered the frying pan, and the royal boy's spirit—happy, healthy, chuckling merrily—sat beside him on the fainting couch, lightly cloaking his mildewed earthly body. The happy phantom drifted gently upward and dispersed like vapor.

Prince Itty-Bitty was gone.

August slumped, suddenly drained of energy.

"Are you all right, sugar?" Hydrangea was kneeling on the floor beside him, her hands on his thigh, her expression filled with concern. "You look exhausted. Sugar, you appeared to be having an entire conversation with a frying pan. I feared you might be going quite insane. But whoever you were talking to, wherever they were, whatever transpired between you . . . well, nephew, it worked."

Hydrangea grimaced, nodding at the small pile of bones and tattered silk on the couch that had moments before been a zombie.

"I believe," said August, nodding, "I may be getting the hang of it. Let's just hope I can do this twenty-nine more times."

He contemplated the undead faces below him. There was a new restlessness to the zombies. Their faces followed him even more obsessively than before, as faithfully as sunflowers follow the sun. Their whispers were growing louder, more urgent, more demanding. Their voices crowded at the edges of August's consciousness, impatient to be heard.

The dead now knew for certain what the boy was.

They knew that he knew too.

And they were eager to be heard.

August contemplated the daunting task before him. Listening to an unsettled spirit, listening with his heart to their feelings, was tiring stuff. How many times a day could one boy do that?

"We should probably," sighed August, forcing himself upright, "set up some sort of appointment system so I can do this—"

August was interrupted by a sudden jarring, metallic clang, which reverberated around the surviving walls of Locust Hole. It was a sound that August had heard only a few times before.

It was the doorbell.

But Mr. LaPoste, the only person ever—in August's lifetime, at least—to have rung it, was already present.

"Why, whoever can have come a-calling?" gasped Hydrangea, mangling her handkerchief. "I don't believe I've extended any invitations."

"I am sure, Miz Hydrangea," said Mr. LaPoste reassuringly, "there is no need for alarm."

"August?" Hydrangea was wide-eyed and rattled.

"I'll see to it, ma'am," said August. "Just stay calm."

What lay beyond the front door was something from another world.

"Leaf?" said August in astonishment, jarred by the unexpected and incongruous presence of the television production assistant.

"Dude!" protested Leaf. "You're late! You were expected on set two hours ago. We said one-thirty Sunday, remember? You didn't leave a phone number, only an address. But Margot was so jazzed by your sister's picture—she *is* your sister, right?—they sent me out to get you. This is some place. I guess I shouldn't be surprised that you two live . . . well, here."

Leaf stood framed against the stricken, blackened frame of the *Lady Luck,* which dominated everything in sight. He glanced around with raised eyebrows and an expression somewhere between disbelief and distaste.

August's mouth opened and closed a few times. He was at a loss for words. Although it was in fact only three days after their meeting on the *Stella Starz* set, so much had happened since then that this young man and his Hollywood world felt like something from a story heard long ago.

And Leaf was not alone. Someone was gingerly mounting the front porch steps behind him.

"I hardly think that you needed to call the police," said August, frowning as he spotted the dark blue uniforms of two law enforcement officers.

"Oh, they're not with me," responded Leaf, stepping aside and nodding politely as the officers passed him.

"We're looking for a girl," said the closest officer, head low, hands on hips.

Between the dark uniforms there was a flash of bright color.

August tilted his head to see a woman standing at the bottom of the steps. Her orange clipboard and gray suit lent her the air of someone official. But beside her was someone else, someone familiar. When he recognized her, August's stomach lurched.

It was Librarian Octavia Motts.

Two police officers. An official-looking woman carrying an orange clipboard. Octavia Motts.

This very particular group of people could only mean one thing.

August turned.

"Marvell!" he screamed at the top of his lungs. "RUN!"

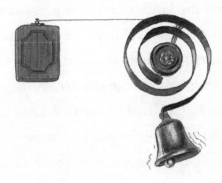

CHAPTER 24

THE PERFECT HAUNTED HOUSE

August opened the window of the small car to release the single butterfly that had made it inside, then closed it and leaned his forehead against the glass.

He watched the little country cemetery sweep by, the one crowded with long-dead DuPonts and Malveaus, the one where he had first encountered his great-great-aunt Claudette. From the back seat, the small zombie grunted softly, recognizing, perhaps, the place she had lived for most of her death.

The mini Roman temple that had served as her tomb still bore a yawning black void in its side where the freshly animated Claudette had smashed her way free.

That had happened on the very first day that August had ventured beyond the safety of Locust Hole, within the first hour.

It dawned on him suddenly that making a zombie was pretty much the first thing that had happened to him.

He just hadn't realized it.

It was like the dead had been waiting for him to come along.

That day, the day Claudette had attached herself to August like a lost puppy, seemed so long ago. He had thought it such a calamity to be saddled with a zombie.

A zombie. One.

Now he had an entire horde of restless undead persons in his basement.

"I hope the bubbles hold out," thought August, "until we can buy more. Mr. LaPoste was on the last bottle."

The little car, which resembled a beige sneaker, progressed along the Old French Highway without obstruction, the county authorities surely having cleared the road of hurricane debris.

The miles of Malveau Industries pepper fields showed visible storm damage, the endless leafy plain interrupted by large bleak patches of flattened, blackened plants. But many others had survived, and some were even spotted with the tiny white blossoms that preceded the fruit.

August remembered how spectacular they had been when he had seen them first, ablaze in all their crimson summer glory.

Back then there had been so much to look forward to, so many firsts for a boy who had spent twelve years sequestered in a flaking ruin. There still were. His very first automobile ride, for example.

He wanted to give the experience his full attention. He wanted to ask Leaf about the make of the car and how it worked.

But it was all August could do to stop himself from bursting into tears.

A plaintive, desperate screech was still ringing in his ears.

The sound of Madame Marvell's boatswain's whistle, shrieking for help from the sheriff's car as it had driven away, had been terrible. But not so terrible as the desolation in the pale face peering bleakly from the rear window, retreating down the lane until he could see it no more.

A sight, he feared, that would haunt his nightmares forever.

"What will they do with her?" he asked, without lifting his brow from the glass.

There was a pause. August imagined Leaf glancing at him sympathetically.

"No parents, right?"

August shook his head.

"No other family? You say she was living on a houseboat by herself? And she's how old?"

"I'm not sure," said August. "I don't know if she knows herself. Younger than me."

"Kids like that, they wind up in the system. Foster homes usually. And hey, that can be a great thing. Estefan, the makeup artist you met? He adores his foster parents. Says he couldn't have wished for a better family. He thinks because they chose each other, they have a special bond."

"Does it always work out that way?"

"Usually."

"Sometimes not?"

Leaf sighed, and August finally turned to look at him. The young man shrugged.

"Some kids find it hard to settle, is all," he explained, smiling comfortingly. "Sometimes they get passed around a bit, never quite landing anywhere."

"Marvell doesn't like to be stuck in one place," muttered August bleakly. "She'll hate wearing shoes."

More silence.

"Cheer up, dude," said Leaf. "Look, I hear you're a *Stella Starz* superfan."

August nodded glumly.

"You're about to meet your heroine, dude. How many people get to do that?"

August considered this.

Though it might take a few days or weeks (he was not yet sure), he did now have the means to rid himself of all his zombies. The development should clear the way for him to finally show up to his own life, to make friends, to belong.

Like Stella.

The thought was brightening his mood a little as Leaf swung the car sharply through high metal gates and into a long dirt driveway flanked by towering oak trees swathed in Spanish moss. The car was forced to stop almost immediately to permit the stately crossing of a glossy jet-black peacock.

"Wait a dang minute!" cried August, sitting forward, suddenly alert. "This is Château Malveau! What are we doing here?"

"We're filming here, dude," said Leaf, startled by the boy's dramatic reaction. "The mansion's standing in for the haunted house we need for the episode. Apparently the owner agreed to let us use it in return for premium spots during the commercials. I guess she owns the company that makes that Malveau's Devil Sauce?"

"She does," confirmed August as the little beige sneaker car proceeded up the driveway, carefully snaking between groups of people gathering up broken branches and bits of blasted pepper plants.

The wedding-cake silhouette of Château Malveau appeared.

"I mean, come on," said Leaf, gazing up at the soaring turrets and darkened windows, "it's kind of perfect, right? The place is eerie as all get-out. Beautiful, I guess, but there's a tangible atmosphere. Gloomy. Weird."

August observed that while the spectacular mansion had survived the hurricane largely intact, there were just enough missing shingles, broken shutters, and castaway palm fronds to enhance its already ominous air.

"I guess the episode we're filming involves Stella's friends daring her to investigate mysterious sounds coming from the basement of a local creepy mansion. She discovers some wizard keeping a horde of zombies in there, and all heck breaks loose."

Leaf rolled his eyes as he shook his head.

"I don't know where the writers come up with this stuff. It's so far-fetched, right?"

August said nothing.

"We're just using the house as a backdrop," Leaf prattled on. "Exterior shots only. We'll film the basement stuff in the studio, back in LA."

Accordingly, they did not come to a stop at the front door. Instead, Leaf's car progressed around the side of the house to park beside several others on a gravel lot. As August and Claudette followed the young man toward the château's back lawn, a wave of apprehension swept through the boy.

It was clear they were headed to the site of August's most crushing mortification, to the place where, several months before, he had been humiliated by someone he had believed to be his friend, where Hydrangea's warnings of the wider world and the betrayals lurking there had been realized.

But no crawfish boil awaited him. No checkered tablecloths

or boot-scooting dancers. In fact, the raucous, bustling film set he found had altered the place beyond recognition, so that revisiting it was less distressing than it might have been. The neatly cut grass was scarcely visible beneath towering spotlights, great canvas reflectors, trundling camera dollies, microphone boom poles, ladders, and pop-up tents.

Leaf responded to a sudden crackling voice in the walkie-talkie clipped to his vest.

"Give me a minute," he said, stepping away to pursue his radio conversation. "Stay right here."

The ground behind Château Malveau fell several feet toward the banks of Black River. Waiting by the house at the top of the rise, August had a better view of the action than he had had on Pepperville's Main Street, and he studied the goings-on below with curiosity.

There were Farfel Katz and Officer Claw, again installed at the craft services table, the cat handler appearing to share a handsome shrimp cocktail with the cat he handled.

And toiling under bright lights nearby was the long-haired makeup artist, Estefan. He was tending to a young woman seated in a tall folding chair, and the pair were laughing freely, sharing some cheerful exchange. So August was astounded when the actress turned to reveal the unmistakable profile of Stella Starz's stepmother, Hedwig. Without her usual scowl and frizzy hair, the woman appeared quite different, lighthearted and friendly.

Beyond them, several young people—not yet in makeup or costume—were chattering excitedly, punching shoulders, and peering into each other's phones. The group had the air of natural togetherness—of belonging—that August had first identified in the *Stella Starz* gang. It still tugged at something deep within him, triggering a surge of longing and envy.

Among them, August spotted Griffin and Abigail, the actors who played Stella's friends Kevin and Morning. Griffin glanced his way and caught August's eye. He grinned and waved.

One of his companions looked up to see who Griffin was saluting.

The companion was Beauregard.

And then August's cousin was leaning in, divulging something to the others, eyes still locked on August, and faces were turning, looking, frowning.

August suddenly felt very conscious of the butterflies that had again gathered around him. It seemed that history was about to repeat itself.

But it didn't.

"Impressive, is it not?"

August turned to see Belladonna Malveau. He half sighed, half smiled, glad of the interruption, relieved to turn his back on the smirking Beauregard, to turn away from unpleasant memories.

"The bus, I mean," said Belladonna, pointing. "It's impressive."

While the lively film set was much the same as that which August had previously encountered, it had one very eye-catching addition. At its perimeter on the banks of Black River stood a long shiny bus of the sort often used by touring rock bands.

And it was indeed impressive.

The entire vehicle was clad in a jumble of vividly colored graphics, one large vehicular advertisement. Groovy purple text reading *"Stella Starz (in Her Own Life)"* was superimposed on a huge image of Stella Starz herself. A smaller decal of Stella's cat, Officer Claw, covered the bus's front door.

It seemed like the kind of bus that might contain a television star.

"You reckon she's in there?" said August in wonder.

"I can't imagine who else might be."

"Marvell would have loved this," mumbled August sadly. "She should be here. Isn't that so, Claudette?"

Claudette grunted in agreement.

Belladonna eyed the zombie lurking at her cousin's shoulder.

"Did you find it," she asked, "the stone that you and Mama are both so crazy for?"

"I did. But then I lost it again, for good this time."

Belladonna grimaced.

"Mama won't like that." She paused. "August, where did you get that copy of the *Croissant City Crier*, the one with the article about the treasure map, the one that sent you off again on your hunt for the Zombie Stone?"

"I found it," said August, "at the top of the carriage-house stairs the morning after the Carnival."

"Do you think our butler left the daily newspaper for you as a courtesy? Did it arrive on a silver tray with a hot pot of coffee and a warm beignet?"

"I doubt," said August with a wry smile, "Escargot thinks of me as *that* sort of guest. So no, it was just lying there all by itself."

"So someone else took the effort to put it there . . . so you would see it."

August followed his cousin's gaze to the mansion's upper floors. He briefly spied something pale at a window, but the glass was ablaze with the rose-colored light of the setting sun, and it was impossible to tell if he'd seen the reflection of a passing bird . . . or a face peering out.

"You think Aunt Orchid wanted me to keep looking, to find the stone for her?"

Belladonna shrugged.

"I wouldn't put it past her. She's certainly been ornery since you left, like she's waiting for something. Better keep a low profile if you don't want to give her the bad news."

Leaf returned, still gripping his walkie-talkie.

"Okay!" he said, smiling. "Margot's ready for you. Let's go."
He nodded toward the chaotic set.

August's stomach turned. Suddenly everything seemed fuzzy
and unreal, like a dream. Was this actually happening?

"Is she really . . . ?" He stared at the bus.

"Yep, she's really in there," confirmed Leaf. "Smile, dude!
You're about to meet your heroine.

"You're about to meet Stella Starz!"

CHAPTER 25

THE DEATH OF STELLA STARZ

August quickly closed the door behind him so no butterflies might follow, then clambered up the steel steps past a well-padded driver's seat to discover a space that, while obviously much smaller than Château Malveau, rivaled it in luxury.

The interior walls of the bus were paneled in gleaming walnut. The ceiling was lacquered midnight blue and studded with sparkling spotlights. Beyond a counter and well-lit mirror—much like the stations in Estefan's makeup trailer—was a plush lounging area with a deep shaggy rug, squishy-looking swivel chairs, and an expansive lilac leather banquette. Beyond *that* was a well-stocked mini kitchen, its counter loaded with flower-filled vases, bottles of fancy sparkling water, and healthy snacks.

"Margie, honey, you want some cucumber juice?" a big voice bellowed from behind the open refrigerator door, although no part of its owner was visible. "Some tiny slivers of carrot, maybe? Got to keep your strength up!"

The fridge door closed, revealing a woman who was far smaller than her voice. Her face was little, but her hair was large. Her fingers were little, but her rings were large. Her body was little, but the shoulders of her sparkly pantsuit were large.

She was, August thought, like an adult who had been slightly shrunk in the wash.

The woman looked up from the pale green bunch of celery in her hands and, on seeing the visitors, gasped, clearly startled at their sudden appearance. It took her only a second to recover, however, and staring at Claudette, she opened her mouth, hugged the celery to her stomach, and let out a fat guffaw.

"Well, I'll be, if that pea-brained production assistant wasn't right for once in his sniveling little life! Now *that,* honey," she declared to Claudette, "is the best zombie makeup on the entire set, *the entire set*! Has casting signed you up yet? Cheese and crackers, you're perfect. Margie! You have to see this. Margie, honey! MARGOT!"

August winced. The woman's yell was jarringly loud. Despite her petite size, her presence seemed to fill the entire bus.

Behind her a door opened, revealing a bedroom beyond.

August's heart was pounding now, his thoughts racing.

Would she recognize him? Would she level an accusing finger at him and scream "Loser!" or, worse, "Monster!"?

Stella Starz emerged.

Or at least a girl who looked just like Stella Starz emerged. But somehow she seemed like an impostor.

This girl's hair did not bob optimistically on her head in two poufy pigtails but curled loosely about her face. She did not wear square, geeky glasses or a patterned scarf or a trim cardigan but simple black leggings and a voluminous sweater that fell off one shoulder.

This girl did not bounce into the room with a zany grin and bright, eager eyes. She did not crackle with excitable energy and move with large, confident gestures. This girl did not seem like the type of person who eagerly placed herself in overwrought situations, where she had no business being.

This girl slipped through the doorway like she was trying not to be seen. Her head was low and her gaze shy. She was clutching a book to her chest.

"Yes, Mom?" said the girl, her voice as small as her mother's was large.

The woman forcefully shook the bunch of celery toward Claudette.

"Are you seeing this? Isn't she perfect, Margie? PERFECT! For the closing scene, the whole zombie-rising-from-the-grave shock ending?"

Margot Morgan Jordan (this girl was certainly *not* Stella Starz) glanced briefly at Claudette. She had not even looked at August yet.

"Yes, Mom," she agreed flatly. "She's perfect."

"You said it, Margie," bellowed Margot Morgan Jordan's mother, snapping off a stick of celery and shoving it at her daughter. She broke off another and took a bite herself. "And what Stella Starz wants," she said, crunching, "Stella Starz gets!"

August was left with the distinct impression that it was Stella Starz's mother who got what Stella Starz's mother wanted.

"What's your name, honey?" the woman asked Claudette, grinning and crunching.

"She's from Lapla— I mean, she's not from round here," said August. "Her name's Claudette. I'm her translator."

This was not, figured August, entirely untrue.

"A foreigner?" said the woman. "She *looks* European, doesn't she, Margie? Got that intellectual, hollow-eyed thing going on. Well, you"—she waggled the celery at August—"tell your client that Stella Starz wants her in this show. And what Stella Starz wants—"

"Stella Starz gets!" said August, finishing the sentence.

Margot Morgan Jordan's mother looked at him—*really* looked at him—for the first time. She nodded appreciatively.

"That's it, kid," she crowed, giving him a celery poke. "I

wish the fools running this circus were half as smart as you. It would make my life half as difficult!"

She thrust the remaining vegetable at her daughter, who had not consumed any of the stalk she held.

"Eat that, Margie!" she ordered. "It's good for you. I'm off to find that dimwit Leaf and make sure this pasty European girl has a contract. Take care of these kids for a minute, honey. I'm sure they'd be jazzed to meet Griffin and Abigail, huh? Why don't you all go hang out?"

"I don't want to," said Margot, lowering her eyes. "I . . . I'm reading."

"Cheese and crackers, Margie, you and the books," cried the small woman with the big rings. "It's not healthy, I tell you, all this reading. You should be out there with the other young people." Her tone turned cajoling. "I saw a couple of cute boys on set!"

"Mom!" Margot frowned, clutching the book and celery closer to her, as if the objects might protect her from her mother's loud voice and strident demands.

"Oh, whatever, girl," sighed the woman, rolling her eyes at August as she strode past. "Whatever Stella Starz wants . . . ," she bellowed sarcastically.

The abrupt departure of Margot's mother left the bus with a sense of emptiness . . . and relief.

August looked up to find the young actress studying him with an air of curiosity.

His heart sank.

"I know you," said Margot thoughtfully. "Where from?"

August did not want to lie. She would find out the truth eventually, and the lying would just make it worse when she did.

"From the Carnival Grand Parade," he said miserably, certain that his relationship with Stella Starz was about to end a sentence or two after it had begun. "I was on the float that crashed. There was an incident with Officer Claw."

Margot's eyes widened with recognition.

"Right!" she said, nodding. "The guy who scared the cat who freaked out the driver who wrecked the pirate ship. I saw you on TV."

"It really wasn't my fault," mumbled August. "If you knew me, you'd understand I'd never frighten a helpless animal deliberately. But I am sorry if he was traumatized."

"Helpless?" scoffed Margot. "Traumatized? Officer Claw? Believe me, that brute is far more likely to do the traumatizing."

August's jaw dropped a little.

"But . . . but you always say," he stammered, "that he's a shining example to feline-kind across the universe."

Margot tossed the celery in a trash can, exited the kitchenette, and placed her book on the coffee table page-side down to keep the place. August noted its title: *Whispers in the Walls*. The young actress drew back the sleeve of her loose-knit sweater to reveal a crosshatch of scratches on her arm, some apparently quite fresh.

"Ouch!" said August.

"If he wasn't so popular," said Margot, "I'd beg them to get Stella a goldfish instead. But apparently Claw is great for ratings. You know he gets paid more than me? You look doubtful. I know it's hard to believe, but ask yourself who they invited to act as the parade's grand marshal: Stella, or Stella's cat?"

"You seemed so mad," said August quietly, "when you were interviewed by Cyril Saint-Cyr and Dixie Lispings."

"Sure, I was mad," grumbled Stella, pointing to a claw mark that was rather pinker than the rest. "He did that when they shoved him into my arms."

She studied her battle scars for a moment, then her head popped up with a sudden realization.

"Oh!" she said, grimacing. "I said some pretty unkind things about you in that interview, didn't I?"

August nodded, eyes downcast.

"I didn't mean them," said Margot in an apologetic tone. "I just reacted how the producers told me to, how they thought Stella Starz would if someone upset her precious Claw."

Her eyes sought out August's.

They exchanged a small smile.

"She doesn't hate me after all," thought August, with a great sense of relief.

"Why don't you want to hang out with your friends?" he asked. "Kevin and Morning are out there."

"Oh, they're not my friends," said Margot, sliding onto the lilac banquette and hugging her knees to her chest.

This response was so bizarre that August did not even fully register it.

"Kevin and Morning are just characters, of course," he laughed. "I know that. I meant Griffin and Abigail."

"We're not friends," repeated Margot.

"I don't understand," said August, utterly baffled. "You're the *Stella Starz* gang. You do everything together. You recover stolen penguins and form rock bands and unmask school librarians as spies or smugglers of exotic animals (although the librarian I know would never do such criminal things). You have lunch together every day. You share kettle corn.

"You belong!"

"*Belong?*" Stella frowned good-humoredly. "Dude, it's TV; we're just acting. Those guys don't much like me; they think I'm stuck-up and boring. They never say it to my face, but I know behind my back they call me 'Stella Snooze.'"

"Boring?" August was incredulous. " 'Snooze?' Why, that's just crazy talk. You dye your friends' hair purple! You hide reindeer in your garage! You baked Hedwig's phone into a birthday cake! You are Stella Starz!"

"*I,*" said Margot, quietly but decidedly, "am Margot! I'm

not wacky or zany. I'm not especially adventurous, I'm scared to death of penguins, and I've never met a spy. That girl you see on TV, that's the girl that they"—she waved her hand vaguely at the activity beyond the window of the bus—"invented. Stella Starz doesn't really exist. Her whole life is just a story."

August staggered backward into one of the swivel chairs. It was as squishy as it looked, but August didn't notice, for his mind was elsewhere.

His head was swimming.

The intimate winks, the shared California rolls at Sushi Yum-Yum, the high fives . . . the belonging: it was all a mirage. A fantasy.

For so long now, August had deeply yearned for something— had been chasing something—that wasn't even real.

It had never been real.

August had, of course, always understood that *Stella Starz (in Her Own Life)* was scripted entertainment, the product of writers in Hollywood. He had always known that the people he saw on the screen were actors with names different from the ones they had on the show.

He had just never imagined that they (and their relationships) were any different in real life from how they appeared on television. Perhaps if he had given it more thought, he might have considered this possibility. But he was so intoxicated by Stella Starz and the life she starred in, it had never crossed his mind.

Spread across the squishy swivel chair, stunned, August felt as he had when staring at that sprite-lit lagoon in Lost Souls' Swamp, knowing that he had lost the Zombie Stone forever.

Something that he had treasured was gone, and it was never coming back.

It was like something had died.

"Margot," said Margot, "prefers reading to roller coasters. I'm especially fond of horror, the creepier the better. I'd rather be in here with *Whispers in the Walls* than out there being Stella Starz."

August nodded, pulling himself together.

There was no Stella. Only Margot.

"But if you don't like acting," he asked, pulling himself up by the arms of the chair, "why do you do it?"

"It's all Mom, really," said Margot. "It's her dream more than mine. She was in a movie once, before I was born, and wanted to be a star. But everyone said her voice was too annoying. She tried to change it, got vocal coaching and stuff, but it didn't take, so nothing more happened for her. She would have loved to be Stella Starz. Now, at least, she's the next best thing."

"Stella Starz's mother?"

"And manager." Margot grinned.

August glanced around at the impressively luxurious surroundings.

"Seems like there are at least some advantages," he said, grinning back.

"Sure, there's the money. One day I will use it." Margot's expression suddenly lit up, and for a second she resembled the spirited character she had made so famous. "One day I intend to visit all the great horror sites of the world: Dracula's castle in Romania, the villa on Lake Geneva where *Frankenstein* was written, the library in England that's haunted by the ghost of a beheaded king."

August brightened at the thought of libraries.

"I just applied for a library card," he said.

"Oh!" said Margot, thrown by this unintended change in the conversation's direction.

"Our local librarian said I should. She seemed real nice at the time. But now I'm not so sure; she helped the authorities find my friend, who didn't want to be found. I guess Stella would agree that librarians are not always what they seem. What are you looking at?"

It was obvious that Margot had stopped listening. She was staring intently through a window facing Black River. She frowned and moved her nose closer to the glass. Now she was on her knees.

"There's something in the water," she said. "Lots of some-things."

The girl started back with a gasp of shock.

"Zombies!" she whispered.

"I know," said August. "There are zombies everywhere.

Although I have to say the makeup is not that realistic. Estefan should probably study my great-great—"

"I don't think," said Margot, removing herself from the banquette, "those are actors."

She turned to August with real alarm in her eyes.

Almost simultaneously they heard a shriek from somewhere beyond the confines of the bus. It was followed by another, and then by a loud crash, and then by another full-blown blood-curdling scream.

August leaped up to join Margot at the window.

Emerging from the river was a small nightmarish army of hollow-eyed, slime-dripping skeletons, their movements sharply angled, jerky, and disturbing.

Many were without skin or faces or hair, but some were distinguished by the elements of their costume: brass buttons, flat caps, kid gloves.

All looked as if they had spent a century moldering in the wreckage of a riverboat lost to the swamp.

"Oh dear," said August. "Mr. LaPoste must have run out of bubbles."

CHAPTER 26

ZOMBIE ATTACK

"Margot!" Margot Morgan Jordan's mother bellowed shrilly as she burst wild-eyed into the bus.

Through the open door behind her came a rising discord of shrieking and yelling and crashing.

"Zombies!" screamed the woman, pointing a little finger with a large ring toward the river-facing window. "ZOMBIES!" She repeated it at full volume, as if—inexplicably—no one had heard her foghorn tones the first time. "*Real* zombies! Don't just stand there, Margie, come with me!"

Margot Morgan Jordan hesitated, flustered, then bumped into the coffee table.

"Leave it!" ordered her mother as Margot reached for her book, which had been knocked to the floor.

"Please don't be alarmed," said August, attempting to explain the situation. "They are harmless; they're simply looking for—"

"*Harmless?*" bellowed Margot's mother, and August thought the diminutive woman might shake him in frustration. "Have you *seen* the things?"

Something suddenly slammed against the window, and all looked around sharply to see two skeleton palms, black with sludge and scum, pressed against the glass. They were shortly followed by a heavily cracked skull, which peered curiously inside as a snail slithered out of its nose socket.

Margot Morgan Jordan's mother screamed at the top of her lungs.

Margot Morgan Jordan screamed too.

In solidarity and confusion, Claudette DuPont let out a guttural but plaintive howl.

"To the mansion!" bellowed Margot's mother.

The woman grabbed her daughter's arm with one hand, August's with the other, and with surprising strength she bundled the youngsters unceremoniously out of the bus. August snatched at Claudette as they went, dragging her with them.

At the foot of the steps, a skin-crawling, skittering sound from above caused them all to glance up. A skeletal form was scampering on all fours across the bus's roof like some grotesque clockwork toy. And suddenly it was leaning over the edge, its bony hand reaching for them.

There was more screaming from the Morgan Jordans as they fled.

"They're looking for me," protested August, trying to break free from Margot's mother. But the woman's tiny, determined, terrified grip was like a vise, and there was no escaping it. Despite all the drama, August found himself wondering if she or Claudette would win a contest in arm wrestling.

"Let me go!" yelled August. "I can stop them!"

But his protests went unheard as everything around them descended into chaos and hysteria. August, Claudette, and the Morgan Jordans were swept up in a tsunami of people surging toward Château Malveau. Most were screaming bloody murder, shoving each other aside and trampling chairs and equipment underfoot.

August could not see much other than the crowd around him, but at its edges he spotted flashes of jerking bony limbs, chattering jaws with rotted teeth, and black, soulless eye sockets, which, although vacant, were searching—August knew—for him.

He caught glimpses of zombies scuttling up scaffolding, leaping onto camera cranes, swinging between trees, all silhouetted against the sunset sky. There were zombies curiously licking microphones, attempting to remove jars of peanut butter from their fists, trying on wigs.

There were zombies everywhere.

A tower of lighting equipment came crashing to the ground nearby. Ladders, reflectors, and booms were toppling. Tents were collapsing. The sounds of screaming, wailing, smashing, and small electrical explosions filled the air.

Château Malveau now loomed large. August stumbled on the back porch steps, but he was buoyed up by Margot's powerful mother and the fleeing crowd. The crush of people suddenly intensified as they bottlenecked into the back door of the mansion in a desperate, heaving mass of impassable buttocks and sharp, poking elbows.

"Please, one at a time!" August heard the condescending tones of the Malveaus' butler, Escargot, although he could not see him. "Sir, where are your manners! Madame, unhand me! I beg of you . . . Ooof!"

August had just caught a glimpse of the toady, wide-mouthed butler as a little hand with large rings landed on his striped vest and shoved him forcefully aside.

"Stella Starz must be saved!" bellowed Margot's mother. "Without her, none of you people would have a job." She barreled forth like a miniature juggernaut, an unstoppable force. "Ow! Ugh! Get . . . out . . . of . . . our . . . *way!*"

August was squeezed tighter and tighter by the bodies around him as they pressed through the span of the doorway (it was a large door, but there were a lot of people). The boy was beginning to wonder if his ribs would make it intact when *pop!*

Suddenly there were soft rugs underfoot and sparkling chandeliers overhead, and his nostrils were filled with the scent of lavender furniture wax.

August was discharged into the grand hallway of Château Malveau.

"Bar the door!" Margot's mother was screaming. "They're coming!"

"But there are still people outside," protested another woman's voice.

"They're too slow. Leave them! Stella Starz must be saved!"

As the great door closed, August spotted a wide-eyed, panic-stricken face beyond the narrowing aperture. It was Leaf's.

"It's fine!" cried August. "They're just lost. Let me out!"

But no one was listening.

August had to get outside. The zombies wanted only one thing: him.

Could he get them under control? He wasn't sure. But he felt certain they would at least follow him away from that place. Well, probably.

August spun around, searching for a route through the crowded hallway. Harried, disheveled refugees sobbed and babbled into their phones, talking loudly over one another.

"They looked so hungry!"

"Will they eat our brains?"

"I can't become a zombie; did you see how they dress?"

Margot caught August's eye. She wore a long-suffering expression, locked in her mother's tight embrace. The woman was
wailing like the Malveaus' peacock.

"Oh, my darling girl," she cried. "I thought I'd lost you,
Stella!"

"Don't you mean 'Margot,' Mother?"

Farfel Katz and Officer Claw huddled behind a large pot-
ted palm. The cat looked like a badly cleaned rug, and his eyes
were saucer-round with outrage. His handler was attempting to
comfort him with the handsome shrimp cocktail, which had mi-
raculously survived the stampede.

A sudden bony impact shook the back door, eliciting a collective shriek. Scrawny twitching forms, skeletal palms, and vaguely
formed faces appeared at the frosted sidelights, accompanied by
a muffled cacophony of wheezing, hissing, and growling.

"Save Stella!" screamed Margot's mother. "Save Stella
Starz!"

Dragging Claudette behind him, August forced his way
through the distraught mob in the direction of the mansion's
front door. He spotted Belladonna near the foot of the staircase,
bending over with her hands on her hips, hair in her face. She
looked up and they locked eyes. He headed for her.

But suddenly she disappeared behind a body, and August
was face to face with the other twin, Beauregard. His sidekick,

Langley, hovered nearby, biting his nails as his head swiveled anxiously from side to side.

"We are all most certainly going to die," whimpered the tall, rangy boy.

"Oh, shut your piehole, Langley," hissed Beauregard. He turned on August. "You, DuPont, are at the bottom of this, I can smell it. Everywhere you go, your foul-breathed, revolting, undead freaks follow, causing destruction and terror. You ruined the crawfish boil. You ruined the parade. Now you've ruined this. You quite literally ruin everything!"

August understood Beauregard now, the insecurity behind the meanness. And the understanding helped him weather his cousin's cruel words. But the assault was so venomous, he faltered a little. Who wouldn't?

Besides, August realized bleakly, Beauregard's accusations were not entirely untrue.

"I am sorry," said August meekly. "I cannot help who I am."

The boy's candor caught his cousin off guard. Beauregard sneered, but with less conviction.

"But," continued August, with a glimmer of optimism in his voice, "I can fix this, cousin. I can. I think."

"And how," inquired a familiar voice, creamy as café au lait, "might you do that . . . exactly?"

Orchid Malveau stood in the open doorway of the Chamber

of Jewels, framed against the ghostly glow of the museum lights that illuminated her priceless collection of minerals and gemstones. One bejeweled hand gripped the doorframe, the other pressed her long, glittering veil to her abdomen in a gesture of anticipation.

"You have found it at last, then?" she said, a smile lurking on her rose-colored lips. "You have recovered Orfeo's Cadaverite, the Zombie Stone. You went in search of the map and tracked Leech down in Lost Souls' Swamp. Oh, well *done,* August! Well done. Where is it? Give it to me. I must have it."

"No," stammered August, distressed at the extent of his aunt's misunderstanding. "No, ma'am, I don't have the stone. It's gone."

"Gone?" Orchid's voice was quiet, dangerous.

"Gone for good," said August. "It's somewhere at the bottom of Lost Souls' Swamp, possibly in the stomach of a giant alligator."

"Gone . . . for good."

The woman's face drained of all color, its skin appearing to sag before August's very eyes. She stumbled slightly and clutched at the doorknob to support herself, as if her legs had lost that ability.

Her mouth twitched as if she were trying to contain a scream.

"But without the stone," she said suddenly, "how can you possibly fix . . . *this*? What do you mean?"

"Well, here's the thing, ma'am," said August nervously. "It is not the Cadaverite that's the Go-Between. It is not the Zombie Stone that controls the dead.

"It's me!"

CHAPTER 27

THE CHAMBER IN THE CHAMBER

Claudette was so obstructive that Orchid eventually yanked the zombie into the chamber too before slamming the door shut behind her. Instantly, the three of them (plus some butterflies) were alone in the gloom, the sounds of panic and chaos stifled like a television heard from a distant room.

"Explain yourself," demanded the woman, spinning to face August and grabbing his coat. Behind fine black lace, black eyes burned with obsession.

Something smashed loudly against the exterior wall, causing August to start and Claudette to grunt. But Orchid scarcely seemed to notice, her focus devoted entirely to one thing.

August recalled Professor Leech's appraisal of his aunt's

fixation during the séance on Funeral Street. "You care," the man had said, "about nothing else. Nothing."

"I am truly sorry, Aunt Orchid," the boy whispered, a little frightened now. "I know your collection is the only thing that brings you true pleasure. I tried my best, I did. I know the thing was valuable, and I can never repay you. But there must be other specimens out there."

"Explain," repeated Orchid steadily, fist tightening on August's lapel, "what you mean when you say that it is *you* who are a Go-Between, that it is *you* who control the dead."

"So, it seems," said August hurriedly, licking his lips, "that the DuPont treasure was never Orfeo's famous gemstone. The treasure is a hereditary trait. Uncle Orfeo described it as a genetic anomaly. The treasure is a gift, he said, the ability to communicate with the dead, to command them, even."

Orchid hesitated, clearly skeptical.

"You?" she said hesitantly.

"Yes, ma'am. Me. Some of us receive the gift whether we want it or not."

"You are a living Go-Between. *You.*"

August nodded.

The lapel was released. Orchid straightened with an expression of revelation.

"So *that* is why Leech's so-called Oraculum revealed your face during the séance."

She emitted a strange little laugh and rubbed her temples with her fingertips.

"So, August. It seems that it is *you* for whom I have been searching all along."

"Me?" squeaked August. "But I can't complete your collection. I am not a priceless chunk of Cadaverite. I doubt I'm worth much at all."

"It was never, August, about the material value of the thing. It was never about its rarity, or even about the collection. Indeed, this entire room"—she delicately waved her open hands around their surroundings—"was contrived to further the search for that which my heart has desired for many years. A Go-Between!"

The woman stared at the boy with a strange, quiet triumph.

"And now, in you, I have found one."

"But *why,* Aunt Orchid?" August was thoroughly confused. "Why do you want a Go-Between so desperately?"

The woman went quite still. She looked down, then nodded slowly in a manner that suggested it was time to reveal all.

Black diamonds glittered as a long, elegant finger beckoned.

August and Claudette obediently followed the woman to the bookshelves that housed her impressive assemblage of minerals: fire opal, meteorite, bloodstone.

The long, elegant fingers lifted a glass cloche from one of the round plinths.

August remembered it well, for it was the only display that

sat empty, the one labeled "Cadaverite." On examining it for the first time, the boy had felt a curious sadness surrounding the vacancy, as if something important was missing.

The long, elegant fingers pressed down on the little stand that would have supported the specimen, had it been present. But rather than toppling over as one might have expected, the squat black cylinder disappeared into the wooden base beneath it.

There was a deep, well-oiled click, and suddenly the entire bank of shelving swung away from the room, revealing at one side a narrow opening.

It was a hidden door.

* * *

The chamber beyond the chamber appeared to have three windows, although no part of them was visible behind the tightly drawn thick velvet draperies. The only light derived from fat candles that flickered in wax-smothered sconces on the wall.

August understood, of course, that candles do not burn indefinitely. He concluded, then, that Orchid must recently have been in the room, possibly (probably) even when the zombies had launched their "attack."

The place was heavily perfumed by glorious creamy gardenias, hundreds of them frothing from several large urns on the stone floor. It was a familiar fragrance, one that August had come to associate with his aunt. He had assumed the scent was that of her cologne, but now he understood that she smelled of this place.

Other than the flowers, the chamber's only contents were at its center: a pair of tables that stood two feet apart, each bearing an identical rectangular box.

"Hello, my darlings," said Orchid softly, gliding between them and laying a palm on the top of each. "The time has come, finally, for us to be reunited. I have found it at last, the Go-Between."

The woman turned to August with a trembling smile.

The boy approached her with a rising sense of dread, a dread that turned to horror as he realized that the boxes were in fact . . . coffins.

Each was topped with glass so that its contents were clearly visible. And what August saw inside caused his knees to weaken and his heart to leap into his throat.

There lay two children, their young hands crossed, pressing withered sprays of gardenias to their chests. Each had a full mouth with curving lips that looked like it had been drawn by an artist. The symmetry and proportions of their oval faces were so perfect, they reminded August of paintings he'd seen in a documentary about the Italian Renaissance. Each head was crowned by tightly waved honey-blond hair.

One was a boy. One was a girl.

The children were twins.

And they were quite dead.

CHAPTER 28

THE ONES AFTER

"*These* are the children in the Funeral Street portrait," whispered August, scarcely able to believe his eyes. "These are your children. Your *first* children. Aren't they?"

His eyes rose accusingly.

But his aunt was oblivious, staring with a distant smile into the caskets.

"This is Antoinette," she said, stroking the glass with the back of her hand. "So like me: willful, smart, adventurous." She turned her head. "But Aubrey, dearest Aubrey, was the sweet one: so kind, so quiet and observant, until . . . the Peruvian flu."

A shadow crossed the woman's face, and it darkened as if divided from the sunlight by a thundercloud. And August saw again the woman he had met many months before, a woman staring at a shuttered window with an expression of unutterable grief.

"You were robbed," he whispered, repeating the words she had said to him at the time. "You would do"—he gulped—"anything . . . to recover what you lost."

He had thought at the time that she had been referring to her husband.

She hadn't.

Orchid nodded slowly.

"Anything," she said.

"What do you mean by . . . *recover*?" August's heart was racing.

Orchid's eyes burned bright and fierce in the flickering candle flame.

"You already know what I want, August. It's what I wanted when I first invited you here to hunt down Orfeo's Cadaverite. It's what I wanted when I permitted you to remain on Funeral Street to search for the Zombie Stone. It's what I wanted when I left the newspaper that revealed the map at the top of the carriage-house steps."

August backed away slowly until he was pressed against the chamber wall.

"You want them back," he croaked.

"I want them back."

"You want a Go-Between to reach into the spirit world and

force them into their bodies. You want to make them . . ."—the word stuck in his throat—". . . zombies."

"I want them back," repeated Orchid, "however I can have them. I want them restored to a form that I can hold, that I can kiss, that I can comfort and keep safe so that nothing ever harms them again."

"But it wouldn't be them, Aunt Orchid. Not really. Just shadows, distorted reflections of the people they used to be." He glanced at the small zombie, as always, at his side. "Like Claudette."

"I don't CARE!" The woman's voice rose with raw emotion verging on hysteria. "I want whatever is left of them, whatever little bit I can wring out of the universe. A ragged fragment of my precious darlings is better than the monstrous nothing they have left behind!"

"This will not bring them happiness, Aunt. I . . . I know this firsthand. The spirit inside a zombie feels trapped, confused, discontented."

"You're wrong! My presence will bring them contentment. They will be happiest in my arms."

"It's not right!" August raised his own voice now, outrage and fear fueling his courage. "I won't do it. I don't even know if I *can* do it; I've never made a zombie . . . not deliberately."

Orchid lowered her chin and stepped toward her nephew with scowling fury in her face. But suddenly her expression collapsed, as did her whole body, as if all energy had been vac-uumed from it.

She crumpled to her knees at her nephew's feet, grabbed his hands in her own, and gazed up with imploring eyes.

"You don't know grief yet, August," she said thickly. "It is . . . it is . . ." The woman struggled to find the right words.

In her heavily burdened shoulders, in the fatigue and frailty of her face, August saw the Orchid who had coaxed a crushingly sad melody from the harp in her music room. He remembered how that music had made him feel.

"It's unbearable," said August.

"Please, August. Please!"

The indomitable, vibrant person who could silence a room with a slap of her fan, who inspired no small sense of fear in August himself, had been replaced by a limp, vulnerable crea-ture, her face shining with tears.

The reversal of dynamic befuddled the boy; suddenly his aunt's happiness rested in August's hands.

He was a kindhearted boy.

He was a confused boy, bewildered by his aunt's desperate pleas.

He relented.

"Do you have anything reflective?" he asked.

* * *

Again Claudette's remarkable strength proved to be indispensable, and the overmantel mirror from the Chamber of Jewels
was brought in. The broad bottom of its gilt frame was placed
on the ends of both caskets, and Claudette was positioned to
hold the thing upright so that the upper halves of the recumbent
children were reflected in the glass.

Orchid stood at Aubrey's head, August at Antoinette's.

The living boy closed his eyes. He quieted his mind, concentrating on the darkly glowing nothingness. He took a deep
breath, inhaling the pungently sweet aroma of gardenia flowers
and the musty odor of dusty velvet. Time slowed.

August heard the soft fizz of melting candle wax. He heard
the faint rustle of expensive Belgian lace and the even fainter
sound of a tear trickling down a powdered cheek.

The coldness of the stone floor penetrated the soles of his
shoes. It seemed to press against his feet. Or was gravity pressing
him into the stone? He felt that powerful, dull, distant throb.

August opened the bridge.

Someone whispered in his ear, and August opened his eyes.

The mirror held the images of two young people, twins. But
unlike the similar reflections that August had observed thus far,
these figures were faint, seeming far more distant than the others had.

Moreover, their garments and hair did not drift and ripple
as if they floated in some ambiguous, flimsy place. Rather, the

children stood rooted, surrounded by an inky blackness, empty but definite.

Aubrey and Antoinette did not inhabit the vague, foggy world between worlds where discontented spirits floated aimlessly.

They were not nowhere.

They were somewhere.

"Can you see them?" August asked his aunt softly; she was as well positioned as he was to do so.

The woman looked at him with wet, wondering eyes and shook her head.

"Here," said August, "take my hand. Close your eyes. Smell the universe around you. Hear the ground beneath your feet. Can you feel a dull, distant throb? You were born a DuPont, Aunt Orchid. There must be just a little of the gift in you. Now . . . look!"

Orchid breathed a quivering, rapturous sigh and slumped forward, reaching across the caskets toward the mirror with trembling fingers.

"My darlings!" she whispered hoarsely. "My dear, sweet Antoinette, Aubrey."

The children smiled and spoke.

"I can't hear them!" Orchid glanced anxiously at August.

The boy squeezed his aunt's hand more firmly, and he listened, not with his ears but with his heart, not to the children's words but to their feelings.

"Mama!" The voices sounded distant and echoey, as if reverberating through many dimensions to arrive at this one.

"Return to me, darlings!" cried Orchid, enraptured.

"We know what you want, Mama." The twins spoke in unison, their voices so intertwined it was difficult to tell one from the other, like a perfect duet. "We have felt your longing for many years now. But we will not return. You gave us wonderful lives, and we left your world too soon, but without regrets. We are happy here, Mama."

"Happy *there*? Alone in the cold and darkness? Why, it will never do. You must come home."

"It is not cold here, or dark." And as the words were spoken, blurred splotches of vivid colors flooded the inky backdrop, greens and golds that one could almost imagine to be sunlit fields. "We are not alone." A fuzzy brown form capered around them, a goat perhaps, or a dog. "We *are* home."

"But your home is with me, darlings," protested Orchid. "You must come home. August, make them come! Command them to come! There are words, magic words." The woman was speaking with increasing urgency and desperation. "My father used to speak of Orfeo's act, of the incantation he would employ. 'Po-na-fantom,' something like that. Say the words, August. SAY THEM!"

"No, Mama, please." The twins' voices were gentle and wise. "Do not force us into a place we no longer belong. Do not turn us into broken, ugly replicas of something that used to be. Remember us as we were, loved and happy. We could never be happy there now. You want us to be happy . . . don't you, Mama?"

Orchid hesitated, blinking, shaking.

"You are *truly* happy there?"

"Oh, it is beautiful here. Sometimes, Mama, it smells so sweetly of gardenias, and we know you are close, we know you are with us."

"But who," said Orchid bleakly, "is with *me*?"

"The Ones After," said the twins. "The ones like us. They live still, in your world."

"Yes, of course," said Orchid, with a small, hesitant smile.

"There is a girl."

"Belladonna. She is like you, Aubrey. Quiet. Creative. A little sad."

"And a boy."

"Beauregard. He is bold, like you, Antoinette. Angry and insecure, perhaps, but I fear that is my fault."

"You have spent so long, Mama, looking for us. But all that time, the Ones After have been looking for you."

Orchid's body was racked with a sudden mighty sob, and she pressed a fist to her mouth.

"I know, I *know*," she wailed. "After you were gone, darlings, the vacant space you left behind, the utter emptiness, was terrible."

"Like a display case," thought August, "with no display."

"So . . . I tried to replace you," continued Orchid sorrowfully. "But Beauregard and Belladonna are not you, and I have caused so much pain to all of us by trying to make them so. I have done a terrible thing, I know that. I doubt they can ever forgive me."

"Give them a chance to, Mama," said the twins. "They love you. You have been so very sad, but you should feel happy, Mama, for you have been loved by so many for so long. Find the joy in living again, for our sake. Will you try?"

"Will you let us go now, Mama?

"Will you open your heart to the Ones After?"

Orchid nodded, weeping quietly.

August could feel the twins' presence fading; their reflections were dimming.

There was no click, no release, no departure. They were not trapped. They were where they belonged.

"We will always be with you, Mama," they said, their voices thin and distant. "Just listen. Listen not with your ears but with your heart, and you will hear us.

"We love you."

Antoinette and Aubrey Malveau were gone.

And their mother turned to the wall behind her and pressed herself against it, covering her face with both hands. Her nephew gently laid his head on her shaking back. Claudette (having clumsily relieved herself of the mirror) drew close, picking her nose with a sympathetic air.

"Have you ever wanted something, August," whispered Orchid, "with all your heart? With your entire being?"

August saw a scene.

A group of friends were gathered at a lunch table, thumb-wrestling, giggling into their phones, sharing kettle corn, and high-fiving one another.

The group seemed happy. Complete.

"I have, ma'am," he said. "But I have recently discovered that it never truly existed."

He moved to the woman's side to see her face.

"I have wasted much time, Aunt Orchid, chasing after something that isn't real."

They exchanged a small, sad smile.

A muffled but massive crash pierced the stillness of the secret chamber, a jolting reminder that there was a world beyond it . . . in chaos. More clamorous noises followed, sounds of destruction—smashing and shattering—and screams of terror.

There was a slam, much closer, as if the door to the Chamber of Jewels had burst violently open.

"Mama!" The fearful cry was scarcely recognizable as Belladonna's; August had never heard the surly girl so lacking in composure. "Mama, where are you?"

"The zombies are inside!" The second voice—shrill and hysterical—was Beauregard's. "They're out of control. Mama, please! Help us!"

Orchid Malveau started up as if shaken from a dream, her expression alert, her posture invigorated.

"The twins!" she gasped, blanching. "*My* twins need me. Belladonna!" she screamed. "Beauregard! Mama's coming!"

Like a lioness, the woman sprinted toward the secret door, barreling through it into the Chamber of Jewels beyond.

Belladonna and Beauregard stood there, faces filled with alarm and surprise at their mother's sudden and unexpected emergence from the bookshelves. Beyond the entrance behind them, catastrophe was unfolding; people were running and shrieking, vases were smashing on the gleaming mahogany floors, and scrawny, ragged figures were swinging from the sparkling chandeliers.

A zombie suddenly appeared in the doorway. He was a large and particularly gruesome fellow, having retained one bloodshot, shriveled eye and a mouthful of blackened, festering teeth. Rotting flesh hung from the skeletal fingers that gripped the doorframe, and the creature wheezed and growled in the most unsettling manner, gray saliva bubbling and dangling from his slack jaw.

He appeared to focus on the twins and, with a savage look

of hunger, launched himself at them, fingers outstretched like monstrous claws.

"No one," bellowed Orchid Malveau, "eats my children!"

She lunged between the twins, grabbed the airborne zombie by his sludge-coated ribs, and, using his own momentum plus a good twist, hurled him across the room so that he landed, a tangled mess of withered limbs and damp rags, impaled on an andiron in the fireplace.

"Aunt Orchid, stop!" cried August, stumbling to place himself as a barrier between living and undead. "They're not dangerous, I promise."

Orchid hesitated, then retreated, protectively encircling each twin with one arm.

"I won't lose them, August," she warned him. "Not these ones."

"You won't, ma'am," the boy assured her. "Zombies, I promise you, do not eat people. Not even their brains. They're simply lost. They are looking for help, not for trouble."

"Well, they're certainly *causing* trouble," said Orchid, nodding toward the mayhem in the hallway. "*Something* needs to be done. What is the solution?"

August glanced at the zombie behind him (who was attempting to liberate himself from the andiron) and at Claudette, who waited faithfully, ready to assist.

"I am," he said simply. "*I* am the solution.

"At least I think I am.

"As I told you, Aunt Orchid, I am a Go-Between.

"I am a necromancer."

CHAPTER 29

AUGUST OF THE ZOMBIES

Thunder rumbled and lightning flickered across the group of skeletons: a gruesome, silent roster of grim gamblers, slimy sailors, and hollow-eyed chorus girls. Skulls gleamed. Skinless faces grinned madly. Bony fingers extended toward the lone living boy before them.

The boy who had made them.

They weren't just skeletons, you understand, they were zombies.

And the boy wasn't just a boy, he was a necromancer.

* * *

"I hear you. I can hear you all," cried August, holding up his palms to placate the restless horde. "Calm down; everyone will get their chance to speak."

Hydrangea and the mailman, Mr. LaPoste, exchanged quizzical glances. From their vantage point at the edge of the hole in the parlor floor, the drama in the basement below seemed to be unfolding in near silence.

To them, the only audible voice was August's.

August, on the other hand, could scarcely hear his own thoughts for the clamor of babbling and chattering in his head.

His gift had fully materialized.

The bridge between worlds was fully open.

But August was learning, slowly, how to close it when he chose. Which was just as well, for the dead were loud, and they would not shut up.

"Please be patient," he pleaded. "I can't handle you all at once. I'm sure Gaston will be back at any moment."

The volume of the rain outside suddenly increased as Locust Hole's front door opened, then slammed closed. August looked up to see Gaston's face appear beside Hydrangea's and the mailman's, droplets of water falling from his ginger curls.

"It's raining something awful out there," he said, brushing off his wet coat. "Here you go," he added, handing LaPoste a brown paper bag. "Essential supplies. Managed to get about thirty."

From the top of the bag the mailman withdrew a bottle of bubbles.

"Grosbeak's had a few," explained Gaston. "The Admiral

donated the rest. She said it's a gift. Think she's taken a shine to you, August. Says you're a good influence on me."

"Well, that should keep us going for a couple of days," said Hydrangea. "Though I confess my cheeks are growing weary from all that blowing."

"Which is why," crowed Gaston, "you'll like this, ma'am!"

From his coat pocket the boy produced a large plastic contraption, lime green, shaped vaguely like a hair dryer.

"It's a bubble gun!" he announced, pumping the trigger to produce an instant flurry of gorgeous quivering orbs.

Only August (and Claudette, of course) heard the collective "Ooooooh!" of wonder and delight that rose from the zombies as the delicate spheres drifted down toward them.

"And for you," added Gaston, looking at August, "I got this."

He tossed something into the hole. August caught it. It was a copy of the *Pepperville Prophet*.

"You made the front page, DuPont."

August unfolded the local newspaper.

" 'August of the Zombies,' " he said, reading aloud. " 'Local recluse plays Pied Piper to the undead, saving television's beloved Stella Starz.' "

Below the cover story's title was a photograph that filled much of the page. It showed a boy in a cloud of butterflies exiting the high metal gates of Château Malveau, followed closely by a ghoulish parade of zombies, frightening yet compliant. In the background, a disheveled crowd scratched their heads, and a little woman with big hair clung to the unmistakable form of Margot Morgan Jordan.

"August of the Zombies?" said Gaston.

August looked up.

"I don't hate it," he said, shrugging.

In the distance, thunder rumbled. The storm was receding.

"Well, August of the Zombies," said Hydrangea a little impatiently, "exactly how long will it take to be rid of our . . . *guests*? How many bottles of bubbles will we require?"

"It is getting a little easier, ma'am," said August. "It is moving a little faster. I managed two yesterday, and today I have dispatched another two before lunchtime. But it is very tiring, ma'am, listening so closely with one's heart."

"I know, sugar," said Hydrangea, smiling sympathetically. "You are doing a fine job."

"Besides, they're not *so* troublesome, are they, Aunt? It's not like we have to provide them with meals or anything of that sort."

"I suppose not. But they are hardly the most"—Hydrangea dropped her voice to a whisper—"*fragrant* individuals." She held the hankie to her nose, nodding apologetically at the zombies.

"I'll go as quickly as I can," said August. "It would be helpful if you and Mr. LaPoste could distract some of them in the kitchen; it's so difficult to hear just one of them when they are all trying to be heard. And, Gaston, could you entertain the others down here? A bottle should last a few hours, perhaps less with the bubble gun."

August turned back to the restless figures swaying between the pepper barrels on the basement's dirt floor.

"All right!" he said smartly, slapping his palms together with purpose. "Who's next? How about you? Yes, you with . . . with the thing." He circled his finger vaguely around his own scalp.

A bedraggled creature lurched forward, clad in a ragged bandanna and the remnants of what had once been overalls. The top of his skull was missing, his dried and shriveled brain exposed.

"Engineer?" asked August.

The zombie nodded.

"Looks like you were pretty close to the boiler room explosion."

The zombie nodded again.

"Unfinished business in this world?"

The zombie nodded once more.

"All right. Your appointment is in five minutes, upstairs"—August pointed to the hole above them—"in my office."

* * *

From her post at the entrance to the parlor, Claudette emitted a guttural alert. August looked up and smiled at the engineer, who waited, shuffling nervously from foot to foot.

"Thank you, Claudette," said August. "You may show him in. Now, there is nothing to be frightened of, sir. You sit right here beside me." August patted the seat of the fainting couch. "And if you'll kindly hold up this frying pan . . . in front of your face. Yes, like so. Perfect!"

August lifted a notepad and pencil.

"If you'll give me just a moment, I have to concentrate, get in touch with the universe, that sort of thing. It's my process," he added helpfully.

The boy closed his eyes and grew very still. The nostrils of his small nose flared just a little, and a crease appeared on his brow.

The engineer glanced anxiously at Claudette as the faintest filament of blue light crackled at the edge of the pan. The smaller zombie offered up a lopsided shrug.

"Ah! There you are," said August, opening his eyes and gazing into the flat copper surface. "That's quite a head of hair you have, sir." He glanced at the wrecked zombie skull beside him and grimaced. "You must miss it. Now, you are . . ."—he scanned the notepad with the tip of his pencil—". . . the one who's been whispering, let me see, ah, yes, 'Clementine.' You're the Clementine fellow. Now, tell me, are we talking 'clementine' like the fruit or 'Clementine' like the name?"

August nodded with a look of concerned concentration.

"Uh-huh. Mm-hmm." He scribbled something on his pad. "Yes. Yes, I'm listening . . . with my heart."

The frying pan helped.

Without it, the voices of the dead—when August permitted them entry—were loud and many and nearly impossible to comprehend. The pan's reflection helped August focus on just one spirit, to hear that one and that one alone distinctly; and more, it helped them hear him.

And the thing was growing ever more reliable: for they were growing together, the boy and the pan.

With every use, the bright filaments of energy became more vivid and active. The thing was leaching up the boy's magic and conforming slowly to his gift, as a baseball glove will, over time, take the shape of its wearer's hand. The old copper frying pan was becoming to August what a priceless hunk of Cadaverite had become to his great-great-uncle, what a dime-store crystal ball had become to a slippery professor of limited talent.

A talisman.

And in its coppery reflection, several zombies had now shared their heartaches with the young necromancer. They had, with his gentle encouragement, revealed what regret or frustrated goal had been preventing them from quitting the world of the living.

Some remained to wreak revenge. Others to forgive, or to seek forgiveness. Many were loath to quit their loved ones. Most would never find the thing they sought, for the people that had filled their lives were also long gone from this earth.

But they could speak of them.

And August could listen.

And when he could not hear their words, he could listen to their feelings.

And by listening with his heart, he could *feel* their feelings.

And somehow, in the speaking and the listening and the feeling, the restless souls found that the boy had unburdened them. Somehow, in the speaking and the listening and the feeling, the young necromancer had quietly helped them lay down their troubles. And freed from the weight of them, most of the spirits— who were, after all, less substantial than air—rose up and up and left this place, headed with purpose for somewhere else.

Most. But not all.

As Orfeo had predicted, some poor creatures had spent so long wallowing in their own darkness—in envy or grief or anger—that it had consumed them entirely. The emotion was all that was left of them, so there was no load for them to set down. August could not send them onward, for their sorrow was so heavy, it anchored them here.

They refused to leave.

In such cases, the talisman was more than a help; it was indispensable.

By focusing, by channeling every drop of it into the frying

pan, August's gift was amplified, and he discovered that he could not only communicate with the spirits, he could compel them . . . by invoking the ancient incantation.

"Po-na-fantom," he would say. "Bridge of Ghosts, I call upon thee."

He did not shout the words or adopt a theatrical voice as had his great-great-uncle and Professor Leech, both—in their own ways—showmen. August was not attempting to impress or entertain, merely to assist, so he uttered the spell in his everyday quiet, even way.

August wasn't sure if the words in themselves had much power. But he felt the age in them; they had been spoken since words were spoken. Perhaps, over millennia of being applied to magic, they had gathered some of it to themselves along the way.

He did not enjoy being forced to say them.

He hated to see the zombies' eyes roll back, the visible whites burning with that empty light. He hated the passivity that overcame their posture, leaving them little more than puppets under his control. The sight still recalled the poster for DuPont's Dance of the Dead, a testament to necromancy gone sour, a family disgrace.

But August DuPont was not his great-great-uncle Orfeo. He was not Tiberius Leech. His intentions were not selfish; his heart was not callous.

He invoked the spell only to release a tortured spirit from the broken, rotting cage of its earthly remains. August understood that the ghost would linger still, in that nebulous nearby realm where such phantoms roam. But though foggy and confusing, it was at least a tranquil, soft-edged place, free from all the harsh horrors of a zombie's existence.

Fortunately, the unfortunate engineer with half a skull was not such a resentful, incompliant soul. Indeed, August found him to be a big-hearted man with one simple regret: that he had—on the morning of his death—risen too early to bid his little girl a happy seventh birthday.

"I know how very sad that must make you," said August kindly. "But, sir, the engine of the *Lady Luck* exploded in 1911. Clementine is either real old . . . or she is already waiting for you in the forever place. Either way, Mr. Furness, you will see your little girl very soon, and you can wish her a happy birthday for every year of her life."

Click and release.

Lift and depart.

Pile of bones.

And so passed the rainy day, with August DuPont, necromancer, unmaking the zombies he had himself unwittingly made. The light outside was dwindling when the boy collapsed back into the fainting couch. He was wan, and there were bags beneath his eyes.

"Empathizing is an exhausting business, Claudette," he said. "I have the energy for only one more today. Who have we got?"

With elbows on his knees and head in his hands, August rested his brain and his heart. He heard the familiar step-drag-shuffle of zombie footsteps on the parlor floorboards. A pair of old-fashioned high-heeled boots with buttons on their sides came into the boy's line of sight. He knew those boots.

He looked up with a tired smile.

"Now, as it happens," he said, "I already know *your* name. Are you aware that the Pepperville Public Library has an exhibition devoted entirely to you, and that we are distantly related?

"Please take a seat, Miz Bouquet."

CHAPTER 30

DRAGON'S KISS

LouLou Bouquet's coppery reflection was especially vivid, as if she was more alert and present than the average ghost. In the world of mirror, with the lower half of her face restored, she was far less frightening. In fact, the wide, generous smile and distinct, endearing dimples beneath the dapper ribboned hat were not alarming in the least.

"At last you have come," said LouLou Bouquet's reflection, her speech crisp and distinct. "I have words that may be spoken only to DuPont ears."

August was taken aback, for this was an unusual opening to one of these conversations. There was something about Lou-Lou's familiarity that reminded him of Orfeo; all three of them were, after all, related.

"Have you been waiting, by any chance," August asked, "to inform me about the DuPont treasure? Because, ma'am, I already know the gift is inside me. Or it *is* me, however you care to put it."

"Why yes," chuckled LouLou, "and no. I have not lingered, child, to tell you of your gift, but rather to take advantage of it. You see, I have important information to share, and only a bridge between worlds—a person like yourself—has the ability to hear it."

"But you have been dead for many years, Miz Bouquet," protested August. "Surely there were others like me who came before."

"Only my nephew Orfeo. But he was a flighty young man, with no interest in my family secret. After the gift had flowered in him, to Orfeo my spirit was no more than a tool to furnish him with acclaim. Like it or not, I was forced to perform in his grotesque Dance of the Dead."

"I have talked with Uncle Orfeo," said August. "He does, I believe, truly regret his past. Having resided so long inside a large reptile with unsavory habits, he understands how it feels to be trapped in a place one doesn't belong. I promise you, Miz Bouquet, I would never use the gift as he did."

"The wise," said LouLou, "learn from the mistakes of their forefathers. And I can see, child, that you have wisdom within you. And kindness. That is why, August, you are a deserving recipient of my legacy."

Although fatigued from a day of listening not to words but to feelings, August perked up. "Legacy" sounded like something interesting.

"Orfeo did not want it, so I have been forced to wait these many years for someone who does."

"Oh," said August eagerly, "I want it!"

"It comes with a story."

"All right."

"This story begins in the century before last, before this house even existed. My father, Pierre DuPont, and his cousin, Maxim Malveau, left their faraway home to seek their fortunes in this country."

"I have heard this story before," said August politely.

LouLou Bouquet frowned and held her finger to her lips.

"You have not heard all of it," she said. "No one has. My father arrived with a pepper plant uprooted from his mother's garden and a hot sauce recipe concocted in her kitchen. With these, Pierre founded a hot sauce empire. Why, DuPont's Peppy Pepper Sauce could be found in every fine dining room and restaurant from Croissant City to Paris, France.

"You have learned, no doubt, that Maxim stole this recipe, and with it he launched a rival product. His novelty bottle—the one with the horns—was a phenomenon. You might expect that my father was consumed by anger or despair after that. But he was strangely unconcerned.

" 'Lou,' he said to me once, 'fear not. Malveau's Devil Sauce will never compare to ours. DuPont's Peppy Pepper Sauce is fiery yet sweet, complex yet simple. Malveau's is merely fiery and simple.' I asked my father why this was so."

August held his breath, awaiting Pierre's long-ago reply.

"He told me," LouLou continued, "that while Maxim could use our recipe to reproduce our method and blend of aromatics, he would never lay his hands on our sauce's most essential ingredient, a unique type of pepper plant.

"Oh, Maxim tried every possible variety, but could never replicate the flavor of that known only to our family, the one that originated in my grandmother's faraway garden.

"Do you know the name of this variety, August, the DuPonts' very own pepper plant?"

"Hydrangea has never told me," said August. "But I think I can guess. Is it . . . Dragon's Kiss?"

"Dragon's Kiss peppers," said LouLou, beaming, "are what earned DuPont's Peppy Pepper Sauce the awards and accolades and what has made it the choice of hot sauce collectors worldwide. They are a source of family pride, the rock upon which the DuPonts' fortunes have rested."

August observed the woman's glowing pride with saddened, guilty eyes.

"I fear, Miz Bouquet, our family has not been real good at keeping things up. Only a few of the plants have survived, clinging to life. I tried to save them. I harvested their seeds, propagated new plants, and was even growing a fresh crop in the front yard. It was doing pretty well . . . until recently. There was a hurricane. And the embankment collapsed. And there was an incident with a ship-wreck." August winced, hating that he must deliver such bad news. "I am afraid, Miz Bouquet, Dragon's Kiss peppers are no more."

"I know," said LouLou gently. "I was there, child. I'm sure you can imagine that hurricanes are less fun for a clumsy zombie than they are even for the living. But, August, that is precisely why our meeting could not have come at a more fortunate time."

August waited.

"I see," said LouLou, "or rather, my human remains see a clock over there in the form of a small porcelain goatherd. He has lost his head. Would you fetch it, child?"

The chimes clinked inside the broken object as it was lifted from the mantel.

"I must confess, Miz Bouquet, that it was me who broke it," admitted August, returning to the couch and the spirit's reflection in the copper pan, "when I was small. Did it belong to you?"

"It was my mother's. But the clock is far less important than what it conceals. Reach inside, August, behind the works; your fingers are yet small enough to fit."

Beyond the tiny brass gears and levers August felt an angular yet flexible corner, like that of an envelope. After some twisted expressions and frustrated grunts, with two fingers he was finally able to extract a small package of folded brown paper; it was no wonder that the clock's chime had always sounded so strange and pained.

"Open it!" urged LouLou. "Go carefully now. Yes, like that, in the palm of your hand."

On the unwrapped paper lay a handful of dried seeds.

August guessed immediately what they were—as have you, no doubt.

"Dragon's Kiss pepper seeds?" asked the boy.

"From Pierre's original plant," confirmed LouLou. "Hidden away for such a time as they might be needed. That time is clearly now. Think of this, August, as a gift from beyond the grave. What you do with it is up to you."

Click and release.

The shimmering form of LouLou's spirit clung loosely to the zombie beneath. She smiled one last time as her image rose and the figure beneath began to crumble.

"It may seem daunting," said LouLou, her voice little more than a memory. "But it has been done before, so why not again? From a handful of tiny seeds, August, you too could choose to build an empire!"

CHAPTER 31

HER OWN PEACOCK

"Come, Aunt," said August gently, from his sunny seat on the porch steps. "It is the very last one, and one cannot harm you. Besides, you have the protection of your helmet."

Hydrangea's attention was fixed on the solitary butterfly perched on August's outstretched finger. She twisted her handkerchief, hovering just inside the porch's net curtain, but would not venture through.

"I understand," said August, speaking into the frying pan he held before himself and the insect. "Your mother thought you would not amount to much, so you spent your life trying to prove her wrong. But really, Professor Leech, that's no excuse for your behavior. I appreciate that being consumed by an alligator is most unpleasant; I've heard that before. But you really only have your-self to blame."

August glanced over his shoulder at his aunt and rolled his eyes.

"Are you sure I can't persuade you to move on to the for-ever place? I am certain you would be much happier there. Your human remains have by now been digested, and I have heard from a reliable source that it is quite tiresome hopping out of one butterfly and into the next every few weeks or so. Well, I'm sorry to hear that, Professor. I wish you could set down your bit-terness. But you leave me no choice."

August heaved a heavy sigh.

"Po-na-fantom," he said, his tone resigned, and the corona of flickering filaments surrounding the frying pan suddenly in-tensified. "Spirit that is Tiberius Leech, I command thee to quit this innocent creature and let it live out the rest of its short life in peace!"

There was a brief pause before the insect fluttered from Au-gust's finger with a confused air, as if it had no idea where it was or how it had gotten there. It flapped its wings for a moment or two, weaving about as if it were drunk, before finally hurrying off into the blue sky.

"Leech will return next week," August muttered to Clau-dette beside him. "He cannot set aside his desire to be a famous necromancer. I do hope he tires of being a butterfly and decides to move on, but I fear it may take some time."

The boy turned to his aunt. "There, Aunt. You see? All gone. No butterflies. Not a single one."

He rose and approached the curtain.

"And even if they return, ma'am," he said gently, "they cannot harm you now. They are just butterflies, not betrayals. Yes?"

August pulled the netting aside and held out his hand. A bee-keeper's glove emerged slowly, and its fingers curled around the boy's. The hand inside was shaking. A tentative toe in a dainty shoe ventured into the sunlight.

"You came outside before," August quietly reminded his aunt. "And that was during a hurricane, not on a lovely day like this."

"You were hurt," protested Hydrangea. "You needed me."

"I need you now, Aunt. Miz Bouquet's seeds have sprouted, and I cannot farm these peppers by myself. I cannot run a hot sauce empire all alone. At least not yet. I am, after all, twelve years old!"

The boy stepped up beside the woman. He slipped his arm around her waist.

"I'm here, Aunt Hydrangea. I will not leave you. I will never betray you. I'm your August."

Hydrangea looked at her nephew with glistening eyes.

"Can you ever forgive me, sugar, for hiding you away all

those years? I was so afraid that what happened to me would happen . . ."

"You were trying to protect me. I understand. I forgive."

"Look at you, sugar. So grown up. So brave."

"It's easier to be brave," said August, "when you are not alone."

And together, the wilted pageant queen and the strange, owlish boy stepped outside to join the small crooked zombie.

Hydrangea took a trembling breath.

"Oh, the smell," she whispered. "The marsh grass. The tupelo trees. The wild iris. I had forgotten." She pushed back the long sleeve of her glove and studied her exposed arm. "Sunlight. So warm." She looked around. "And oh, August, just look at those seedlings! So strong and green. You are a natural pepper farmer. Have they been given compost yet? No? Well"—she pulled off her gloves altogether—"we best get started. Claudette can fetch the manure easily enough, I'm sure."

Hydrangea stopped and looked up sharply.

"Now who might this be?"

A taxi was creeping down the lane. Its brakes squealed as the vehicle stopped beside the mailbox. A girl emerged, stepped over the destroyed gate, and advanced along the paths of the Italian garden.

Her expensive-looking dress and high socks were black and oddly formal for a sunny weekend day. But around her neck hung a large dramatic necklace, formed from manicotti lacquered to a high gloss in an eye-popping shade of sunflower yellow.

As she grew closer, August grinned.

"Belladonna Malveau," he said affably.

"I wondered if you'd recognize me," said Belladonna, self-consciously running a hand through her gleaming chestnut hair.

"Your natural color?"

The girl nodded.

And Hydrangea coughed politely.

"I," she announced, "shall retire to consult *The Capsicum Compendium* on the best sorts of fertilizer. Miz Malveau." She nodded graciously at Belladonna and withdrew discreetly into the house.

"You've got some nice green seedlings here," observed Belladonna, scanning the Italian garden's flower beds. "I heard around town that you had got yourself some big old shipwreck in your front yard."

August nodded.

"The county," he explained, "used some of the larger timbers to repair the dike." He pointed at the dark restoration in the embankment. "Claudette cleared up the rest, didn't you, Claudette? She's awful strong."

Claudette twisted back and forth a little, clearly pleased with herself.

"We still need to fix the fence," said August, glancing past his visitor. He observed the idling taxi. "Are you going somewhere?"

"To the airport," said Belladonna. "I just stopped to say goodbye."

"You're going to *fly*? In the *air*?" August was immediately envious. He thought of the ospreys that soared overhead on great pale outstretched wings and how wonderful that must feel, the view that they must have. "How marvelous."

"I suppose." In spite of herself, the naturally surly girl smiled. "I'm planning to stay with some relatives up north. There's a branch of Malveaus up there, the Van Malveaus."

"Up north sounds like a long ways off."

"There's a school, you see. One of those artsy kinds of places. They saw my jewelry and found it irresistibly depressing. They think I'm a good fit for them."

"Cyril Saint-Cyr must be selling a lot of Belladonna Malveau originals. Sounds like you're becoming famous."

Belladonna laughed with a lack of reserve August had never seen in her.

"Not quite. Remember when I couldn't watch your zombies—back on Funeral Street—because I had an appointment? It was actually an interview with the school's admissions office. Even Mama didn't know."

August smiled proudly.

"So, Belladonna Malveau," he said, "you are growing into your own peacock at last."

The girl—utterly out of character—blushed and lowered her eyes.

"I said you were annoyingly wise," she muttered.

"Have you . . . have you forgiven her, your mother?"

Far-apart eyes the color of breakfast tea stared off somewhere else, perhaps into memories.

"Yes?" she said. It was more question than statement. "I think. But we are very different. Perhaps when I am older, things will be better between us."

"Still, I am sure she will miss you."

"She has Beauregard, who, after all, is much more like her. Since Langley left for Europe with his grandmother, Mama and my brother have become the best of friends. Beau is even teaching Mama to fence. They slash and jab like two wasps fighting over the last sugarplum, like they're trying to kill one another. But they seem to enjoy it. I think it uses up all the energy they normally put into being insufferable, because believe it or not, they've become more agreeable lately. Well, relatively; they *are* still Malveaus."

Belladonna pointed to an orderly stack of fruit crates piled beside the porch steps. A thick black marker had been used to label each with a name: Captain Poisson, François Furness, Lou-Lou Bouquet.

"What are those?"

"Zombie remains," said August with an embarrassed shrug.

"I've got the hang of unmaking them. But they do leave behind something of a mess. Mr. Goodnight—you know, of Goodnight's Funeral Parlor—has been collecting them and returning them to the graves they came out of. I think he might be sweet on my aunt Hydrangea; he's doing it for free."

"Ah!" said Belladonna knowingly. "I had heard that you finally solved your small zombie problem. And"—she waved a finger at the empty space above August's head—"the skin condition . . . that was never a skin condition."

"No butterflies," said August, grinning. "No living dead. I am officially zombie-free."

"Well . . ."—Belladonna tilted her head quizzically—"not quite."

"Yes," August assured her. "It took me several days, but all the zombies are finally dispensed with."

"Well . . . not *all.*"

August turned in the direction of Belladonna's finger, and his heart skipped a beat.

He was looking at Claudette.

CHAPTER 32

PEARLS

"I have told you: they are not up there," insisted August.

The boy and the small zombie had been standing for an hour beside the crooked remains of Locust Hole's gazebo, squabbling via the shiny underside of August's frying pan. Claudette was still pointing stubbornly toward the structure's roof, which looked even balder and more ravaged after the assault of Hurricane Augusta.

Of all the zombies, Claudette alone had remained reticent, able to communicate only one word, over and over. August had trouble concentrating sufficiently to truly listen to her feelings.

One might have suspected the boy did not really want the small zombie to leave.

"But, Claudette," August protested, "your pearls are somewhere in the Gardner's Island lagoon. I understand that they have something to do with your being here, although I can't imagine what; you had them, after all, when I met you. Well, when I *made* you. But I am sorry, they're gone."

"Pearls!" demanded Claudette more urgently, her reflection and her body still pointing upward.

"You can be a very obstinate zombie," grumbled August. "I am telling you: they are not up there. But you are obviously not going to give it a rest until you see for yourself. So I guess let's take a look!"

Lifting his knee high, August placed the sole of his shoe on a surviving fragment of the gazebo's handrail. Using the vines twining around the adjacent post as leverage, he hauled himself up, clambering onto a collapsed section of the roof, then reaching back to hoist the undead girl behind him. From there it was a short scramble up to that part of the structure which remained relatively solid and stable.

As he gingerly straightened, August's eyes fell upon the window of his garret bedroom. From this angle he could see the telescope sitting on his desk, the same telescope through which he had first spied a certain makeshift houseboat moored in the canal. Ten feet below him lay that same canal, empty now but for a hundred darting minnows and the shadow of something that looked like an old propeller.

"Is that what severed your arm, Claudette?" asked August,

grabbing the frying pan from where he had flung it before their ascent. "Why were you even up here? And how did you come to be killed? It's only ten feet down."

"Pearls!"

With some frustration, August searched what remained of the gazebo roof, checking the gutters and gaping cracks for the sake of appeasing his persistent undead relative.

"There are no pearls up here, Claudette," he said gently.

"Pearls!" She was still pointing. Upward.

"So, *not* the roof? Farther?" August followed Claudette's finger to the high overhanging branch of the nearby oak tree. And as he squinted into the sunlight, he saw something in a crook of the bough, something that glinted. "Is *that* it? Is that why we're up here?"

"Pearls!"

The heavily gnarled trunk was only feet from the gazebo roof. It was not hard to gain a foothold. And the branches were not so widely spaced as to make the climb impossible—though it was not easy either.

"Madame Marvell," muttered the boy as his scrabbling shoes peeled shards of bark from the tree, "would have been a better choice for this."

But after navigating the stump of the branch that, ripped off by Hurricane Augusta, had nearly drowned him, August wriggled onto the higher bough, straddling it like a pony. It seemed much loftier from above than it had from below. The canal was far beneath the boy's feet, the minnows scarcely visible.

"A person could break their neck if they fell from up here," said August. "Is that what happened, Claudette? It is, isn't it? But you were way too small to be climbing so high. What on earth were you doing?"

Carefully, inch by inch, his heart fluttering, August edged his way along the spanning limb toward the glimmering treasure.

"Well, I'll be," he gasped quietly.

There, curled beneath a leafy twig in a woody crook, lay a skeleton, that of a cat. It was surrounded by faded flower petals and an assortment of small offerings: blue candles, a mouse formed of sackcloth, a rusted can of sardines. The tightness of the crevice had protected the shrine (for shrine it clearly was) from the ravages of time and hurricanes.

August reached for the glittering thing.

It was a silver name tag, attached to the shredded remains of a leather collar.

The name tag was engraved with a name.

And the name was "Pearls."

"This is the cat in the photograph of you and your brother in the parlor?"

Claudette nodded.

"You laid her to rest here in her favorite tree, the one Orfeo mentioned. You brought her all these things, things you knew she would like. Until one day you fell." August paused. It was suddenly all so clear.

"You've come back . . . for *her.*"

The descent was even trickier than the ascent, especially while gently cradling fragile feline remains in the crook of one arm. August accrued several scratches and a tear in his pants. But in minutes he was handing the delicate prize into Claudette's eagerly outstretched arms.

And as he did, everything changed.

The zombie was almost lost to the shimmering vision of the young girl August had come to know through her reflection. So too the skeleton cat was cloaked in a gauzy version of its living self. August beamed at the sight of the rapturous reunion. It seemed as though Pearls might knock Claudette's head from her shoulders, so powerfully did the cat rub its ears against the girl's chin.

The frying pan lay facedown on the roof, but such was the connection between them, the young necromancer no longer needed it to hear this particular small zombie.

"Pearls!"

The pretty, flush-faced Claudette—the real Claudette—raised her eyes.

"Thank you, August," she said, her voice sweet and clear but a little shy. A far cry from the guttural grunts of her zombie remains. "Thank you for everything. I am sorry I was such a problem. I would have gone home earlier if I had been able to."

At these words, the blood drained from August's face. Indeed, it felt like it was draining entirely from his body.

"Home," he said. "You're leaving? Now?"

"Of course," said Claudette with a regretful smile. "Don't all my kind leave when you help us finish our unfinished business? Mine was Pearls. It was always Pearls."

"But, well . . . *you* can't leave," August scoffed. "Not *you*. I mean, the others, sure. But *you* . . . you are . . ." His mouth opened and closed, but no more words came.

"But you have wanted me gone," Claudette said, half laughing, "ever since I arrived."

It was true, thought August, that his recent life had been devoted to finding a way to rid himself of this small zombie. But suddenly the prospect of a world without her seemed like a very empty place. A place with something missing. Something important. Something that it would be difficult for him to live without.

Without the small zombie, Orfeo's alligator might well have eaten him when their canoe sank.

Without her, he might have been trampled to death on the streets of Croissant City.

Without her, who would have powered Gaston's makeshift raft, or cleaned up the remains of the riverboat, or assisted the young necromancer in releasing more than thirty restless souls from their zombie cages?

Without her, August would never have been given the

opportunity to meet Stella Starz and come to understand he was chasing a mirage.

Without her, without Claudette, who would be ever present at his side, a patient, loyal, silent source of support, protection . . . companionship?

It was painful to imagine turning to find nothing where the zombie had been, where she *should* be. It was almost as if she had become part of him.

"Don't go," whispered August. "Please."

"I can't stay here, August," said Claudette. "You know that. I don't want to be a zombie anymore. I want to go home."

August DuPont had lived most of his life in a dusty mansion, sequestered from the world, denied its joys but also sheltered from its pains. Only a few months earlier he had walked through his front door for the first time, and had immediately been subjected to more emotions than he could have imagined existed: humiliation, anger, elation, fear.

But none of those feelings compared to this one.

This feeling was dark and heavy and brutal. It was a feeling that made him want to flee to his garret bedroom and slam the door in an effort to keep it away from him. It was a feeling that he thought, if he let it in completely, might tear him to bits.

"I'll *command* you to stay," whimpered August. "I know the words. You know I know. I'll keep whatever part of you I can. Whatever ragged fragment is left behind is better than nothing."

"Like Orchid would have kept her twins," said Claudette, "if you hadn't shown her how cruel that would be?"

August nodded.

His lip was trembling. He felt stupid, babyish.

But he was past caring.

"Like Orchid," he whispered.

And suddenly there it was. He knew her, his aunt Orchid. He understood her. He knew what she had done and why she had done it.

Because he wanted to do the same.

"Goodbye, August," said Claudette. "You won't forget me, will you?"

August shook his head. But he couldn't really see her anymore.

Because of the tears.

"Take this," said Claudette. The dank zombie hand folded something round and wet into his fist.

Click. Release.

August felt a rising sensation, like a feather on a warm summer updraft.

Then the hand was gone.

Pearls was gone.

Claudette DuPont was gone.

And as far away as Pepperville, people could hear the sound of a young boy's heart breaking.

CHAPTER 33

THE FOLLOWING AUGUST

Later that year—by August, in fact—those who arrived at Locust Hole expecting a forsaken scene of isolation and ruin were disappointed. You see, August is the month when the chili peppers ripen in Hurricane County, and the flower beds of Locust Hole's Italian garden were bursting with pepper shrubs aflame in crimson, orange, and gold.

Moreover, from beyond this fiery crop there rose a house much altered. Where the ruins of Hydrangea's quarters had been, a sturdy skeleton of timbers was forming beneath the noisy saws and hammers of sweat-browed workmen. The roof was less bald and less saggy, the shutters hung fairly straight, and the unchecked vines and moss had been trimmed and tidied. It is true that the clapboards were still in need of a coat of paint, but it was easy now to imagine how transformative that could be.

In another month or so, Locust Hole might even qualify as a lovely home.

This was the setting that greeted the Malveaus' limousine as it crunched upon the lane that ended at Locust Hole, purring to a halt at the new garden gate. As she was handed from the back seat by Escargot, the butler (and sometime chauffeur), Orchid Malveau's mouth fell open in surprise. So did Escargot's.

August observed their reaction with some satisfaction.

"Aunt Hydrangea." He gently prodded the lady beside him, who was engrossed in raking the freshly graveled paths. "We have a visitor." August pointed toward the mailbox, where Orchid hovered. She was still clad from head to toe in black, but her veil of mourning had been replaced by a large, flat, dramatic hat.

"Hydrangea?" said Orchid, squinting. "Is that you, Sister?"

Hydrangea slowly laid down her rake and straightened. August half expected her to bolt toward the house.

"I'm right here, ma'am," he whispered.

Hydrangea lifted the netting of her beekeeper's helmet, and with August reassuringly close, the pair moved toward the lane.

"I have something for you," said Orchid Malveau, studying her sister with aloof curiosity.

Cautiously, Hydrangea reached out to accept the ribboned parcel offered across the gate.

"We passed the mailman—that grinning, rabbity creature—on the iron bridge. Since I was heading this way, I offered to deliver the mail to save him the trouble. Despite the fact I was doing him a favor, he seemed oddly put out."

"Handkerchiefs," Hydrangea explained, shaking the box gently. "I go through considerably fewer than I used to. But still, the gifts are well intended."

"You have an admirer, then?" said Orchid.

"Two," confirmed August, grinning. "The handkerchiefs come from Mr. LaPoste. Mr. Goodnight, the undertaker, sends freshly made beignets." He nudged Hydrangea mischievously. "They are competing for my aunt's affections. Are they not, ma'am?"

"Phfttt!" muttered Hydrangea, swatting at her nephew while suppressing a smile.

"They should think themselves fortunate," said Orchid indignantly, "that their advances are even considered; a DuPont would represent a catch for either man. Not to mention," she added suddenly and quietly, with uncharacteristic shyness, "they are courting a former Miss Chili Pepper Princess."

"We both know, Orchid," said Hydrangea, "that I have never held that title. I appreciate that you have indulged my fantasy for years. But the sash and tiara are rightfully yours. August, go fetch them; they are packed up inside."

"No, August, stop!" said Orchid. "Keep them, Sister. You were not crowned that day, but should have been. Something won by cheating is not truly won at all." She paused, looking stiff and uncomfortable. "Hydrangea, I regret my actions during the pageant. And after. It was not my objective, but I have caused you much suffering. If it is of any consolation, I have paid a price for my betrayal that day . . . the day of The Incident."

"But the price you paid was too high, Sister: your husband, your children, lost to the Peruvian flu. I would never have wished such a thing upon you."

The women gazed at each other for a moment silently, sadly acknowledging thirty years lost to jealousy and resentment.

But their unspoken communion was interrupted by the sudden buzz of an electric saw, which sharply drew Orchid's eyes to the roof of Locust Hole.

"It seems"—she gestured to the construction site—"you have had some financial good fortune. There were rumors in town that Pelican State Bank had designs on foreclosing."

"I found something of value," explained August. "Jacques LeSalt's presidential pardon. Mrs. Motts at the Pepperville Library said it was a priceless fragment of national history. I guess she was right, because an important museum in the capital paid a lot for it."

"So, August," said Orchid, "you are the DuPont to rescue Locust Hole. Your mother would have been very proud of you. Would she not, Sister?"

"Yes, she would," agreed Hydrangea, gazing at her nephew fondly. "Dearest Lily. She was the best of us, was she not, Orchid?"

"She was. You look so like her, August. Our papa called her his little owl."

"Lily always knew you were special, sugar," said Hydrangea. "That's why she named you August."

"But I'm named for the month I was born," said August. "My birthday just passed. I turned thirteen."

"You did indeed," chuckled Hydrangea. "But the month was named for the emperor Augustus. 'August' means eminent. Exalted, even. Special. I think she must have guessed at something of your gift."

"You refer, I assume," said Orchid, "to his gift of necromancy. Or is it perhaps his gift for farming?" She jabbed her palmetto fan toward the large basket at August's feet, mounded with glorious, freshly picked peppers, then surveyed the healthy, fruited shrubs beyond. "I confess that I am surprised by your success. And impressed. By both of you. Tell me, have you started production?"

"We have mashed a partial crop," said August. "And mixed the peppers with salt. The oak barrels in the basement are nearly full. But it will take three years before we're ready to add the vinegar and strain it to make hot sauce."

"At which time," said Orchid good-naturedly, "you will most likely put Malveau's Devil Sauce out of business."

"We will never," chuckled Hydrangea, "compete with the mighty Malveau Industries; it is, after all, just the two of us. Indeed, our little operation won't support this big old house for terribly long. The proceeds from Jacques LeSalt's pardon will not last forever. But they should be sufficient at least"—she ran her hand through August's hair—"to keep a roof over this young man's head until he graduates."

"Perhaps," suggested August, looking from one aunt to the other, "there is a solution, a way for the DuPonts to remain at Locust Hole. It would involve . . . working together."

The women exchanged guarded glances.

"A new hot sauce," announced August eagerly. "Made with your money, Aunt Orchid, and our peppers, Aunt Hydrangea. A hot sauce superior to Malveau's and more modern than DuPont's. A hot sauce that will win awards and be found in every dining room and restaurant from Croissant City to Paris, France."

Turning the latch, Orchid opened the gate and stepped onto the gravel.

"A new hot sauce for a new era?" she suggested, approaching her sister. "For a new partnership? What do you say, Hydrangea? Co-owners? Partners?"

"I . . . ," Hydrangea stammered. "I am not sure what to say. I suppose it might work. But what would this brave new sauce be called?"

"Well, *that,*" said August, grinning, "is obvious."

The women turned to their nephew with puzzled expressions.

"The name of our new hot sauce is right in front of you," laughed August, lifting his basket. "Dragon's Kiss!"

It was perfect, and they all knew it.

EPILOGUE

August lowered the copper frying pan, and the butterfly (a particularly pretty one, a cloudless sulphur, perhaps, or a sleepy orange) rose and fluttered off through the open garret window, weaving groggily from side to side as if it had just awoken from a long nap.

"Professor Leech again?" asked Gaston.

"No, actually," said August, turning, coming off his knees, and slumping onto the bench that sat beneath the window. "It was a boy, about my age when he died. He lived so long ago that his body has turned to dust. He got separated from his tribe and has been seeking them ever since. I explained he'll find them in the forever place. I think he understood."

"You can really talk to the dead," asked the girl August had always known as Madame Marvell, "in a *frying pan*?" She was straddling August's desk chair, her arms crossed across its back.

"It must seem strange, I guess," said August, "but I can. We could try contacting your mawmaw later. You must miss conversing with her through Delfine."

Marvell nodded with bright, squirrely eyes.

"I'd like that," she said. "And the butterflies? How often do they come?"

"Used to be all the time," replied Gaston. The sturdy, freckled boy was sprawled across an old tapestry loveseat, curiously inspecting a model skeleton dressed like a circus ringmaster, with a cork for a hat and a chopstick for a baton. "Less often now. What do you reckon, August, one every other day?"

"I figure there must have been a backlog," said August. "A whole century's worth of restless spirits circling my head, trying to get me to help them. Seems like there are still a few stragglers. But of course, no matter how many I send on their way, there will always be more trying to get home." He brightened at a sudden thought. "Speaking of home, how's your new place, Marvell?"

"Our house is big—well, at least compared to mawmaw's and mine. It's a little stationary, if you ask me. I like a house that bobs around and creaks a bunch. Sometimes my legs still feel kind of wobbly, like they miss being on the water."

"And Miz Motts?"

"She wants to adopt me."

"Well, that's a fine thing, right? She seems real nice."

"She's nice enough, I reckon. She lets me call her Octavia. And even though they located my birth certificate, she let me choose my own name. I chose 'Marvell' so a part of my mawmaw would stay with me. Octavia thought that was a fine idea. She's not perfect, though, Miz Octavia; I mean, she prefers books to TV, if you can credit it. She would like *me* to prefer books to TV too. That's something we're still . . . let's say *discussing.* Oh, and she dresses me up all fancy."

"I know," laughed August. "You look so different with shoes."

"I hardly recognize *you*," retorted Marvell cheekily, "without zombie drool on your shoulder."

August smiled, but turned away.

"You miss her," said Marvell, with apology in her voice.

August nodded.

The three young people fell quiet, remembering.

But the stillness was not awkward. Indeed, there was something easy and natural about the wordless companionship. There was a cohesion among the youngsters. They formed a group. They were complete.

They belonged.

"Say, August," said Gaston, gently breaking the silence.

"How did you learn to make these things, anyway?" He held the ringmaster aloft.

"The *Stella Starz* show," answered August, grinning. "The very first episode I saw on your TV"—he pivoted to Marvell—"Stella had a new art teacher. The teacher, she turned out to be an agent investigating the librarian, but before all that was revealed, she taught Stella's class how to craft with wire and papier-mâché."

"Oh, right!" said Marvell, nodding slowly. "I remember that one. But I don't recall any skeletons."

"No," admitted August. "I just borrowed the method. Stella made a giant spider, painted it black, and left it in the driver's seat of her father's girlfriend's car. Hedwig fainted."

"I always thought," confessed Marvell, "that Stella was kind of annoying. I kept watching the show mostly to see if Officer Claw would finally bite her." The girl suddenly glanced at her watch. "Speaking of which, it's almost four o'clock. You know, today's episode is the series finale, the very last one ever, they say. I saw an interview with Margot Morgan Jordan. She said she's tired of being Stella Starz and wants to write a horror novel."

Marvell frowned as the boys exchanged glances.

"What's the problem? I'm sure Miz Hydrangea won't mind if we watch in the kitchen."

"Actually," said August, standing and snapping his suspenders with pride, "Gaston and I have a little surprise for you. Come take a look-see."

The trio crossed the garret room, ducking to avoid the raw beams, and gathered at the small dormer window overlooking the canal. There, beyond the freshly repaired gazebo, bobbed a smart wooden canoe, painted a joyful scarlet red.

"My cousin Grizel and uncle Godfrey helped us with it," said Gaston.

"You guys built it yourselves?" Marvell was openly impressed.

"For you," said August. "It's yours. For your wobbly leg problem."

"Seriously?" Marvell stared at him with disbelief. "For *me*?"

August nodded, grinning.

The lid of the old keyless piano crashed shut as the girl promptly rocketed out of the room.

"So, no *Stella Starz*?" laughed August, following quickly. "Gaston, grab the paddle and the fishing pole. They're over there. Looks like we're doing the launch right this minute."

The thunder of six young feet on wooden stairs echoed through the empty cavities of Locust Hole. But after a few seconds, they receded and were gone, leaving the garret room in dusty, sunlit silence.

But not, however, entirely empty.

A large jar stood on August's desk. Once it had held Ping-Pong balls, but now there was a new resident. Well, not entirely new. It had been in that jar before.

Floating freely in clear but vinegary fluid was a sphere. And the sphere was an eyeball.

While August DuPont had been present, the eyeball, of its own accord and unobserved, had swiveled and spun, following the boy's every move. Now that he was gone, it was fixed on the open doorway, awaiting his return. The eyeball watched and waited; for its owner—when she had been on this earth—had loved the boy with all her heart.

You see, while every living thing must one day perish and leave this place, love alone will linger, patient and eternal.

THE END

ACKNOWLEDGMENTS

Although sprouted from the seed of my own idea, the misadventures of August and Claudette DuPont would never have filled these pages without the persistent enthusiasm and seasoned guidance of my editor, Melanie Nolan.

And without my trusty agent, Lori Nowicki of Painted Words, *Zombie Problems* would never have been channeled toward the enthusiasm and guidance of Melanie Nolan.

A special thanks to the warm and welcoming residents of Bayou Teche, to the Nature Conservancy, the Atchafalaya Basinkeeper, and numerous other organizations and persons who invest so much time, money, and energy into preserving Louisiana's rapidly eroding wetlands.

Behind many authors lies a long-suffering yet supportive partner. I am such an author. So, my final thank-you—for all the suffering and support—must go to my husband and most devoted fan, Rick Fields.